AN UNFAMILIAR SOUND PIERCED CARRIGAN'S SLUMBER. . . .

A gentle tug on his IV line followed. The scattered glow through the window backlit a stocky male figure, his arms raised as he jabbed a syringe into the injection port on the IV fluid bag.

The realization of danger gripped Carrigan. He whipped around toward the stranger. His fist crashed into the man's groin.

The stranger dropped with a groan, and Carrigan pressed his advantage. Seizing the IV line, he snapped it over the man's head and jerked it tight around a bearded throat. The sudden jolt ruptured the plastic, reversing the flow. Blood and fluid splashed the swarthy stranger as he lurched away, pawing for his gun.

Though Carrigan wasted only a few seconds freeing his knife and ripping out the IV catheter to keep his life's blood from pouring out on the floor, it was just long enough for the man to aim the muzzle of his pistol right at Carrigan's head. . . .

MICKEY ZUCKER REICHERT
THE
UNKNOWN SOLDIER

DAW BOOKS, INC.
DONALD A. WOLLHEIM, FOUNDER
375 Hudson Street, New York, NY 10014

ELIZABETH R. WOLLHEIM
SHEILA E. GILBERT
PUBLISHERS

To Gary, finally

ACKNOWLEDGMENTS

There are a number of people whose expertise contributed to making this a better, more accurate story: To William Hesson for medicolegal advice; Howard Hilleran and Chuck Herron of Carousel Motors; Porsche Cars North America, Inc.; Mark Moore and Bill Johnson for their command of guns, strategy, and warfare (past, present, and future); Henry and Marilyn at William's Gun Store; Dano of Dillon Precision Products, Inc.; two nameless men from Burt's Tavern who rescued a stranger's car from a ditch; Ahmad Abdel-Hameed and Rabih Zaatar for their knowledge of the Middle East; John Grace for daring to trust a lunatic with his Porsche, Captain Kevin Ran dle, Chris Lucie, Miramar Naval Air Station, and Ray Feist for military information; Dr. Stephen D. Zucker, and too many residents, staff doctors, nurses, and medical students from Thomas Jefferson Medical College and The University of Iowa to name individually. The credibility is theirs, the mistakes my own.

Also, Dave "Axeman" Hartlage, Dwight V. Swain, Sheila Gilbert, and Jonathan Matson who lent their time and their unique talents now and in the past.

Contents

CHAPTER 1

Cardiac Arrest

Doctor Jason Walker kicked open the residents' on-call room door with the toe of his running shoe. A bar of light from the medical ward hallway played over a metal-framed bunk bed, the sheets and blankets crisp and unrumpled. At its head, shelves nailed to the walls held awkward stacks of reprints, journals, and textbooks piled so high Walker suspected his slightest movement would cause an avalanche. Directly opposite the bed, a chair blocked a full-length mirror. A digital clock/radio on the seat blazed 2:17 a.m. Walker flipped on the light, stepped inside, and let the door swing shut behind him.

Walker unclipped the green plastic beeper from the waistband on his on-call scrubs and flung it to the lower bed. It bounced once, then lay still and mercifully silent on a woolly green blanket that looked like something from an army barracks. "Only less comfortable," Walker grumbled, irritable from fatigue. He shrugged off his white coat, swept it from his shoulders, and tossed it to the bedpost amid the rattle and clang of equipment in its pockets. *Tuesday: April 30, 1985. Another Jason Walker "black cloud" night.*

Early in their first year, each resident seemed to

develop a pattern of call. Some, those with the "white cloud," unfailingly managed to be assigned evenings with no patient activity; they slept through the night. Others would keep busy with emergency helicopter transports or brilliant diagnoses of rare diseases. But for Jason Walker, it was always the same. Minor complaints on the ward would keep him awake into the early morning after which a long train of adults with coughs and sniffles would appear in the emergency room.

Walker shouldered through the door in the far wall that led into a bathroom he shared with the intern in the adjoining room. *It's not fair.* Walker rummaged through the pile of residents' toiletries until he found his own shaving kit. Unzipping it, he removed a bar of soap, his toothbrush, and a tube of Crest. *The staff physicians justify the residents having to take call every third night by saying "as it is, you're missing two-thirds of the good cases."* He brushed his teeth with rapid strokes. *Right about now, I'd settle for a single interesting patient.* The only advantage of being in-house at night was that, without the attending staff physicians present, the residents in training handled all emergencies. But, though already into the second year of his internal medicine residency, Jason Walker had never had the chance to lead a code.

Walker rinsed his toothbrush and tossed it back into his kit. He ran a hand through sand-colored curls, trying to ignore the widening semicircle of scalp visible at his temples. His hair felt slightly oily. He glanced longingly at the shower but knew the instant he undressed, an emergency call would come over the beeper. For an instant, he considered doing it for that reason alone. *Stupid, supersti-*

tious nonsense. Fluffing his hair with his fingers, he yawned and returned to his room, pulling the restroom door closed behind him.

Another night kicked to hell. Walker retrieved his beeper and nestled it on the pillow beside his ear, where it would certainly awaken him no matter how deeply he slept. Neatly, he untied his shoes and placed them, side by side, beneath the chair. Removing his wire-rimmed glasses, he put them on the clock, checked the alarm, and found it set for 7:00 a.m. Satisfied he could catch as much as four and a half hours of sleep, he flipped off the light, peeled back the covers, and crawled between the sheets. In the dark, he fumbled at the lowest shelf to uncover a push-button telephone beneath the assortment of residents' reading material. His efforts sent magazines skittering to the floor beneath the bed. *Better there than on my face in the middle of the night.* Walker lay back and tried to sleep.

Instantly, uncertainty crowded Jason Walker. He relived every decision, admission, and complaint. The quiet darkness forced him to pass judgment on each examination, every medication order he had written or spoken that day, and even the amount of research he had performed on his patients. Sleep receded, impossible with his mind jumbled with self-doubt. Questioning his ability had become a nightly occurrence. No matter what method he chose to confront a problem, there was always a higher level resident or attending who would have done it differently and was quick to evaluate and criticize. Now in his second year, Walker had finally become confident enough of his clinical skills to develop techniques to help him disregard the guilt and fear that descended upon him whenever he tried to rest.

Gradually, Walker replaced thoughts of ulcer treatments, blood sugar levels, and hypertension with an image of the new house he had chosen to rent in a town north of Liberty Hospital called, appropriately, North Liberty. The house was an ugly A-frame constructed of materials a grade above thumbtacks and cardboard, but the surrounding six acres of forest made it worth the fifteen-minute drive to and from work. Walker smiled as he recalled his discovery of a beaver living in a lake nestled in the woodlands; the surrounding trees bore the scars of its nightly feasts.

Thoughts of his new home's peace lulled Jason Walker to sleep.

The high-pitched shrieks of the beeper jarred Walker awake. Heart pounding, he fumbled for the plastic and thumbed the button silent. The number dialed in by the caller flashed red across the display; in his startlement, Walker caught only the last digit. He pressed the button again. The numbers appeared one by one: four-eight-zero-eight.

Four-eight-zero-eight. Though the shock of Walker's abrupt awakening had tightened his muscles, exhaustion still fogged his mind. It took his brain an unusually long time to identify the caller. *4808. The E.R.* Groaning, Walker rolled, grabbed the phone, and punched out the number in the dark.

The unit clerk answered on the first ring. "Liberty Hospital. Emergency Room."

Walker's voice sounded more hoarse than he expected. "This is Jason Walker, medicine resident on-call. Someone paged me?"

"Just a second, Dr. Walker. I'll find out who called you."

Walker glanced at the clock. *3:42 a.m. An hour and fifteen minutes of sleep. Record high for me.*

The familiar voice of an energetic emergency room nurse named Nancy came over the line. "He-ey, Dr. J! Sorry to bother you, but we've got a patient down here for you."

A patient, not a question. No avoiding it now. Jason reached up and flicked on the light. He cradled the phone with his chin as he replaced his glasses and reached for his running shoes. "He-ey, Nan-cy!" He tried to imitate her enthusiasm, but his effort fell flat. "What have you got there? Anything exciting?"

"Something ... different." She pronounced the last word in a way that suggested he might find the case amusing. "Don't kill yourself getting down here. See ya." The line went dead.

Walker pulled his laces tight with a sigh of annoyance. He appreciated Nancy letting him know it was not a real emergency. Few things bothered him more than charging recklessly through the corridors, arriving gasping and fluttering at a bedside only to discover a smiling patient with a condition less in need of urgent treatment than his own breathless wheezing was. He paused to run a comb through his hair, wipe sleep from his eyes, and brush his teeth. His chin sported a stiff growth of stubble, but he did not bother to shave. It never seemed fair to blow morning breath on a patient, but anyone who crawled into an emergency room at 3:00 a.m. had to expect his doctor to look reasonably disheveled. Grabbing his white coat amid a metallic clatter of shifting tuning forks, reflex hammers, and penlights in its pockets, he exited the on-call quarters.

The walk to Emergency seemed to take forever. Once there, Walker found it relatively quiet. The unit clerk was reading a newspaper, and most of the other Emergency Room personnel knelt in chairs around the charting table, working on a crossword puzzle. Nancy met Walker by the computer printer beneath the paramedics' call-in radio, her short, red hair immaculate above blue eyes as alert as her manner. She offered him a bowl of warm popcorn. "Cubicle six," she said, pointing to a drawn curtain in the main ward. "His name's George Malaphy. Are you all right?" She caught his arm, genuinely concerned.

This early, the buttery aroma of the popcorn made Walker queasy. "Just tired. What's he got?"

Nancy smiled, removing her hand. "I think you might want to ask him. I'll come with you."

Walker nodded. He knew Nancy worked hard and never shirked her duties. If she suggested he ask Malaphy himself, it was only because she felt the patient's explanation would have a greater impact on his diagnosis.

Nancy set aside the popcorn. As Walker headed toward the room, several of the nurses waved around the crossword puzzle. "Hi, Dr. J."

Walker returned the gesture mechanically and pushed past the curtain into cubicle six.

Clothed in jeans and a T-shirt, George Malaphy sat on the metal Emergency Room table. Walker judged the patient's age in the early fifties. He appeared larger than Walker's slim 5'10" frame by a good three inches and a hundred pounds. A ring of mixed black and gray hair separated his receding hairline from his bald spot.

"Mr. Malaphy, I'm Dr. Walker." Walker extended a hand. "What can I do for you?"

Malaphy accepted Walker's hand in a tight grip, and Walker examined his patient's fingernails from habit. Though dirty, they retained a normal shape and pink color with no evidence of chronic diseases. "Doc, I've got this spot on my scalp, and it don't got no feeling in it." Releasing his grip, Malaphy traced a coin-sized space on the bald area of his head.

Walker glanced at Nancy who shrugged. He cleared his throat. "Numb, huh?" Walker started, not certain what to say. The symptom did not go along with any diagnosis he could conceive of, and he could not imagine how Malaphy would notice such a thing at all, let alone at three o'clock in the morning. "When did you first notice this?"

"Just before I came in. I was sleeping and reached up and noticed it."

Obligingly, Walker walked around Malaphy and put his fingers on the man's scalp. It felt uniformly warm, the indicated site the same healthy hue as the rest of his skin. "Mr. Malaphy, are you on any medications?" Walker braced himself for the possibility of a long list.

"None at all." Malaphy sounded proud.

"Any medical problems? Did you injure this part of your head recently?" He glanced at Nancy over Malaphy's head. "Does he have a hospital chart?"

Nancy and Malaphy shook their heads simultaneously. "I'm fit as a fiddle, Doc," the man said.

Walker massaged the scalp, thinking Malaphy's fiddle might have a few screws loose. "So, as far as you know, there's no good reason why you should have a numb ... skull?" Walker carefully separated the last two words. Even at this time of the morning, it seemed unnecessary to antagonize the patient.

"No, Doc. Don't know why. It's just a numb-skull." Malaphy slurred the words together as if on cue.

Walker turned a laugh into a cough. Nancy struggled valiantly against a smile, loosed a loud snort through her nose, and to Walker's relief, left the cubicle. If she had lost composure in front of him, he knew he could never have reined in his own. "Mr. Malaphy, I don't think it's anything serious. I'd like to try one thing." Without explaining further, Walker unsnapped a safety pin from the buttonhole of his white coat. He tapped the point against the indicated area of Malaphy's scalp.

"Ow!" Malaphy jumped in surprise.

Walker reclasped the pin to his coat and stepped around in front of Malaphy, keeping his manner as professional as possible. "Good. You seem to have regained sensation. Go home and get some sleep. If it happens again, don't worry. Call us the next morning after eight o'clock, and we'll set up an appointment in the clinic." He ushered Malaphy from the cubicle. "Thanks for stopping in to see us."

Walker waited until Malaphy left the Emergency Room, wandered through the waiting room to the main entrance, and the door whisked closed behind him. Then Walker collapsed into a chair by the charting table, laughing hysterically. Across the table, Nancy joined him. Apparently, she had informed the other nurses because soon everyone at the table was snickering along with him.

Regaining control, Walker seized the patient's clipboard from its numbered slot and started writing up the incident for Malaphy's chart. The words came slowly. Walker found it difficult enough writing coherently after twenty-one hours of work, but this one seemed particularly hard to phrase in a way to justify his lack of treatment without making the patient sound stupid. He did reasonably well until he reached the box marked "diagnosis." He had just discarded "deadhead" and a host of psychiatric diagnoses he did not feel qualified to make and settled on "Area of perceived decreased sensation on the scalp" when the paramedics' radio blared once, then blasted static through the Emergency Room.

The personnel fell appropriately silent, and a male voice emerged, thinly, beneath white noise. "Liberty, this is niner-eight-oh. Can you hear me?"

Nancy rose and took the microphone. "This is Liberty E.R."

"Do you have a doctor in the room?"

Walker glanced around. Both of the Emergency Room staff physicians had gone off to see patients, leaving him the only doctor in the room. As a specialty resident, he had the right to refuse the call and insist they retrieve one of the emergency attendings.

Nancy looked questioningly at Walker before answering.

Walker's heart raced. *This is my chance.* He nodded affirmation.

"Go ahead," Nancy said, her usual jovial manner blunted.

"We have an unidentified white male, late twenties, with multiple trauma. Respiratory rate 30; heart rate 120. Blood pressure 60 over palpable . . ."

Shit! Impending shock. Walker rose and walked to Nancy's side.

". . . unconscious, multiple lacerations and burns especially on the face, chest, and upper extremities. Breath sounds absent on the right, diminished on the left. Pupils equal and reactive. We've controlled all external sources of bleeding. Got an IV in on the left running lactated Ringer's at about 200 cc's."

Walker knew the radio was intended for the paramedics to convey information and did not operate well in the opposite direction. *But if they don't increase his blood volume fast, he'll die in their hands.* He nudged Nancy. "Tell them to open that IV all the way and get another one in if they can. It's worth the delay."

Nancy relayed the message.

"It's done. Estimated time of arrival . . ." The voice paused, followed by a flutter of conversation that sounded indecipherable over the radio. ". . . five minutes."

Five minutes! Walker caught at the front of his white coat, suddenly frightened. Multiple trauma victims usually went to the Surgery Service. But the surgery resident took home call; it would require at least ten minutes for him or her to reach the Emergency Room. *You wanted it, buddy, now handle it!* Every self-doubt Walker harbored emerged at once. Not even a vestige of sleepiness remained. *I know my stuff; I'm prepared.* He gathered his composure as nurses rushed to ready the trauma room.

The first thing to remember is not to be proud. I'm not alone. Walker instructed the unit clerk. "Page surgery and neurosurg. Let them know this guy's coming. Call anesthesia, too. We'll need to intubate. Oh, and page beeper 142, Shawna Nicholson, my chief resident." Walker turned to Nancy as the unit clerk responded. "We'd better order some O negative blood, say two units for now. I don't think we'll have time for a cross-match."

Nancy gripped Walker's shoulder. "You're doing fine," she said before grabbing a telephone to make the necessary call to the blood bank. Walker paused, glad for the calm competence of the Emergency Room nurses. Their support and faith in him would do more toward making the experience successful and smooth than anything else. Quickly, he entered the main hallway, trotting past the empty waiting room and around the corner to the trauma room.

Walker had scarcely reached the threshold when, down the corridor and to his left, the electronically controlled emergency doors slapped open, admitting damp, summer air. Red light from the ambulance strobed across metal and glass. Three paramedics maneuvered a gurney through the entryway, and the glass panels slid closed behind them.

The cart wheels sounded thunderous on the tile. The clang and slap of the IV bottle against its pole rose faintly beneath the hubbub of conversation. A portable EKG monitor made rapid, steady beeps, indicating the patient's heart rate. Three Emergency Room nurses joined the paramedics as they raced through the hallway. Walker stepped out of the way. No matter how severe the patient's injuries, he knew the nurses needed to transfer the patient from the gurney to the table, secure lines and bandages, and wire the patient from the portable to the stable monitor before treatment could begin.

Walker slipped into the room behind the gurney as the nurses fell into their skillful routine. He found one paramedic near the door. His name badge identified him as Douglas. "What happened?" Walker asked.

Douglas tore his gaze from the patient to look directly at Walker. "Well, Dr.—" He glanced at Walker's name tag. "—Walker. We're not sure. A fellow in one of the houses out by City High said he heard something that sounded like a 'muffled bang.' He got worried some kids might be vandalizing the school, ran over, and found this guy lying in the field."

Walker's eyes traced the constant blips of the patient's heart as the nurses hooked him to the overhead monitor. The complexes appeared normal aside from a rate of about 130.

"Luckily for him," Douglas inclined his head to indicate the patient, "the insomniac was smart enough to stop some of the bleeding before he called 911."

As the nurses finished their tasks and moved aside to draw up medications, Walker found a space at the bedside. The patient seemed close to his own age, in his mid to late twenties. *Certainly no high school kid.* His skin appeared doughy and ghostly pale. Despite a multitude of gashes and pressure dressings, Walker noted the features appeared handsome, almost aristocratic, the hair thick, black, and clotted with blood. Walker clamped his fingers to the patient's neck and felt a pulse, rapid and thready. A wave of pity enveloped him. The appropriate treatment for impending shock rose naturally and, with it, a less professional thought. *Why do we always feel so much sorrier for the young, good-looking ones?*

Douglas had followed Walker to the patient, still talking. "Some sort of explosion . . ."

Walker noticed two large bore IVs in place with satisfaction. The nurses were replacing the nearly empty bottles of Ringer's lactate. Nancy appeared in the doorway with the bags of O negative, and Walker motioned her to use them instead. *He's bleeding somewhere.* A rapid examination revealed no external source. The paramedics had done a fine job of bandaging. *If it's internal, we need a surgeon and fast.*

The pulse disappeared beneath Walker's fingers. For an instant, Walker thought his own heart had stopped with it. Then the EKG monitor alarm screamed through the room, and the picture went flatline. "Start CPR," Walker said, his calmness surprising him. Familiar with the nurses, he delegated responsibilities easily. One clamped a mask over the patient's face, using an ambu bag to breath for him. Another compressed his chest at a rhythm about two-thirds Walker's own speeding heart rate. The blood bags were opened fully. Another IV was slipped into a collapsed vein while blood was taken for studies from another.

Douglas' words seeped between Walker's shouted orders. ". . . definitely an explosion . . . fragments through his chest. I was a medic in Nam . . . grenade or a homemade explosive . . . attempted suicide or killing . . ."

"Type and cross for ten units!" *Fragments in his*

chest? Walker shook his head. *If something hit a great vessel, he wouldn't have made it this far.*

"Should we give epinephrine?" one of the nurses prodded, trying to help.

Walker hesitated. Usually, epinephrine was the first and most appropriate drug to give in a code situation. It stimulated the heart to work harder. *But, in this case, the heart's working fine. He just doesn't have anything in his veins for the heart to pump. Epinephrine will only make him bleed faster.*

"Hold the epi," Walker said. He looked up to see a female staff anesthesiologist had taken over the airway. With the ease of long practice, she removed the mask and slipped a plastic tube into the trachea.

Recalling the absent breath sounds, Walker informed the anesthesiologist. "I think he's got a pneumothorax on the right."

The anesthesiologist inched the tube backward. By anatomical design, an endotracheal tube pushed in too far would slide down the right main stem bronchus. In this case, that would mean ventilating only the bad lung.

"Can someone get a blood gas?" Walker asked.

"I got it." Walker recognized the voice of Shawna Nicholson, his chief resident.

The surgery resident, Robert Sharmin, appeared immediately behind her. "Has anyone given this patient epi?"

Walker seethed. *Typical goddamned surgeon. Wanders in the door in the middle and decides to take over by throwing treatments at an unidentified problem.*

A nurse prepared to inject the epinephrine, immediately halted by Nicholson's words. "Dr. Sharmin, I believe Dr. Walker has control of the situation. I think he has a task for you, too."

Walker found it amazing how, in the midst of chaos, Nicholson could not only remain collected but resist the urge to wrest control from a less experienced house officer. Somehow, she had managed to restore responsibility to the youngest, least seasoned resident without insulting either party. Taking his lead from Nicholson, Walker said, "I think he's got a right pneumothorax, and he's bleeding somewhere. Can you get a chest tube in?"

Sharmin grabbed a kit and set to work, jabbing a trocar and tube between the patient's ribs and into the lung sac with the brutality the procedure required.

The unit clerk stuck his head through the door. "I have the blood gas results."

"Go ahead," Walker said anxiously. The numbers would indicate, in undeniable and vivid detail, the success or failure of his resuscitation efforts.

The unit clerk read each digit slowly. To Walker's surprise, they revealed only a mild decrease in respiratory function, attributable to the pneumothorax. In a cardiac arrest, he expected far worse and had to wonder if the lab had made a mistake.

Sharmin echoed his concern. "That's impossible. They must have mixed him up with another patient."

"I'll get another." Nicholson said, grabbing another heparinized syringe.

Walker waited only until she had finished and passed it to the unit clerk. "Stop compressions." He placed his fingers against the carotid artery.

Obediently, the nurse stopped pushing on the patient's chest, her hands remaining in position for the order to resume.

A pulse thrummed beneath Walker's fingers. *Thank God.* "He's got a pulse."

The nurse backed away. Sharmin unclamped the chest tube and a whoosh of air trapped in the lung sac escaped, allowing the patient's right lung to re-expand. A rush of blood followed. "Shit. Hemothorax. We've got to get this guy to the O.R. right away. Do we have a type and cross?"

"Ten units," Walker confirmed.

The unit clerk appeared. The results of the second blood gas were the same as the first. At Sharmin's insistence, the clerk rushed off to call the Operating Room and staff surgeon on call. Within seconds, the nurses had the patient on a portable monitor, and the bed rolled toward surgery.

The trauma room emptied, leaving only Walker and Nicholson. Walker shoved aside syringe wrappers and the empty chest tube kit, and hopped to the ledge by the sink. He picked at a piece of dried blood on his fingers. "Think he'll make it?"

"I don't know," Nicholson replied truthfully. "It depends on what the surgeons find. But if he survives the knife, he's got you to thank for any remaining brain function. His pupils were equal and reactive the whole time."

"Really?" Walker looked up, aware the indicator boded well for the patient's neurological system. *No guarantee, but a good sign.* He smiled at Nicholson, studying her in the too bright examining room. Like most of the female residents, she wore her reddish brown hair in a short, easy to care for style. The harsh light revealed a simple beauty, even without makeup, and an athletic body beneath tattered jeans and a Disneyland T-shirt she had apparently thrown on in her haste.

"Really," Nicholson did not seem to notice Walker's stare. "You did a great job with the code. Come on. Let's get some coffee. I'll buy."

Walker leaped to the floor. "Thanks." Then, realizing the single word did not convey enough gratitude, he continued. "For the compliment and the coffee. Thanks, too, for not letting Sharmin take the code from me."

Nicholson ushered Walker through the door. "How are you going to learn if people take over for you?"

Walker and Nicholson wandered past the emergency waiting room and down the long hallway toward the main hospital. Briefly, Walker wondered why Nicholson decided to stay in-house rather than hurrying home to her live-in boyfriend and a final hour of sleep. Then he vaguely recalled a rumor that her lover, an ophthalmologist, had taken a staff position in Berkeley, California, and had broken their relationship. "Sort of a Catch twenty-two. I have to learn for the sake of future patients, but I wouldn't want my relative in the hands of a second year resident running his first code."

They reached an intersection in the corridor, and Nicholson turned right, toward the cafeteria. "Now's the time for you to make your mistakes, while you still have backup. If I thought you did something wrong, I'd have said so."

Walker nodded. *She would have, too. But she would have suggested it in such a way to make it seem like my idea.* In his mind, Nicholson made the perfect chief. She was competent, friendly, and dealt well with doctors and their egos. Her patience surprised him. Walker found it difficult enough not to take over when medical students fumbled with needles and IV catheters. Yet Nicholson was flexible enough to allow the residents to develop their own methods of dealing with problems, without forcing her techniques upon them the way many of the staff physicians did.

At 4:30 a.m., they found the cafeteria nearly empty. Walker sat at a vacant table, watching Nicholson stroll toward the counter for coffee cups. Her jeans hugged taut curves, and Walker had to admit, from his angle, her ass looked very nice. If the rumors about her boyfriend were correct, Walker knew he would have a lot of competition if he tried to date Nicholson.

As adrenaline dispersed, fatigue crowded Walker. He lowered his head to the table, his thoughts turning to the patient whose life had rested in his hands. *God, I hope he makes it.* The sincerity of the sentiment nearly overwhelmed Walker. The bond of blood that had formed between him and an unidentified patient within a matter of seconds frightened him. It was the other who should feel grateful; yet, oddly, Walker felt obliged, as though the stranger had rescued him instead of the other way. Walker raised his head to discover Nicholson had taken the chair across from him, two steaming styrofoam cups before her.

Walker curled both hands around one, feeling its warmth against his palms. The aroma of the coffee seemed pleasantly familiar. "Do you really think he'll pull through?"

Nicholson sipped at her cup. "If those blood

gases were correct, that guy's tough as nails. Jason, if anyone's got a chance, he does."

"Yeah." Walker hefted his cup thoughtfully, recalling the speculations of a paramedic named Douglas. "If and when the guy wakes up, I think he'll have one hell of a story to tell."

CHAPTER 2

The John Doe

The man awakened to the clank and whoosh of machinery, and pain that racked his entire body. Instinctively, he went still, searching his mind for some memory of where he was and how he had gotten there. No enlightenment touched him. Even his own name lay beyond recollection. Nauseated and light-headed, he sucked a deep lungful of air, tasting plastic. A mechanical flutter of low-pitched sound accompanied his effort. He tried to exhale, but something jammed more air into his already expanded lungs. Crushed by a feeling of suffocation, he tensed, setting off a sharp wash of pain. Before he could fight against it, the pressure disappeared, and he exhaled comfortably.

Calm, the man reminded himself. *Don't let your enemy know you're awake.* Another blast of air was forced into his lungs. Surprised, he strained against it, reflexively trying to close his windpipe. He choked on a piece of plastic lodged in his airway, startled again by a rapid chorus of the ratchetlike noises he had heard earlier. Pain shocked through his chest, severe enough to make his eyes water.

Desperate for air, he grabbed at his throat. His fingers brushed a tube jutting from his mouth and taped to his upper lip. Seizing it, he jerked. The tape ripped painfully from his skin, the plastic slid free, and he opened his eyes to a dimly lit room. He realized he lay in a bed. A jumble of lines and wires ran between him and several metallic devices and screens he did not recognize.

A second later, an earsplitting whistle cut through the chamber. He heard a distant shout. "It's the ventilator! Room three!"

Footsteps rang on the floorboards. Between the machines, the man caught a sideways glimpse of a female figure dressed in baggy greens. "He's extubated himself," she shouted above the din. "I need some help in here!" She pushed aside the blaring device. A jutting bolt snagged her shirt. She jerked free with a tear of fabric. "Shit." Reaching, she caught a clear plastic mask with an attached bag and clamped it over his face.

The man gasped in a lungful of cold, odd-tasting gas. Urgency gripped him. He lashed out at the woman with a hand, felt wires impede the movement before breaking free. Then, his fist crashed into her shoulder. His blow staggered her. She fell against an IV pole and brought it with her to the ground. Tension on the line ripped the IV catheter from his hand, and blood splashed his arm. He rolled to rise, assaulted by pain that dropped him back to the bed. Alarms of varying pitch added their cries to the ventilator.

Abruptly, the room was filled with people. Someone hit a switch. Light flared overhead; its suddenness blinded the man. A sea of hands descended on him, pinning his limbs to the bed. The mask was smashed over his nose and mouth again. His consciousness retreated, leaving him awash in dizziness. A memory sparked. He recalled hours locked

in a confinement cell so small he had to sit with
his face crushed to his knees. The cramps returned
to him now, the ache of knotted muscles unable to
move, the interminably constant pressure of concrete walls against flesh. Then, he had tried to
amuse himself by talking, attempting to fool his
numbed brain into believing he was not alone by
using various languages. He remembered violent
hands dragging him from the cell, accented voices
demanding information, the pain of their clubs and
knives a welcome release from imprisonment. By
concentrating on physical anguish, he knew he was
still alive.

Still alive. The reference to pain jerked the man
back to the present. He sifted through the voices
that beat against his ears, selecting one from the
hubbub. "Dr. Sharmin's in surgery. How about the
medical resident on call? I think it's Jason
Walker?"

"Get him. Fast. And for God's sake, someone
turn off that ventilator alarm!"

The persistent shrilling stopped as if choked,
leaving the less annoying alarms of the monitors. A
nurse reconnected the appropriate lines, and those
sounds died as well. Excitement caused the nurse
with the oxygen mask to squeeze the bag harder
than necessary.

Forced to breathe at an uncomfortable depth, the
man struggled madly. Weakened by blood loss, he
could not break free, and the realization of being
irrevocably trapped brought the panic of claustrophobia. He howled, his wordless protest muffled
beneath the mask. Another blast of air was driven
into his lungs.

A young male voice cut authoritatively above the

noise. "Back off. Let him breathe on his own. He's scared to death."

Mercifully, the mask disappeared from the man's face. A few sets of hands backed reluctantly away, though he could still feel his captors' stares on him. The world seemed distant. His head buzzed. He sank back to the bed and let his eyes sag closed while he caught his breath. *Enemies. Surrounded. Got to get free.*

"Let me talk to him," the newest arrival said.

Another male responded. "Jason, I don't know if that's a good idea."

Apparently undaunted, Walker pressed forward. The man snapped open his lids to stare into eyes colored a muddled combination of green, brown, and blue, slightly magnified by glasses' lenses.

"Easy, it's all right," Walker said soothingly. Though still looking at the patient, he addressed the nurses. "Give him a dose of Valium. Does he still have an IV?" He glanced away.

The man seized on Walker's carelessness. Fast as a striking snake, he grabbed the doctor by the throat and yanked him into the bed.

Walker fell across the man hard enough to splash pain across every part of the patient's body. His fingers tightened around Walker's windpipe.

Someone screamed. Several pairs of strong hands grasped the man's arms, tearing Walker free. The doctor fell to the floor gasping while the patient fought desperately against his captors.

Gradually, a feeling of peace sifted through the man's panic. He stopped struggling and let the nurses ravel padded restraints around his wrists. The world receded behind a curtain that muffled sound to a whisper. He closed his eyes, his last conscious memory the sound of Jason Walker's hoarse lament:

"Four billion people in this world, and I have to save the life of a fucking homicidal maniac."

The number sounded distinctly low.

The man awakened to a quiet chorus of bubbling and humming machines and the distant sound of movement. He kept his eyes closed, attempting to assess his surroundings without revealing his awakening to anyone who might be watching. He tried to simulate the deep, rhythmical breaths of sleep, but pain forced him to take short, shallow gulps of air. A shaped piece of plastic was wedged uncomfortably into his nostrils, blowing cool, dry gas into his nasal cavity. *Oxygen,* he guessed, but the unnatural clouding of his sensorium and his continued inability to recall even his own name made him less certain.

He opened one lid a crack. Seeing no one in his immediate vicinity, he slowly widened the area of his vision until it encompassed the entire room. He lay on a bed, in a private cubicle. The wall at the end near his feet was composed of glass windows and a door that stood ajar. Faded orange curtains covered all but one pane. Through it, he caught a glimpse of calm activity in a hallway and a marble desk stacked with charts, papers and strange-looking plastic and metal equipment.

Only after he assured himself of the absence of any hovering threat did he turn his attention to himself. From the feel of the sheets' weave, he knew he was naked. His covers lay peeled back, leaving his chest exposed. Thick, clear tubes jutted from either side of his ribs, their insides filmed with old blood. He followed a line of suture knots along his breastbone and noticed smaller, sewn areas on his shoulders where someone had closed superficial lacerations. He discovered gauze patches; and, from the tingling beneath them, he knew they covered burns. A reflection from the IV pole granted him a warped, stretched view of his face. He appeared reasonably young. Black hair singed to varying lengths made him look crazed, though someone had apparently taken the time to wash and comb it for him. Another crooked stretch of sutures marred one cheek.

His quiet assessment took seconds. Satisfied no one would see him move, he reached to brush away the prongs in his nose. His hand rose an inch, then jarred still. His heart quickened. He tried to use the other arm but met the same resistance. Involuntarily, he tensed. *Trapped.* he flushed, suddenly tremulous and sweaty. *Calm down. Can't let them know I'm scared.* The urge to flee became an obsession, and the realization that he could not swirled panic down upon him. *But—who the hell are "they?"* He fought to contain his fear. Then, claustrophobia inspired a certainty of imminent death that shattered his control. He howled, thrashing against the restraints like a madman. The pain of every movement faded beneath the need to break free.

Indecipherable shouts rose above the sudden buzz of an alarm. A young woman in greens slid into the room. She flicked a switch on a display monitor above his head, and the alarm stopped. "It's all right," she soothed, her tone routinely smooth. "You're going to be okay. The doctor will be here in a minute."

Doctor? The man went still. The woman's platitudes did not comfort him, but her voice broke through his panic. *Control,* he reminded himself. He lay still, cursing his trembling, and forcing his lids partially closed in an attempt to look interested rather than afraid. But he could not hide the monitor tracing, a swift red line that betrayed his racing pulse.

The nurse wiped sweat from the man's brow with a gauze pad. He reached to stop her, his inability reinforcing his helplessness. He fought another wave of panic, jerking at the padded restraints on his wrists to break the ties holding them to the side rails.

Footsteps heralded the arrival of a young surgeon dressed in scrubs stained with blood and iodine. He wore paper booties over his shoes and a white hat wrapped around his hair. "Be still!" he commanded, gripping the patient's arm in a cold hand. "You'll rip out the chest tubes."

The doctor's touch and condescending manner enraged the nameless man. Awkwardly, he clawed for a hold on the doctor's hand.

The surgeon addressed the nurse. "Give him a sedative. Whatever he's got ordered."

The nurse turned as a commanding, female voice contradicted from the door. "No, wait. Let me try something first."

The familiarity of the new voice surprised the patient, and he stopped reaching for the surgeon. A memory rose, more vivid than the reality of a hospital room. He crouched in an abandoned building, back pressed against the wall. Rotted beams hung jaggedly from the ceiling, and the odor of mildew assailed his nose. Wind howled through shattered windows; and, beneath it, he heard the almost imperceptible whisk of passing cars.

Relief filled him, its source beyond his ability to comprehend. A small hand gripped his firmly, and he turned his head to see a well-endowed, long-legged woman. Though wind-whipped and tangled, her honey blonde hair in no way diminished her desirability. *Katry.* Mired in memory that seemed to belong to a stranger, he could not grasp how he could recall her name and not his own. An emotion accompanied the thought, the recognition of a finely developed love. And with it came a deep sadness he could not fathom. Curiosity blinded him to the possibility of nearer dangers, and he allowed the recollection to unfold like a movie.

"They're gone," Katry said, her voice strong, a perfect duplicate of the woman who had last entered the hospital room. "What now?"

The man heard himself respond with a confidence he did not recognize. "We'll have to hide out for a few hours at least." Fondly, he studied Katry's curves, hugged by the thin fabric of a standard issue, dark jumpsuit, and the impression of her nipples against the fabric. Pulling her against him, he teased. "I don't think we'll die of boredom." The feel of her excited him more than he expected, and he knew he was the one who would pay for his joke.

Katry shook him off as he knew she must. "Not now, Carrigan. We have to keep running...."

She called me Carrigan. The word did not sound familiar nor, oddly, did he care. For reasons he could not fathom, he held little interest in knowing his name. Nevertheless, it was the only clue he had to his identity, so he had no choice but to consider it him. Coming from the lips of a lover, it seemed certain to be his given name or a strange endearment. *Or an alias.* The last idea jarred him to a frightening realization. *Running, she said. Running from what?*

Wrenched back to the present, the man who now thought of himself as Carrigan stared at the woman whose voice had inspired the memory. He recognized the familiar boldness in her stance, a slim, attractive figure, and Katry's widely-set eyes. But there the comparison ended. Katry sported long, golden locks and green irises while this woman had mahogany-colored hair clipped short, and her eyes were deep brown and trusting. The doctor that Carrigan vaguely recalled attempting to strangle followed her into the room. He recognized fear in a visage creased with exhaustion.

Carrigan concentrated on the woman's words.

"I'm Doctor Nicholson. This is Doctor Sharmin." She indicated the surgeon in the paper booties. "And Doctor Walker." She inclined her head toward the other, more timid man. Then she met Carrigan's stare directly as if waiting for him to reply.

Carrigan said nothing. Uncertain who to trust, he pretended he could not comprehend their language. *At least until I have a better idea of who I am and what's going on. Damn it, why am I on the run?*

Nicholson continued. "You had an accident. You're at Liberty Hospital, in the Intensive Care Unit. We're doing everything we can to help you. Do you remember any of this?"

Carrigan gave no sign he understood. *An accident? What does she mean an accident?* He felt certain he had been hurt before, and this did not look like any hospital he could recall. The machinery appeared unnecessarily enormous and ungainly. He could not fathom why someone would sew him up like a piece of cloth. *And why would doctors tie me to the bed?* He pulled at the restraints.

Nicholson glanced at the other doctors. "We want to call your family and get them here to help you. You need to tell us who you are."

Claustrophobia crushed in on Carrigan again, and he ripped harder at the restraints.

Apparently grasping his concern, Nicholson explained. "You got a little wild. We put those on so you wouldn't hurt yourself. I'll take them off if you promise not to fight."

Carrigan considered nodding but decided against it. Touched by paranoia, he wondered if his enemies had chosen Nicholson knowing she would remind him of Katry. He dismissed the possibility. *If so, they certainly would have made her look like Katry, too. A blonde wig, green inserts, a little makeup. Simple.*

Nicholson's lips twisted in a parody of consideration. "Let's take the restraints off."

"No!" Sharmin insisted. "If he pulls out those chest tubes, cardiac surg will have your head."

The look of annoyance that crossed Nicholson's face amused Carrigan, and it impressed him that none of the emotion leaked into her tone. "He can tear them out thrashing as easily as using his hands. He seems calm, and he wants them off. If anything happens we're here to stop him. Come on."

When no one volunteered to help, Nicholson unfastened one of the ties herself.

"I wouldn't do that," Walker warned, his voice betraying fear. "He might try to kill you, too."

"Jason!" Nicholson snapped.

From Walker's and Sharmin's startled expressions, Carrigan guessed impatience was uncharacteristic for Nicholson and something larger and more personal troubled her. As soon as his hand came free, he pressed it to Nicholson's fingers in gratitude.

Apparently content Carrigan would not pull out his chest tubes, Nicholson untied his other hand.

Sharmin removed his paper hat, releasing a mop of strawberry blond hair. He shook his head to settle it in place. "Why isn't he responding to your questions?"

"I don't know." Walker shuffled closer, still keeping the other two doctors between him and Carrigan. "Maybe he's a foreigner. The nurses said they found some weird money on him."

"Then why isn't he trying to talk in whatever language he speaks?" Sharmin pressed.

"Maybe he's deaf," Walker suggested.

"Maybe we should as *him*." Nicholson patted Carrigan's hand reassuringly, as if to remind him she, at least, had not forgotten he was in the room. She shook his arm.

It seemed a fairly universal gesture for attention, so Carrigan met her gaze. Freed, he began to relax, and the doctors' antics amused him.

"Sir, can you understand me?" Nicholson gazed intently, as if to extract the answer from his eyes. "If you're having trouble speaking, just nod."

Not yet willing to abandon his act, Carrigan made no sign. *There's still too much that doesn't fit;*

and once I reveal myself, I can't take the knowledge back from them.

Sharmin moved closer. "Jesus. Last time I saw eyes that color, I was looking at a Siamese cat. Did anyone check to see if this guy's wearing contacts."

"Of course," the nurse replied icily, obviously annoyed by the insinuation she might not have done her job.

Nicholson continued to stare. Her intensity alarmed Carrigan, but he met her gaze without flinching.

"What did you find in surgery?" Walker asked conversationally. "The op note was kind of vague, and I couldn't read cardiothoracic's handwriting."

Sharmin sounded excited. "Ruptured spleen. We took that out. Pieces of metal and plastic all through the lungs. Pathology still hasn't identified ..."

Nicholson interrupted. "How about a little discretion?" She nudged Sharmin toward the door.

"He doesn't understand us." Sharmin defended himself, but he and Walker headed toward the hallway anyway.

Nicholson rose and followed, throwing a last glance over her shoulder. "I wouldn't be too sure about that." The doctors left the room.

The nurse neatly rearranged the wires and gauges, pulled up the sheet to preserve Carrigan's modesty, and snapped off the overhead light shining into his eyes. "Anything else I can do for you?"

Carrigan said nothing.

She placed a square of plastic near his hand. "Press the call button if you need anything. Your things are in the drawer." She patted a narrow table standing on a metal stalk from a wheeled base. It held a clipboard of papers. "We had to confiscate the knife. The pocket knife, too. You'll get those back when you're discharged." She sighed, obviously unsure whether he had understood any of what she said. As she exited, she pulled the door along until it remained open only a crack.

My things? Glad for the privacy, Carrigan reached out and nudged the clipboard close enough to read. The chart on the top of the stack recorded his temperature, heart rate, respiratory rate, blood pressure, and several, less obvious parameters against time. In the space marked "name," someone had written "John Doe;" and the blank below it read "multiple trauma."

John Doe? that name sounded no more familiar than Carrigan. Shrugging, he opened the sliding drawer beneath the table. He came first upon a watch. No time showed through the smashed crystal. Beneath it, a tiny speaker lay dented beyond use, and Carrigan believed it had once served as a radio. Despite its condition, he fastened it around his wrist with the Velcro strap. Next, he discovered a handful of paper bills with odd, maroon writing and an unrecognizable, bearded face pictured in one corner. He brushed them aside and found a black, plastic device the size of his palm. It held a single button, a blank display, and a gently pulsing red light. *What the hell is this?*

As if in answer, memory flooded him again. Darkness replaced the dull glimmer of hospital light, its pattern interrupted by the crisscrossing pattern of a fence. The blips of the monitors and low-pitched bubble of the chest tubes gave way to the patter of blown sand against metal, the crackle of electricity, and the soft breaths of another man. Dressed in a lightweight tan uniform, his hair tucked beneath a matching cap, Carrigan crouched, awaiting something. The device that had triggered the recollection sat in his hip pocket, its presence soothing. He clutched a machine pistol to his chest, and a portable torch in his hand. Beside him, his companion appeared almost invisible in the darkness.

The memory shocked Carrigan. No doubt, he was planning to breach a security area, and the implications of such an action frightened him. The inhuman composure of the seeming stranger who was himself only scared him more. *What am I doing? Why would I carry a gun? Am I going to kill someone?* Fragments of previous memories returned to him. *Tortured. On the run. My God, please don't let me be a murderer.* Apprehension tightened his nerves to coils. Memory receded, and he reveled in its withdrawal, hating himself for calling it back. *Damn it, I have to know.* He caught halfheartedly at the recollection, allowing it to fill his mind with images.

Strangely, the self of Carrigan's past seemed unaffected by anxiety. On the opposite side of the compound, red light streaked the night sky. He heard a garbled cry of surprise from inside the fence. Then, an explosion rocked the ground beneath him. *The diversion.* The smile twitching across his own face bothered Carrigan. He watched himself raise the hand-held torch as another round of mortars barraged the far side of camp. Footsteps thudded across sand, running toward the disruption. The chop of helicopter blades followed almost instantly.

Carrigan's side of the compound went quiet. He pressed a button. White flame hissed to life from the torch, its beam knife-thin and sharper than diamond. In seconds, he cut a hole in the fence amid the sputter of fire and electricity. "Let's go."

Carrigan clipped the torch to his belt as he and his companion ducked through the opening. A siren blared, and towers lit the perimeter like day, revealing the hulking shapes of three buildings. Carrigan dodged into the shadow of one, his companion close beside him. He fumbled the strange, boxlike device from his pocket. The light winked, red against the darkness. He redirected it, watching the flashes quicken; then, as he pointed it toward the building, the signals merged into a steady glow. A yellow number appeared on the display: 0.0113 K.

"Inside," Carrigan hissed.

"You get this one. I'll go for the other."

One what? The other what? In the hospital bed, Carrigan tightened his hands to fists, trying to understand. The meaning eluded him. He could not remember what he had been after, but something else came to him instead, the grim and absolute certainty that his companion would die.

The Carrigan of memory nodded, devoid of the curiosity and fear that haunted his real self. There was a coldness about him, an indifference to death. As his companion slipped off into the semidarkness, Carrigan found himself pinned in the beam of a helicopter's light. He wheeled aside and skittered around a corner. A voice chased him, amplified to distortion. *The door. Where the hell's the door?*

Carrigan paused. He looked down to a pinpoint of red gliding toward his chest. *Laser sight!* He dove, rolling. Gunshots hammered the place where he had stood, pelting him with sand. *Ten gauge fully automatic shotgun.* His mind mechanically identified the report of the weapon. *If they've got flechettes, I'm a dead man.* Gaining his feet, he dodged around another corner as bullets clanged against the overhanging gutter. He nearly collided with another man in front of the solid, metal door. Dressed in the same tan costume as Carrigan, the stranger squinted, trying to identify him in the irregular lighting. In that instant of hesitation, Carrigan jabbed the barrel of his machine pistol into the man's chest and pulled the trigger.

Just before the guard collapsed, Carrigan spotted another man over the corpse's shoulder. Using the dead man as a shield, Carrigan snaked his arm around and squeezed off another round. The bullets crashed through the guard's head before he could fire an answering shot. He toppled over backward. Carrigan shoved aside the other corpse. Ignoring the bodies, he ran to the door.

Constructed of a single, continuous piece of steel-4, the door appeared imposing and inviolable. Undaunted, Carrigan searched the nearby wall. Discovering a box, he prodded it open to reveal the colored, plastic buttons that coded the entry. He raised the torch in his left hand, the pistol still clamped in his right. A quick glance over his shoulder revealed no one nearby for the moment. Overhead, the helicopter maneuvered, still some distance away. Igniting the torch, Carrigan used the flame to cut around the front of the control panel. The console fell against his forearms, dangling from a chaotic jumble of wires. Substituting a utility knife for the torch, he selected a blade and set to work.

The first cut brought a screech as penetrating as the hospital's ventilator alarm; and, suddenly, there was no longer just the assurance of his companion's death, but of his own as well. Oddly, anger and urgency, not fear, accompanied the realization. He worked faster, cutting, stripping insulation, and re-connecting bare wires until the door slid open with a sound like a giant sigh of relief.

Scattered light trickled faintly into a square chamber. The room contained one object, a long rectangular machine similar to an ancient telephone booth or a coffin on its edge. Still shocked by the murders, the hospitalized Carrigan lay still, fasci-nated by his own memory. He could not recall the nature of the device, only that he had found what he had broken in and killed for. *Killed men wearing the same uniforms as myself without so much as a touch of remorse. So I'm not just a hired gun, I'm a traitor, too.*

The Carrigan of memory tucked the utility knife back into his pocket and, again, retrieved the object he had discovered in the hospital drawer. He touched it to the booth. The light flared a steady red, and the display read 0.000 K. *Right on target.*

Despite the persistent screech of the alarms, his excitement-enhanced hearing picked up the sounds of distant shouts. And by the volume of the rotors, Carrigan knew the helicopters were approaching. Quickly, he replaced the utility knife and the tracker, exchanging them for a tube and timer. He unscrewed the cap with his teeth, squeezed out two globs of explosive plastic, reached up, and secured them to the top of the booth. Dropping the half-empty tube, he stabbed the timer's wires into the putty.

Glancing through the doorway, he saw figures in the darkness, approaching far too quickly. He cranked the timer to thirty seconds, then, from necessity, back to twenty. He wasted five of them taping the timer into place on top of the machine. He turned to run, skidded in front of the exit, only to have a half dozen laser sight pinpoints appear on his shirt. He ducked back out of range, scarcely daring to believe he was not already dead. Apparently men, not machines, controlled those triggers. ... *13-12-11* ... *Can't let them catch me alive.* Desperately, he sought an escape. *Better to die with the target.* Catching the handle of the booth, he wrenched the door open and sprang inside.

... *8-7* ... A light snapped automatically, revealing a circle of padded benches and a slick computer console with the name Macintosh in blazing green. The eye-appealing blue on yellow letters on the monitor screen directed: "Touch enter when ready." *Ready for what?* Carrigan hesitated as the last few seconds ticked away.... *4-3-2* ... *What the hell have I got to lose?* He punched the indicated button. Abruptly, pain shocked through him, an agony beyond his endurance. He thought he heard himself scream before darkness enveloped him.

A closer alarm shattered Carrigan's vision of past reality. He looked up to the hospital monitor to see the electrical complexes of his heart flicking onto the screen at twice his normal cadence. Consciously, he unclenched his muscles and slowed his breathing, and the tracing slackened to a rate below the upper setting of the alarm. *Thievery, destruction, killing without thought or compunction. Please, God, let this be someone else. A dream. A movie.*

Carrigan's twisting movement slammed the

drawer closed on his fingers, and a neatly folded pile of tan fabric swept the corner of his vision. Pulling his hands free, he turned. Behind him, the clothing sat on a table beside a heavy, push-button telephone looking as much like an ancient torture device to Carrigan as any of the equipment in the room. He seized the cloth. The blood-splashed trousers came undone as he dragged them into the bed and returned to a more comfortable position on his back.

He stared. The light fabric made even the hospital staff's cotton scrubs appear cumbersome. Recognizing the pants as the ones he had worn in the memory, he wadded them between his fists. *No denying it now. That murderer was me.* He tried to think, but the medications the doctors had given him to dull pain blunted clarity of thought as well. *Got to get out of here. Got to go before I hurt someone. Before they find out who and what I am. Before I find out who and what I am.*

Carrigan dismissed the last thought. *Can't escape myself. On the run. Can't stay in one place. Can't let them catch me.* Defying the pain, he jammed the trousers beneath the sheet and worked them over his legs. He met the resistance of a catheter wedged through his penis into his bladder. Seizing the rubber tubing he jerked it free. The air-filled balloon that held the catheter in place ripped through with a sharp agony he could not ignore. He stifled a yell, waiting until pain died to an ache, then yanked the waistband into its proper place. Despite the insubstantial feel of the garment, he found the pockets sturdy. He tucked the tracking device and the bills inside.

Next, Carrigan ripped out his IV catheter, oblivious to the blood trickling through his fingers and the steady wash of fluid across the tile. He grabbed wires by the handful and jerked them. The EKG patches peeled from his surgery-shaven chest. Forgetting the chest tubes, he staggered over the lowered side rail amid the mechanical belling of the monitors.

Dizziness struck hard as a physical blow. He fell to one knee as vertigo buffeted him into blindness. The sensation of spinning nauseated him. He clawed to rise, no longer certain which direction was up. Sounds came to him smothered, indecipherable from sight and touch. He tried to speak, but he couldn't hear his own voice. The darkness that trapped him seemed tainted with menace. He struggled against it as his limbs went cold and all strength left him. He toppled into oblivion.

CHAPTER 3

Fever Dreams

The horror of Carrigan's memories haunted him into his dreams, and unconsciousness dragged them beyond his ability to control. For two days and nights he slept beneath a grim parade of murder that seemed endless. A spectator in his own past, he watched his fingers strangle. Knives and stilettos, crusted with strangers' blood, jabbed into vitals with a doctor's knowledge of anatomy. Pistols, rifles, and shotguns claimed their share of lives; and even ordinary objects seemed to become weapons in his hands. Mired in emotionless killings, Carrigan watched, aching with revulsion, as he slaughtered with a beer mug, an ax, and a car; and he broke a man's neck with a well-aimed punch and a fire door. At least two of his victims were women.

Between remembered acts of brutality, Carrigan encountered a sea of platitudes, voices insisting, "You'll be all right," until the familiarity of the words took all sincerity from them and they became as constant and meaningless as the blips of the cardiac monitor. Snatches of conversation spiraled through as well. "... chest tubes out ... cardiothoracic signed off the case ... need to identify ... next of kin ... hospital lawyer says ... lower the dose of morphine ..."

50

Carrigan lost count of his murders during the second day. On the morning of the third day, a different, more lucid recollection assailed him. Where the others had appeared as flashes of action devoid of motive, setting, or passion, this one contained all the elements the others lacked. He found himself chatting with a pair of flat-faced, bearded men in a garishly comfortable room. Trophy racks lined stain-proofed walls; the antique wood supported weapons that ranged from fossilized clubs to early matchlock rifles to machine pistols and flechette-firing shotguns with laser sights to a failed prototype crew-served antitank maser without its tesla-coil power pack. This time, Carrigan believed, he championed the cause of a group; but its nature and bent still eluded him. He knew, without right to question, it had taken an inordinate amount of time to infiltrate and to gain the trust of the men beside him, and the smallest error would cost him and others their lives. Even devoid of details, the knowledge soothed; it introduced doubt, allowed Carrigan to believe he might be some sort of spy rather than a wanton killer.

A disturbance outside the room of his memory interrupted their talk. A moment later, the door swung open; and three men entered, pinning a struggling Katry between them. "Do you know this woman?" one of her captors asked.

Carrigan stared. Sudden concern sapped him of strength, and it took all his training and an effort of will not to break his cover. Pleased by the realization of emotion, the dreamer tried to elicit the particulars of its cause. The depth of his devotion to Katry was obvious, but it took time for Carrigan to recognize the source of his urgency. Somehow, he realized that to admit kinship with Katry would destroy the mission and lose the cause he fought to win. To deny it would condemn Katry to death.

Painfully, Carrigan hid his thoughts behind a mask of indifference, aware hesitation would doom him as completely as a confession. *An instant to decide, a lifetime to suffer the consequences.* The sleeper ground his fingernails into his palms, wishing he had access to the same information he had had at his disposal the last time he lived this experience. The life of a loved one must take precedence over any cause, but the Carrigan of memory did not see things the same way. "Never seen her before in my life," he said in a perfect simulation of sincerity, the words and their coldness a death sentence and the last ever spoken to the woman he had loved.

Terror mobilized Carrigan, and he attempted to amend the memory the way a light sleeper will rework the ending of a nightmare. "Katry, no! I take it back!" He tried to picture himself grabbing her hand, fighting through the five strangers and the defenses that surrounded the home of a man who used an arsenal to decorate his living room. The image evaded him. He chased it, half-rising in the hospital bed, but was slammed back by the restraints that wrapped his wrists again.

A young nurse back-stepped with a gasp, apparently startled by his sudden movement. "You're all right. Everything's okay." Her tone suggested she spoke the words as much to calm herself as him.

The nurse snatched the call button and pressed for help. Carrigan heard a musical note, followed by a raucous sound at the nursing station. A speaker clicked, and a voice came over the room intercom. "What can I do for you, Jody?"

"Bed three's awake. Didn't Walker and Nicholson say they wanted to be called as soon as he woke up?"

"Dr. J and the chief?" The other voice sounded confused. "Neither one's on ICU service."

Carrigan concentrated on the conversation to avoid thinking about rising claustrophobia inspired by the restraints.

"I know," Jody replied. "But they're real interested in the case. They're the ones who coded him when he came in."

"I'll page them." The woman at the desk clipped off her last word with a snap of a lever, and the intercom went silent.

Jody turned her attention to Carrigan. "What can I do to make you more comfortable? Anything you want to know?"

Still not ready to reveal his understanding, Carrigan made no response other than to tug at the restraints.

Catching the hint, Jody frowned. "Oh, no. Those don't come off until I'm sure you understand me."

Carrigan pulled a few more times, then let his hands sink to the sheets. He tried to delude himself that he kept his hands near the side rails out of comfort rather than necessity.

Gently, Jody slid a plastic-coated thermometer beneath Carrigan's tongue. Shortly, a high-pitched beep sounded, and she removed it. She scribbled numbers on the bedside clipboard, peered at the overhead monitors and wrote some more.

Within a few minutes, Jason Walker and Shawna Nicholson hurried into Carrigan's room, accompanied by an unidentified physician and a trio of nurses, one of whom was male. Walker wore a dress shirt and trousers beneath his white coat, his tie tucked into a buttonhole. Nicholson leaned over the bed, and Carrigan caught a glimpse of cleavage despite the conservative cut of her dress. Under ordinary circumstances it might have pleased him, but the memory of his nightmare remained strong within him.

"Feeling better today?" Nicholson asked.

Recalling she had taken off his restraints before, Carrigan yanked at the ties.

Nicholson disregarded his efforts. "We want to help you. People are worried about you. Tell me your name."

Carrigan continued his charade.

Behind Nicholson, the nurses and doctors exchanged silent glances. Nicholson's tone changed abruptly. "Listen, buddy. I don't know what kind of game you're playing. We're trying to help, but you're fighting us every step of the way. Now for the last few days you've been shouting things. In English. I know you can talk, and I know you speak the language."

Horror stole over Carrigan as he wondered how many murders he had confessed to in his sleep. He swept a glance around the room, briefly meeting every stare. Nicholson's straightforward manner impressed him. *She cut through the crap while everyone else tried to placate me. I'm caught, and I've got no choice anymore but to trust someone.*

"All right," he said, his voice dry and more hoarse than he expected. "I'll talk to you. Alone."

No one moved. Turning, Nicholson waved the others from the room, and they obeyed with obvious reluctance.

Carrigan waited until the door closed behind

them, then strained for the sound of someone activating the intercom. Hearing nothing unusual, he met Nicholson's gaze. "What did I say in my sleep?"

Nicholson licked her lips, hiding a smile. "Nothing. I lied. I was certain you could speak."

"You bitch!" Carrigan grinned despite his annoyance, amazed he had fallen for such a shallow and transparent trick. "Tough, commanding, and sneaky. I like that in a woman."

"Damned with faint praise," Nicholson shot back. "Now, tell me your name."

Recalling the writing on the clipboard. Carrigan feigned knowledge. "John Doe," he said with conviction.

"Ha, ha, very funny." Nicholson's manner changed, obviously unamused. "Your real name?"

"John Doe," Carrigan repeated. Having committed himself to the lie, he tried to justify it. "Why do you find that so hard to believe? From what I hear, they call your friend Jaywalker."

"Jason Walker," Nicholson corrected. "Some of the staff call him Dr. J because he's a doctor and from Philadelphia."

The connection escaped Carrigan.

Apparently noticing his confusion, Nicholson explained. "You know, after the Philadelphia basketball player, Dr. J."

Though still bewildered, Carrigan played along. "Uh-huh."

"Enough about Dr. Walker. Could you at least tell me if you have any allergies, chronic illnesses, or conditions. Any drugs taken on a routine basis?"

"None that I know of," Carrigan answered truthfully.

Nicholson seemed relieved, and Carrigan guessed she appreciated the directness of his answer rather than its content. "Age?"

From the blurred glimpse of his image in the IV pole, Carrigan suspected late 20s, but he had no way to know for certain. "How old are you?"

Nicholson picked up the pen from the clipboard and tapped it impatiently on the pages. "My personal life is none of your business."

Carrigan raised his eyebrows to imply the same statement worked for him as well. "You tell me, and I'll tell you."

At an impasse, Nicholson sighed. "Thirty."

"What a coincidence. I'm thirty, too." Recognizing the pun, he clarified. "That's thirty, also, not thirty-two."

"Birth date?"

Trapped, Carrigan bluffed. "Tomorrow."

Nicholson read him easily. "Tell me the date, including year of birth."

Annoyed by his inability to field even simple questions, Carrigan grumbled. "Tomorrow's date and the year appropriate to make me thirty."

Nicholson slammed down the pen. "Why are you being so goddamned hostile!" Anger added color to her cheeks, and the impatience in her voice made it sound even more like Katry's.

Carrigan chewed at his lip, saying nothing.

Nicholson whirled to leave.

"Wait!" he called.

Nicholson turned.

"Could you take these off?" Carrigan rolled his eyes to the restraints. "Please."

"You've got to be kidding. I got hell when you

ripped out the first set of chest tubes, not to mention everything else."

Fear stripped Carrigan of his confidence. Despite attempts to prevent it, he began to tremble, and sweat beaded his forehead. To his surprise, the first stirrings of abject panic actually drove tears to his eyes.

Apparently noticing his distress, Nicholson returned to the bedside. "Talk to me," she said. "Give me a reason to trust you."

Carrigan pacified himself with the silent assurance he could talk Nicholson into removing the restraints. "All right. But you have to promise you won't tell anyone else."

Nicholson shook her head. "When I was a third year medical student working in the psychiatric ward, a young man with a psychotic depression was admitted. He shuffled around the halls and wouldn't talk to anyone. Then, one day, he took me aside claiming he wanted to tell me something and made me promise not to reveal his words to anyone else." Nicholson fidgeted with the clipboard. "I was so excited and impressed that this patient chose to speak with me, I made that promise. Do you know what he said to me?"

Carrigan shook his head.

"He said, 'Dr. Nicholson, I'm going to kill myself.' Then he walked away, aware I couldn't put him on suicide precautions or ask the advice of an attending without violating his confidence."

"What did you do?" Carrigan asked, genuinely interested.

Nicholson tapped the pen on the table as she spoke. "I watched him like a hawk. I was afraid to go home at night; and when I did, I couldn't sleep.

I made the nurses keep close tabs on him without explaining why. Luckily, he never acted on his threat." She regarded Carrigan directly. "Despite what I did to get you to talk, I'm honest. Patient confidentiality is important to me, but my Hippocratic oath is equally so."

Carrigan lowered his eyes. He had no choice but to rely on his instincts, and they told him to trust Nicholson. "So nothing I tell you can remain confidential?"

"Everything you tell me remains confidential," she clarified. "Nothing will leave the hospital. But if you give me a piece of information I think the other members of the health care team need to know in order to help you, I have to put it in your chart. Only the doctors, nurses, and technicians working with you have access to my notes. Anything else you tell me is between the two of us. Will that do?"

Carrigan considered.

"I suspect that's the best deal you'll get."

If nothing else, I think Nicholson will be honest. "Deal," Carrigan agreed.

Nicholson wound the pen between her fingers with a soft noise of relief. "Now will you tell me your name?"

Carrigan cleared his throat, not because he felt the need, but for the moment of delay. "I would, but I don't know it." Carrigan expected anxiety to accompany his confession, but he actually felt more comfortable sharing the secret.

Nicholson blinked through a thoughtful hush. "No idea at all?"

Carrigan did not mention his only lead. A woman with Katry's voice calling him by the name she had used might drive him deeper into memories he had no further interest in exploring. He knew now he did not ever want to discover who and what he had once been. He moved, and the touch of the restraints against his skin made him feel like a cornered animal. "Doctor, I'm deathly claustrophobic. If I swear not to attack anyone or break equipment, will you let me free?"

Nicholson winced empathetically. "Sure." Leaning over, she untied the restraints without extracting the actual promise.

Carrigan unraveled the fabric from his wrists, immediately far more at ease.

Nicholson pressed. "Can you remember anything? A friend's name? The date? How you got here? The president of the United States?"

"Which united states?"

"I'll take that as a 'no.' Do you know where you are?"

Carrigan recalled Nicholson's earlier explanation. "Liberty Hospital."

"That's a start."

"Wherever that is."

"Liberty, Iowa," Nicholson clarified. "Does that help?"

"Not much," Carrigan muttered.

Nicholson patted his hand reassuringly. "Don't worry about it. Sometimes a bad accident can do that to people, especially when it involves a head injury. It'll come back to you. In the meantime, we're all here to help you. With your permission, we'd like to release some information to the press and see if your family comes forward. They're probably worried to death."

"Press?" Carrigan did not like the sound of her

suggestion, and the word carried no meaning for him.

Nicholson wiggled her fingers as if to jog his memory. "The media. You know, television, newspapers."

The suggestion ground terror through Carrigan. "No!"

"No?" Obviously confused, Nicholson prodded. "Don't you want to know who you are?"

"No," Carrigan said, intending the word to address Nicholson's question as well as reinforce his stand.

Nicholson tucked a strand of hair behind her ear. "That's ridiculous. Why not?"

Frightened by the implications of his thoughts, Carrigan grew sullen. "Do I have to have a reason?"

"No, but . . ." Nicholson waved her hand as if to imply her point was so obvious as to defy words. "I just can't imagine anyone not wanting to know who he is. Aren't you the least bit curious? What do you want us to do, call you 'bed three' the rest of your life?"

Unwilling to admit his fear, Carrigan shrugged. "John will do. And if you suddenly woke up knowing only that you'd been involved in some sort of explosion and you tried to strangle a doctor, would you want to know who you were?"

"John, people do strange things when they're scared and confused. I once got cussed out by an eight-year-old girl recovering from insulin shock. You're just stronger than most of the patients who try to kill their doctors. It's not like you succeeded or anything. Dr. Walker's fine. He forgives you."

Carrigan picked at a suture on his arm, saying nothing.

"Don't do that." Nicholson caught his wrist to stop him. "Are you afraid you're some wanted felon?"

Carrigan looked up quickly, her question closer to the truth than he liked.

"Would it help if I told you you're not?"

"Only if you can convince me."

Nicholson set Carrigan's hand on the sheet. "When you fell unconscious, our need to know your identity took precedence over confidentiality. The police took fingerprints."

Carrigan continued to stare, feeling violated though not certain of the implications. "And?"

Nicholson rattled off the list. "Nothing. You're not a convicted criminal. You've never served in the military or obtained security clearance for a job." She considered. "Oh, and you apparently didn't take the requisite second grade trip to FBI headquarters."

Carrigan greeted her revelation with mixed feelings. *Not a convicted crook, a cop, a spy, or a soldier.* Sudden realization clamped down his throat until he could no longer speak. *No denying it any longer. If I'm not with the law, I've got to be against it, and a murderer never caught is the only option left.*

This time, Nicholson seemed oblivious to Carrigan's trepidations. "Somewhere there's a family out looking for you. Parents and siblings. A wife and children."

Carrigan withdrew, converting his fear into anger. Even without the restraints, he still felt trapped. "I'm not married."

"How do you know?"

"I just know, all right!" Carrigan fought tears, and his weakness seared rage through him. "I think we've talked enough for now. Please leave me alone." He turned away, not wanting Nicholson to notice his lapse.

For several seconds, Nicholson hovered silently. She patted his shoulder gently. "You get some sleep. We'll finish this later." She added carefully, "John, we can't do anything else without your consent. We'll get through this." She turned amid the rustle of fabric.

Carrigan listened to her footfalls on the tile, followed by the closing click of the door. Control lost, he sobbed into the pillow, certain this was his first cry in an immeasurably long time.

Carrigan did not recall drifting off to sleep; but, when a nurse's voice cut through his room, he nearly jumped out of the bed. His sudden stiffening jerked the skin of his incisions, and he loosed an involuntary gasp of pain.

"Oh, God, I'm sorry." A middle-aged woman in the accustomed, ICU scrub suit set a tray on the narrow table and approached Carrigan's bedside. "Are you all right?"

Carrigan waited until his discomfort faded to a tolerable level. "I'm fine. You just startled me." He looked at the tray and its assortment of maroon plastic cups and bowls. "What's this?"

"Food." The nurse swept Carrigan's wrist into her hand and checked his pulse against the monitor. "Your doctors decided to let you eat today. Don't get too excited. It's just clear liquids." She released his arm and met his gaze with long-lashed, gray eyes. "I really am sorry I scared you."

"No problem." Carrigan tried to identify the mingled smells arising from the tray. His stomach felt pinched and empty. Uncertain where to start, he simply stared.

"Let me help you." The nurse reached across Carrigan and peeled white plastic caps from two cups and a bowl. "Coffee. Tea. Chicken broth . . ."

All three solutions shared an unappetizing, gray-brown color. The nurse revealed one other object, a smoothly cut, translucent cube the brilliant green of an infant's toy. *What the hell is that?*

Apparently noticing Carrigan's hesitation, the nurse identified it. "Lime Jell-O. Doesn't look much like food, does it?" she added apologetically.

"Right now, anything will do." Even this meager fare reminded Carrigan he had not eaten in days. Finding a napkin, he unrolled it to reveal packets of salt and sugar and a matched set of silverware: a fork, butter knife, and spoon. Seizing the spoon, he delved into the broth. It tasted bland. *Better than nothing, I guess.*

The nurse pulled up a chair and sat with Carrigan while he ate. "You'll be leaving us pretty soon."

"Leaving?" Having finally relaxed to the routine of the hospital, the thought of going elsewhere re-awakened Carrigan's fears.

"You're not sick enough for intensive care anymore," she clarified. "They're sending you downstairs to the regular medical ward."

Carrigan took a sip of coffee. It tasted bitter enough to raise the possibility of poison, so he shoved it aside. "What's the difference between up here and down there?" The tea suited him better.

Retrieving the packet of sugar, he dropped it into the liquid, then raised the cup to drink.

The nurse caught his hand. "What are you doing?"

Carrigan glanced into his tea at the half-submerged paper square. "I just wanted the extra calories. Did I use too much?"

She pried the cup from his fingers and stared inside. "You forgot to open the packet. You can't drink this." Taking his fork, she retrieved the soggy paper with the tines. It tore, spilling sugar into the tea. Replacing the mug on the tray, she shook the tattered paper into the garbage can and loosed a friendly laugh. "Why did you do that?"

Carrigan did not have a ready answer. "I don't know. I just expected it to dissolve or something."

She continued to smile. "Well, for future reference, you have to open it and pour the sugar out. Want me to get you another cup?"

Carrigan examined the tea. Most of the sugar had settled to the bottom, and only a few shreds of paper floated on the surface. "Don't bother." He downed the tea, the final swallow so sweet it set his teeth on edge. "The difference between here and the medical ward?" he reminded.

"You'll still get quality nursing care, just a little less personalized. We'll take you off the monitors." She indicated the circular EKG stickers on his chest. "And you'll have a new doctor."

I finally found someone to trust, and I won't lose her. Carrigan slammed the mug down on his tray so hard the silverware jumped.

The nurse backed her chair away defensively. "Not new, exactly. Dr. Walker's down on the ward, and I think he's planning to take your case."

"I don't want Dr. Walker."

"We have other residents." The nurse rose. Carrigan's sudden mood change apparently made her uneasy, and she no longer seemed interested in chatting.

Carrigan tried to soften his tone. "What about Dr. Nicholson?"

"She's the chief. She doesn't usually take patients." She studied Carrigan in the examination light. "Let me find her and let her talk to you."

Carrigan nodded agreement, and the nurse left his room faster than decorum demanded. He stared at the green lump of Jell-O, its surface dancing with every movement of the tray. Since the nurse had awakened him, his mind seemed clearer, though his past still mercifully eluded him. He felt fairly certain the memory that had made him believe he was "on the run" was distant, but he could not shake the urge to flee and dodge, to arm himself, to watch his tongue and whom he chose to trust. Nicholson had inspired a comfort no one else came near to matching. *If not for her, I'd bolt from here in a second. I'd rather take my chances alone than rely on someone whose judgment I question.*

Carrigan's gaze fell on the knife. Though dull, it would serve better than no weapon at all. He palmed it. Then, checking to make certain no one was watching through the glass windows, he scratched the blade along the cinder block wall. The edge carved paint from the surface, a poor substitute for a diamond hone.

The sound of approaching footsteps warned Carrigan to cease his activity. He slipped the knife beneath the sheets as the nurse reentered his room. "Dr. Nicholson's with an emergency. She said to move you downstairs and she'll meet you there when she's free."

Guilty for his surliness, Carrigan swatted the Jell-O with his spoon. "Is this stuff really edible?" he asked conversationally, trying to make amends.

The nurse grinned. "You wanted calories. Try it. It can't taste any worse than that little bit of tea you drank with your sugar."

Carrigan tasted a spoonful and found its fruitlike flavor and fluid texture more pleasant than he expected. From the doorway, the nurse watched him finish the Jell-O, then entered and took his tray. Carrigan held his breath, waiting for her to notice the missing utensil; but, if she did, she gave no sign.

A moment later, two grizzled men arrived, each wearing an overlarge, blue shirt with a breast patch identifying him as a hospital volunteer. "We're supposed to take you downstairs, sir," the taller one told Carrigan.

The nurse skittered back into Carrigan's room with a floppy book of bound papers. She set it on the sheets covering Carrigan's knees. Though the lettering was upside down from his position, he could make out the name "John Doe" in black magic marker and, beneath it, a sticker reading "Volume 1 of 1."

The men rolled the table out from in front of Carrigan, stepped to either side of his bed, and locked the side rails into the up position. The nurse handed him the lightweight, tan pants, with his tracking device and some odd-looking bills still tucked into its pockets. The doctors had replaced the catheter in his bladder after he lost consciousness on the floor. They had left the watch fastened to his left wrist and inserted a new IV catheter in his right arm. The nurse snapped off the cardiac monitor and unclipped the lead snaps from his EKG pads.

One of the volunteers transferred Carrigan's IV fluid bag from an overhead rack to the pole attached to the bed. "Hands and feet inside," he instructed in a routine monotone. "Let's go."

Carrigan grasped the half-sharpened knife beneath the sheets to keep it from sliding free during transport. His other arm encircled his belongings as he prepared for the ride.

A short roll in silence brought Carrigan and the volunteers to the elevators. The doors lurched apart to reveal dented, yellow walls and a ring of chrome handrails. To Carrigan, the opening appeared far too small. He watched in horror as one of the men pressed a button to hold the device and the other wheeled his bed inside.

Carrigan shot upright. His shoulder smacked the IV pole, and it teetered dangerously. Before he could launch a protest, the door slid closed, trapping him into an enclosed space with the volunteers.

"You okay, young fella?" one of the men pushed on Carrigan's woodenly stiff shoulders, his efforts less noticeable than the sough of movement and the feeling of gently falling.

Carrigan's heart slammed in his chest, and he concentrated on the changing display of numbers with fanatical intensity. 6 ... 5 ... 4 ... 3 ... 2. A bell rang, and the doors rumbled open on a hallway. The volunteers wheeled him free. Relieved, Carrigan sank back to the bed. Unintended threat entered his tone. "Don't ever, *ever*, put me on one of those things again."

The men exchanged glances. "I'm sorry," the shorter one said. The apology sounded genuine. "We had no idea you didn't like elevators. I'll let your nurses know."

Carrigan made no reply, trying to produce saliva in a mouth gone uncomfortably dry.

The volunteers rolled Carrigan through the corridor, around a corner, past a nurses' station, and into a room numbered 230. On the ward, visitors and personnel wore street clothes, aside from a preponderance of starched, white pants and jackets among the latter. The room appeared much like the one in the ICU except for the addition of a bedside chest of drawers and padded chairs in two of the corners. Instead of the cardiac monitor over the head, a television jutted from the ceiling at the foot end of the bed.

A woman dressed in a sweater, crisp white slacks, and spotless white shoes followed the volunteers into Carrigan's room. A red stethoscope rested across her shoulders, a patient identification band and a hemostat dangling from the earpieces. "Welcome to 2 West, John. My name is Karen, and I'll be your nurse until 3:00 this afternoon. My friends upstairs said you might want a sponge bath and a chance to get out of bed."

Carrigan raked singed hair from his forehead. "A shower and scissors would be nice."

She nodded. "I can set you up with the barber later today. No showers until your sutures come out."

The volunteers edged toward the door. "Anything else you need?"

Karen waved them off without looking.

"Just want to tell you young John, here, doesn't

care for elevators." The men exited, closing the door behind them.

Karen raised her brows in question.

The thought of making his fears public bothered Carrigan, but it seemed preferable to another caging in that airless death trap the volunteers called an elevator. "Claustrophobia," he explained simply, suspecting Nicholson had already written the diagnosis on his chart. He steered the conversation to more mundane matters. "Why do the sutures have to come out before I take a shower?"

"Water's not good for them." She did not offer a better reason. "Besides, you may find it difficult to stand long enough to take a shower. They said you passed out upstairs."

Briefly, Carrigan wondered why the surgeons had not closed his incisions with some sort of waterproof adhesive or plastic staples. He stretched his limbs, aware they seemed far stronger than they had during his attempt to escape. "I'm fine. Let's take a walk."

Karen shook back a head full of dark curls. "One step at a time. Try standing. If you do all right, I'll ask Dr. Walker if we can take out the Foley." She indicated the bag half filled with pink-tinged urine. "Then, I'll give you a wheelchair tour of the unit."

Without awaiting further encouragement, Carrigan thrust aside the sheets and stood, barefoot and naked, on the cold tile of the floor. His movement pulled at the incisions, but he did not find the accompanying pain significant enough for concern. Light-headedness churned down on him. A mixed pattern of spots unswirled his vision, then gradually resolved until he felt as normal standing as lying down. "Now, about that tour . . ."

Karen laughed. Opening the bottom drawer of the chest, she handed him a flimsy, feminine garment and a blue and white striped bathrobe. "Put these on. I'll talk to Dr. Walker and get someone to watch the rest of my patients. If you run into trouble dressing, hit the call button." She indicated a device beside the bed controls. Turning, she left Carrigan alone.

Carrigan dressed swiftly, using the snaps on the gown to maneuver the sleeve over his IV line. He placed the knife and tracking device in the robe pockets, arranging them unobtrusively. Neatly folding his pants, he tucked them into the top drawer beside a wrapped bar of soap and a fuzzy, white towel. A concrete window ledge attracted his attention, and he suspected it would prove better for blade-sharpening than the painted cinder block of the ICU walls.

Karen returned. "Foley comes out, and we're on our way." She gestured for him to lie down.

Carrigan complied.

Using a syringe to remove air from the internal balloon, she whisked the catheter free and tossed it into the garbage. "You may have some bleeding and pain the next few days."

Carrigan stood, certain he had inflicted the trauma on himself when he ripped out the previous catheter. He watched as Karen transferred his IV bag from the bedside to a portable pole.

"I've got a wheelchair for you outside."

"I don't need it," Carrigan insisted. The tightness of the sutures made him walk slightly hunched. The pain seemed tolerable, and he felt sound.

"We'll bring it just in case." Karen used the tone of one who knows better but has grown accustomed to protestations. They emerged into the hallway, Carrigan pushing the pole before him and Karen rolling the wheelchair at his side. "Where to?"

Tired of stale air and buildings, Carrigan pointed away from the ward. "Outside. Or at least near a big window."

They passed the nurses' station, amid stares and encouraging smiles. "Main entry, then. Oh, but we'll have to take an elevator down a flight."

The idea spoiled Carrigan's mood. "No stairs?"

"Not that'll accommodate a wheelchair and an IV pole."

They exited 2 West and came upon a fire door directly across the corridor. "I'll handle the pole, and I already told you I don't need the chair."

Karen shook her head. "I don't think I want you trying those steps. They're cement. If you fall, you're my responsibility."

Afraid to lose his chance for fresh air, Carrigan pressed the bar that opened the door. "Tell them you couldn't stop me." Quickly, he shoved the panel open, surprised by its weight, and, hefting the metal pole, started down the concrete steps.

"Hey!" Abandoning the chair, Karen chased Carrigan. "John, come on. Don't play around."

Carrigan reached the first floor amid her fading objections. Once there, she pulled the door open and ushered him through it. "I've never seen anyone move around this soon after surgery." She exited behind him and let the door swing shut. "Where do you get your endurance?"

"Endurance School." The memories that accompanied Carrigan's quip took all humor from it. He recalled treading frigid, polluted waters with nothing but a bathing suit and his wits to find his way home. "Where's the entrance?"

Karen pointed to the right, and they continued their walk. Shortly, the acrid odor of smoke pinched Carrigan's nostrils. He stopped, alarmed. "Something's burning."

Karen ushered him on. "There's a smoking area near the entrance. You a smoker, John?"

Smoker? Carrigan shook his head; the word carried no meaning for him.

Taking his gesture as a negative answer, Karen said, "Good. Dirty habit. I would have guessed you did, though."

"Why's that? I look like the dirty habit type?" As Carrigan and his escort turned a corner, they emerged into a waiting area filled with stuffed chairs connected in rows. Beyond them, ceiling to floor glass windows framed a huge, doorless exit that supplied Carrigan with a glimpse of the outside. Gray-white haze settled over the entryway where several of the milling people clutched or puffed on cigarettes. Carrigan stared, wondering why anyone would want to suck burning gases into his lungs.

"No offense. It just seems like the cute guys always smoke, drink, take drugs, or beat their girl-friends." Karen laughed. "I think it's God's way of balancing things for the plain ones."

Pleased to discover that at least one woman found his appearance appealing, Carrigan momentarily forgot he had a habit dirtier than any of the ones she had mentioned. Then they reached the entryway, and the wonders of the outdoors usurped other thoughts. Everything looked so exciting, Carrigan did not know where to stare first. "What's that?" He pointed out a building near the hospital, its architecture strikingly plain and open and its five levels surprisingly low to the ground compared to his expectations.

"Parking garage for staff and visitor cars. There's another over there." She indicated a site to the right of the first.

Carrigan turned to follow her gesture, but the vastness of the area beyond the macadam driveway and highway arrested his attention. A field with neat rows of plants stretched as far as Carrigan could see. A distant blur of trees rose to the sky. The spacious serenity promised by the scene sent a shiver of excitement through Carrigan. Unable to contain his awe, he stared. "What's that?"

Karen followed his gaze, squinting as if to discern a speck amid the wonders that attracted Carrigan. "What's what?"

"That whole thing." Carrigan made a broad wave, encompassing all the area across the road. "The open space with the green things."

Karen gave him the same incredulous look as the nurse who had fished the paper from his tea. "Some farmer's cornfield."

Carrigan resisted the urge to insist corn came in cans, not fields, struck by the implications of her words. "You mean, some guy owns that land? Owns it? The way I own this watch." He shook his wrist. "And the hospital owns this stupid-looking gown." He pulled at the fabric. "And you own . . ." He turned to meet Karen's quizzical expression and broke off, suddenly defensive.

"Of course," she said. "Why? You want to buy it?"

You mean I could buy it? Carrigan kept this

thought to himself. He covered neatly, with the same false composure as an overzealous cat who, after rolling off a wall, pretends it fell on purpose. "Yeah. Get me a box, and I'll take it back to the ward." Resisting the almost overpowering urge to further study the land, he spun toward the waiting room. The hospital seemed cramped, the air choked with smoke and dust. "I'm tired," he lied. "I'm ready to go to my room."

"I'm not surprised." Karen herded Carrigan through the crowd. "I think we've done enough walking for the moment." Her tone turned wry. "Never seen a cornfield before, huh, John. Are you a city kid?"

Carrigan shrugged, having neither the knowledge nor inclination to answer her question. His mind filled with the image of tall, streamlined dwellings hitched together like train cars, a dark skyline of towers closing in on rushing passersby. Overhead walkways capped the horizon, and subways shook the sidewalks until the very earth seemed ready to vanish beneath his feet. Sleek automobiles threaded between the buildings, claiming the final empty spaces. Carrigan banished the memory, concentrating instead on a leisurely stroll between open rows of growing corn. The vision soothed him, and Carrigan/John Doe guessed he was going to like Liberty, Iowa. A lot.

CHAPTER 4

Secondary Gain

By the time Chief Medical Resident Shawna Nicholson, arrived in Carrigan's room, he had already bathed, gotten his hair washed and cut, and suffered through two plotless soap operas. The latter paraded affairs and paternity suits like summer fashions, reminding Carrigan he had not been with a woman in a long time, a situation unlikely to change soon. He had watched the news with trepidation, learning more than he wanted to know about pesticide and herbicide runoff in well water. The mentioned date, Saturday, May 4, 1985, confirmed the newspapers he had nervously scanned over the past few days. Uncovering no stories of murder in Iowa did not appease his conscience. The nameless felon whose killing sprees frightened him lounged in a sickbed in Liberty Hospital.

When Nicholson entered his room, Carrigan dialed off the television sound, allowing its picture to provide a flickering background to their conversation. Inexplicably, the format of the news had seemed no more familiar than its content; and Carrigan could not shake the ludicrous belief that the copy of *The Des Moines Register* a nurse had given him was the first newspaper he had ever seen. One thing seemed certain. Whether reading or listening, the news terrified him; and avoiding it seemed the best policy until his mental status stabilized.

Nicholson dragged a chair to Carrigan's bedside. "So, I see you got the dental room. Two-thirty. Tooth hurty. Get it?"

Carrigan studied Nicholson, relieved to find a new focus for his attention. She wore corduroy dress pants and a rumpled, button-down blouse. A partially washed-out blood spot discolored the fabric in a circle above her left breast. Her red-brown hair looked as if she had not run a comb through it since the morning. Oddly, Carrigan found her disheveled appearance more attractive. "I get the joke. It's just not funny. Or original."

"Sorry. I'm a doctor, not a comedienne." She glanced at the television screen where a newscaster repeatedly shoved a microphone in the faces of men leading horses around a paddock. "The nurses said you wanted to see me. I apologize for taking so long. I got tied up with an emergency in ICU. In fact, the patient who took your bed."

"What's he got?" Carrigan asked, more out of politeness than interest.

"She," Nicholson corrected. "And I can't tell you. That would violate patient confidentiality."

"Of course." Nicholson's answer pleased Carrigan and made him even more comfortable with his decision to trust her.

"What can I do for you, John?"

Carrigan staunched the impulse to make a suggestive comment. "I understand you're giving me away to another doctor."

"Giving you away?" Nicholson raised her brows questioningly. "I've got news for you, John. I've never been in charge of your case. Upstairs, you were a surgery and TCV patient. Dr. Walker and I just helped out of interest."

"TCV?"

"Thoracic cardiovascular surgery."

"Sorry I asked." Carrigan glanced up to a screen filled with names of horses, owners, and jockeys. "And down here? Who owns me?"

Nicholson ignored his obvious sarcasm. "You're Dr. Walker's patient."

"I don't want to be Dr. Walker's patient."

Nicholson crossed her legs, revealing a pair of boldly patterned, argyle socks. "Dr. Walker happens to be one of the best residents we have. He saved your life, you know."

"I've heard that." Carrigan remained relentless. "And I'm not questioning his skills. I just don't trust him."

"I don't see the difference." From the tone of Nicholson's voice, Carrigan could tell she was trying to be diplomatic despite an arduous day and whatever personal matter still troubled her.

"First, he's scared of me."

"He'll get over that."

"Second . . ." Carrigan found the concept difficult to frame, and frustration made him curt. "Doctor, I haven't a frog's idea what makes me believe in one person and not another. The fact is, besides you, there's no one in this place I trust."

Despite the seriousness of the topic, Nicholson chuckled. "A frog's idea? Where did you come up with that?"

Carrigan shrugged, annoyed by Nicholson's mirth. "Your guess." Thinking the expression completed, he wondered why Nicholson hesitated as if to let him finish.

When Nicholson spoke, she restored the sense of earnest consideration to the conversation. "Why me?"

"I don't know." Carrigan paused thoughtfully. "Okay, I can guess. I like the way you take control, even in a situation that involves a patient you claim isn't yours. When I asked you to keep our conversation secret, a lot of people would have agreed just to get me to talk, then violated my confidence at the first opportunity. Hell, if they did it careful, I wouldn't ever find out. You wouldn't promise. You told it straight." He added gently, "And that depressed patient you mentioned, the one who said he'd kill himself."

Nicholson nodded encouragingly.

"I'm willing to guess most doctors would have put him on suicide precautions. For his own good, they'd claim."

Nicholson hitched her chair closer. "Sure. And they'd probably be right. If he had committed suicide, I'd be responsible, legally and emotionally."

Carrigan seized on Nicholson's point. "But, right now, I need a doctor whose word is more important than concern for my welfare. I can look after myself. What I need is a confidante."

Nicholson shifted, apparently distressed by his words. "I'm not paid to listen." She went suddenly pensive, as if recognizing her words as an opening to some matter on hold. "But I know a man who is, and I asked him to wait outside." She rose. "I think it's time you met him." Trotting eagerly to the door, she nudged it open and yelled into the hallway. "Harry, come here."

Carrigan ran a hand through his straight, black hair, pleased by the feathery feel of its cleanness after days without a shower. He folded his legs, sitting upright on the sheets. On the screen, he watched lathered horses prancing, slight jockeys in checkered costumes perched on their backs.

Soon, Nicholson returned with a long-faced, bearded man in tow. His manner and crisply ironed suit and tie gave him the appearance of a salesman or a professional liar. Carrigan took an instant dislike to the stranger.

Nicholson introduced them. "John, this is Dr. Ferguson."

"Nice to meet you." Ferguson stuck out a hand.

Carrigan accepted the handshake without returning Ferguson's greeting.

Ferguson took Nicholson's chair while she hovered in the background. "I'm from the Department of Psychiatry. Dr. Nicholson tells me you need some help regaining your memory."

Carrigan met Ferguson's gaze solidly. "Then Dr. Nicholson misunderstood. I have no interest at all in regaining my memory."

Ferguson attempted to keep his features steady but surprise flashed across his face. His brows flicked upward. "Oh? Would you like to talk about it?"

"Not with you. No." Carrigan turned his attention back to the announcer on the television screen.

From a corner of his vision, Carrigan watched Ferguson give Nicholson an apologetic shrug.

"Thanks, Harry." Nicholson walked the psychiatrist to the door. Once he had left, she whirled, slammed the panel, and turned on Carrigan. "You're starting to annoy me, Mr . . ."

"Doe?" Carrigan supplied.

The quip eased Nicholson's tension. By the

twitching at the corners of her mouth, Carrigan could tell she was struggling to maintain her anger. "Why did you do that?"

The question was beginning to sound familiar to Carrigan. "I didn't trust him. I told you I won't talk to anyone I don't trust."

Nicholson dropped back into her chair. "Why not? What's your obsession with trust? We're all here to help you."

Absently, Carrigan massaged the knife beneath the fabric of his robe. He knew the answer but could not decide whether he was ready to share his emotions with Nicholson. Then, seeing no way around it, he sighed. "The truth?"

Nicholson placed her hands on her knees. "I think I've earned it."

"I'm scared." The confession made Carrigan angry at himself; fear was a weakness he knew he should not tolerate.

"Scared of what?" Nicholson challenged.

Of murdering more people. Of being locked in a cell so small, my own panic will kill me. Carrigan shook his head, trying not to focus too hard on either thought. He revived the picture of the cornfield. "I'm not ready to tell you yet."

"For someone who claims to trust me, you don't."

"Give me some time. In a few days, maybe I'll be ready. I can tell you one thing." Carrigan returned to the original topic. "It'll take months for me to learn to trust Dr. Walker. Years for Ferguson. So will you take my case?"

Nicholson sighed. "With conditions."

"Those are?" Carrigan reminded himself her

honesty and commanding manner were two of the qualities that had gained his trust.

"Jason remains the physician of record; I just supervise. That way, if I'm not available, you're not left without a doctor. Second, I have the right to discuss your case with any hospital personnel I trust and think can help. That includes a psychiatrist."

Carrigan considered. Though displeased, he saw no means around Nicholson's conferences. "So long as I don't have to speak with these people, it's a deal."

They both loosed sighs of relief, and the ensuing quiet swiftly grew uncomfortable.

Nicholson indicated the television picture of horses capering and snorting toward the starting gate, each accompanied by a more placid animal wearing the same stable colors. "Who do you think's going to win?"

Carrigan followed her gesture. "Win what?"

"The Kentucky Derby. Which horse do you think will win."

The screen filled with the post positions, odds, and owners of each animal. Carrigan scanned the list, selecting the only familiar name. "Spend A Buck."

Nicholson seized the call button and turned up the television sound. "What about Chief's Crown? He's the favorite."

Carrigan chewed his lip. "No. I think it'll be Spend A Buck."

"You sound pretty certain."

Carrigan rolled his gaze to Nicholson. "Certain? You're talking to a guy who can't remember his own name."

Undaunted, Nicholson pressed. "You still sound

sure. Want to put your money where your mouth
is?"

The expression was unfamiliar to Carrigan.
"My what?"

Apparently misunderstanding his consternation,
Nicholson laughed. "I guess that was a dumb thing
to say to a penniless man. Do you want to make a
bet? You're being advanced to full liquids tonight.
If I win, you owe me your ice cream. If you win,
I'll order you a full diet and make you a batch of
chocolate chip cookies. That is, if my health nut
roommate will let me."

"Deal."

Nicholson scooted her chair around to face the
television. Carrigan settled back to watch the race.

That evening, the elevator doors hissed open on
the fifth floor, and Shawna Nicholson stepped into
the single, straight hallway of her apartment building. It had been a long day, especially for a Saturday; and she harbored mixed feelings about
returning to the comforts of her two room apartment. Though her new roommate's sports para-
phernalia had replaced Randy Oakley's tasteless
bowling trophies and college awards, memories of
her live-in boyfriend still haunted every corner.

Nicholson pushed the thought aside and trotted
past rows of doors from habit. Three apartments
before the heavy door to the staircase, Nicholson
stopped. She pressed her back to the blank stretch
of wall across from apartment 512, careful to avoid
the oblong, red shape of the fire alarm. Fishing her
keys from her pocket amid a jingle of change, she
rose, selected the correct one, and jabbed it into
the keyhole. The lock gave with a click. She shoved

open the panel, freeing her key with a practiced motion.

The smells of pine cleaner, mahogany, and carpet potpourri greeted her, mingled with a greasy, less familiar aroma. Ignoring the tiny kitchen to her left, Nicholson sprawled across the striped couch in the living room. She sighed, not bothering to flick on the Oriental lamps that occupied matching end tables. The brass-framed, glass coffee table held a bowl of mixed nuts. A handmade entertainment center supported the television, its bottom shelf crammed with cassette tapes for the stereo system on the table beside it. Nicholson could not help recalling that Oakley had recorded most of the albums for her, introducing her to groups such as "Pink Floyd" and "Genesis."

Tracy Harlowe leaned over the counter that separated the kitchen from the main room and also served as a dinner table. "Got tied up with a patient?"

"Yeah. The one I can't tell you about." Nicholson looked up. Though only roommates for two weeks, she and Harlowe had grown up together in Liberty, Iowa. As children, they had lived two houses apart, and their friendship had endured years of separation by jobs, colleges, and medical school. Both girls had been raised in families of brothers, and Harlowe had never lost her interest in physical pursuits. She worked as a fitness instructor at a local health club. After a full day of teaching aerobics and besting members at racquetball, she spent her spare time playing basketball with the medical students or swimming.

Always awed by Harlowe's boundless energy, Nicholson appreciated it as an athletic vigor rather than the bouncy, annoyingly cheerful enthusiasm of a prom queen. Harlowe wore her natural blonde hair short and harbored an affinity for athletics and for healthy foods with taste rather than the stereotypical berries and twigs. Her ceaseless activity had resulted in a tight figure that goaded all the single males in the building to borrow cups of sugar or stop by with other, equally transparent alibis.

Nicholson crossed her ankles over the arm of the couch, easing off her shoes with her toes. She spoke over the thunk of their landing. "What's for dinner?"

"Burgers."

"Really?" The answer surprised Nicholson. She had grown accustomed to the lack of red meat in her diet.

Harlowe turned away amid the hiss and sputter of hot fat. "Don't get too excited. It's 85% lean and half soy."

Better than nothing. Spotting her chance, Nicholson said, "Good. Glad you're in an open-minded mood about food. I need to whip up a batch of chocolate chip cookies. I made a bet with this patient on the Kentucky Derby. I choose the favorite, right? He takes one glimpse at a field of thirteen and picks out the winner at six to one."

Harlowe made a disgusted noise and returned to the counter. "Here I am feeling sorry for you, having to work late on a Saturday. Then I find out you're watching TV with the Incredible Hunk."

Nicholson sat up. "Who said the guy's good-looking?"

"You did, back when he first came in."

Nicholson shrugged. She recalled discussing the case with Harlowe before John had sworn her to secrecy. Hospital policy allowed her to discuss cases as long as she withheld the patient's name and identifying features. "The TV was just part of his therapy. He's driving me crazy."

"What's the matter?" Harlowe teased. "You swooning every time you walk in his room, so you can't get your work done?"

The comment rankled, reminding Nicholson of her recent breakup. "Ha, ha. Very funny." Several nights of introspection had uncovered an avalanche of emotion and motivations. Raised in a Catholic family and by a series of religious, private schools, Oakley had more than the usual male hunger for a sexual relationship. He had claimed Nicholson was his first love, and his early hesitancy in bed convinced her of his inexperience. Nicholson and Oakley had shared the apartment for three months before Oakley's mother agreed to meet Nicholson. The mother had acted openly hostile. To Nicholson's surprise, Oakley never discouraged his mother, and their relationship deteriorated from that day onward. Oakley left for Berkeley promising to write; but, in the ensuing two weeks, he had not bothered to answer any of Nicholson's letters. Now, Nicholson felt certain Oakley had followed the advice of his mother to "dump this slut and find himself a nice, Catholic virgin to marry." Nicholson punched at the cushion, sending dust skittering through the artificial light from the kitchen. "I get enough grief at work."

Harlowe went silent, apparently stunned by Nicholson's hostility. For once, she seemed to lose her chronic, fun-loving composure. "Geez. Awfully sensitive, aren't we? You get a scalpel caught sideways?"

Nicholson cursed her temper. Before Oakley's departure, she would never have snapped at a facetious comment. "I'm sorry." She returned to the original subject. "The patient needs a psychiatrist, but he refuses to see anyone but me."

"Ah ha!" Harlowe tapped a spatula on the counter, then whirled to tend the burgers. "That explains the phone call from young doctor shrink. He ought to be arriving just about . . ." She paused to glance at the clock. ". . . now."

Harlowe's words reminded Nicholson she had called Tom Bercelian before leaving the hospital. Now in the last year of his psychiatry residency, Bercelian had become a close friend of Nicholson's in medical school. He lived on the third floor of her apartment building. "Oh, shit. I forgot all about him." Studying her wrinkled, blood-splashed shirt, she wondered if she had time to change.

A knock at the door banished the possibility. Harlowe reached around the kitchen entryway to open the door for Bercelian.

"Hi, Tracy." Bercelian stepped inside, peering around Harlowe as the door swung shut behind him. "Hey, Shawna." He smiled, his dark eyes piercing beneath a wild head full of curls, his expression perpetually friendly.

Nicholson waved Bercelian to the couch. "Sorry to pull you away from your wife."

Bercelian perched on the arm of the sofa. "No problem. Sue got called in to the hospital to anesthetize an appendectomy."

"Let's hope she anesthetizes the patient as well as his appendix," Nicholson said. Bercelian's information appeased her conscience. It never seemed fair to wrest a resident from his family on a night off, especially when the resident's spouse was also a resident with an even busier schedule. "I just wanted a curbside consult. Can you stay for dinner?"

Bercelian glanced over his shoulder at the kitchen. "Depends. Who did the cooking?"

"Jerk." Harlowe's face reappeared over the countertop. "I did. But they're burgers, and they're ready. I think you can handle it."

"Date nut burgers, no doubt," Bercelian whispered to Nicholson.

"I heard that!" Harlowe called back. "Now get over here and eat."

Nicholson and Bercelian obeyed, hauling stools to the counter as Harlowe presented three plates with steaming burgers on whole wheat buns accompanied by crisp carrot and celery sticks.

"Hmm," the psychiatry resident teased. "How do you get granola to stick together this well?"

Harlowe shot Bercelian a dirty look.

Smiling to himself, Bercelian added a generous helping of ketchup to his burger. "Is this personal?"

"Personal? Hell, no." To Nicholson's chagrin, her voice clearly radiated her annoyance.

Bercelian raised his burger but did not take a bite. "Hey, *you* called *me*, remember? Don't chew my head off. I just thought you might want to discuss this strange mood you've adopted since Randy left."

The implication of Bercelian's words further angered Nicholson. She flushed. "I'm not in a strange mood," she said, immediately realizing her tone betrayed her again.

Bercelian and Harlowe exchanged knowing

glances, a gesture that only served to fuel Nicholson's growing rage.

"Oh, I forgot," Harlowe said with rampant sarcasm. "My buddy Shawna always invites friends up here to attack them for asking simple questions." She snapped a carrot stick in half. "Childhood quirk."

"You never liked Randy." Nicholson glanced sharply from Harlowe to Bercelian. "Either of you."

"I'm certain he has his qualities." Bercelian spoke with infuriating calm.

"Don't give me that pseudo-psychology crap." Nicholson pursed her lips, feeling patronized.

Bercelian set aside his burger. "Are you asking for honesty? You won't like my answer."

"I can handle it." Nicholson trusted Bercelian's opinions, though she hated to admit it even to herself. It was his eye for human responses and relationships that had driven him toward psychiatry.

"In psycho-technical terminology: the guy's a dork. Aside from being spoiled and manipulative, Randy has the personality of a doormat. If he didn't look like he belonged in a Marlboro ad, women wouldn't give him the time of day."

Great, he thinks I'm shallow. Though insulted by Bercelian's implications, Nicholson did not forget she had pressed him for a response. Instead of arguing, she channeled the conversation away from her personal life. "I didn't call you up here to talk about me. I want to talk about a patient." She glanced at Harlowe, aware she should not discuss the case in front of her roommate but certain Harlowe would not repeat the details to anyone.

Catching the hint, Harlowe seized her plate.

"I've got some reading to do. If you need me, I'll be in the bedroom." She wandered into the opposite half of the two room apartment.

Nicholson knew Harlowe could still hear the conversation, but she appreciated her roommate's gesture.

Bercelian swallowed a mouthful of burger. "About this patient?"

Nicholson crunched a celery stick, not certain where to begin. "The paramedics brought him in four days ago. He had a cardiac arrest in the Emergency Room."

Bercelian stopped her. "I've heard about this guy. Amnesia. You consulted us already."

Nicholson slouched as her interest in the case dispersed her anger. "John refuses to talk with any of your people. He wants me to play psychiatrist. What's the current treatment for memory loss?"

Bercelian took another bite and waited until he finished chewing to speak. "Hypnosis. Interviews with sodium amytal. The goal is to delve into the unconscious and spark enough memories to trigger a complete recall."

"No good." Nicholson lifted her own burger. "I don't know how to do that, and he's not going to allow someone else to hypnotize him. I'm certain he'll refuse drugs, too, at least one most people refer to as 'truth serum.' "

"Can't talk him into it?"

Nicholson considered. "I doubt it."

"Then you'll just have to talk to him. A lot. See if you can't stimulate his memory that way."

A short pause ensued, the silence broken only by the sounds of chewing. Nicholson cleared her throat. "A few things bother me. John seems pretty cool about the whole thing. He claims he doesn't want his memory back, and he seems to mean it. If I couldn't remember who I was, I'd be going out of my mind."

Bercelian finished the last piece of his burger and brushed crumbs from his hands. "Actually, his behavior goes along with the diagnosis."

Surprised, Nicholson questioned. "Really?"

"Sure." Bercelian picked up a carrot stick. "Despite what you see in soap operas, amnesia's rare as hell except in alcoholics; and it doesn't inspire panic. Usually, the patient is fully aware of his memory lapse but not generally disturbed by it. Did he hit his head?"

"There're signs of head trauma." Shawna fiddled with a celery stick, too intrigued to eat.

"That's probably the instigating event, but usually there's an emotional basis as well. I'm willing to bet he's got some traumatic event in his past he doesn't want to remember, whether it's the accident or something else." Bercelian ate the carrot. "You said a few things," he reminded. "What else bothers you?"

She tried to frame the concept into words. "He doesn't seem consistent. He has no recollection of anything before waking up in the hospital, yet he remembers everything I tell him. He speaks fluently and uses some common objects, yet he seems to have no idea about other normal things. Things like sugar. Money. Cornfields."

"Inconsistent. You think he might be faking?" Bercelian guessed.

"Do you?" In classic psychiatrist style, Nicholson turned the question back to Bercelian.

"Not necessarily. Some forms of generalized amnesia fit what you described. Watch for patterns. It's all right for him to recognize an object today he didn't know yesterday. But if he starts forgetting things he already knows, I'd challenge him." Bercelian pushed his plate aside. "Any secondary gain?"

Not having practiced psychiatry since her third year of medical school, she reassured herself of the terminology. "You mean does he have any underlying reason to pretend? Trying to worry family, gain attention, that sort of thing?"

"That was the definition last time I checked."

Shawna gnawed at the celery stick as she considered. "Not that I can see."

"How about his insistence on a gorgeous, female doctor tending his every need? Do you feel like he's manipulating you?"

She blushed, embarrassed by Bercelian's compliment. "If he is, he's good. He seems genuinely frightened, and he didn't try to make me feel guilty when I took four hours to answer his summons. Besides, the guy looks like Mel Gibson with muscles. There're plenty of prettier nurses, techs, med students, and doctors on the ward, ones who won't give him the hard time I do."

"Frightened?" In true psychiatrist fashion, Tom picked up on the inconsistency in Nicholson's description. "I thought you said this guy didn't seem concerned by his memory loss."

Shawna nodded agreement. "That's the other thing I wanted to discuss. He's scared to paranoia about something. I'm pretty sure he thinks he's a criminal ever since he woke up confused and tried to strangle Jason Walker."

Tom laughed. "He tried to strangle Jason? Good for him. Jason needed a good shaking up."

Shawna stared, appalled by Bercelian's levity. Accustomed to protecting her charges, she defended Walker. "What is this, trash Jason Walker day? He's a damned fine doctor. Conscientious as all get out."

Bercelian regained his composure masterfully. "The word is compulsive. The guy's tight as a rectal thermometer. I'll bet he spends his free time reading medical journals. For God's sake, Shawna, most of the interns shed those stupid white coats in their first half year. The last time I saw a tuning fork, it was in the pocket of a medical student."

"Could we talk about John, please?" She returned to the subject, tired of Bercelian insulting Walker because of his dedication. "If he's unconsciously repressing all his bad memories, why's he so scared?"

"Does John strike you as a schizophrenic?"

She drew on the memories of her psychiatry rotation. She recalled the chilling sensation of abnormality that seemed to radiate from unmedicated schizophrenics, a phenomenon one of her fellow students had referred to as "go-away ions." "No. Definitely not."

"A hysteric?"

Nicholson shook her head. John's suave self-assurance did not fit the picture. "Huh-uh."

"Then I'd like to conjecture." Tom laced his fingers on the tabletop. "Now, since I haven't met the patient, I can only go on what you've told me. John's head injury probably induced an organic amnesia. As he healed, his mind took advantage of the lapse and continued to repress the memory."

Bercelian met Nicholson's gaze. "Now I stress that this is an unconscious process. I don't think the guy's conning you. Fortunately ..." He paused. "Or unfortunately, depending on how you look at it, John's a nonhysteric attempting to use a defense mechanism that falls under the heading of hysterical disorders. His attempts to thwart memory are starting to fail. Struggling against them induces vague remembrances of whatever he's attempting to suppress. And that causes fear."

Her mouth hung open. "That's amazing. You put that mess together neatly."

Tom rose, his expression bland but his eyes sparkling at the compliment. "Neatly, not necessarily correctly. Of all the inexact sciences comprising medicine, psychiatry is probably the most ambiguous."

"How about some parting advice?"

He smiled. "You mean like how to *part* the Red Sea? Sorry, one miracle per customer."

Shawna cringed. "I thought you gave up puns for Lent. If you didn't, you should have. That was awful. And you know I meant ideas for dealing with John."

"Keep trying to talk him into hypnosis. Barring that, just jar his memory in conversation." Bercelian walked to the door. "Oh, and keep me posted. It's not often we get a patient this interesting."

Shawna followed Tom to the entryway. "The word is frustrating, and I'm really glad you're curious. Dr. Bercelian, I believe you just unwittingly committed yourself to many nights in conference."

Despite Nicholson's bold assurance, six days passed before she found another opportunity to discuss John Doe's case with Tom Bercelian. This time, they met in the apartment coffee shop amid the multicolored boxes of vending machines and the distant bumps and hums of washers and dryers in the laundry room next door. Shawna sipped her coffee. Uncomfortable with her last session with John, she kept up small talk longer than Tom's spare time allowed. She did not feel like discussing the incident with Bercelian, but she knew it was in the patient's best interests, no matter how cruelly Bercelian chastised her psychiatric techniques.

Apparently sensing her reluctance, Bercelian did not press. "How're things at the hospital?" he asked vaguely.

"Quiet," she admitted. "The new interns come in July, you know. I scheduled my last two rotations empty in case I needed to fill in for sick residents or staff. It's been a healthy year, so I'm just teaching and working on some research. I've only got two patients, a terminal carry-over from last month and John."

Spotting his opening, Tom asked the inevitable question. "So, how is our mystery patient?"

Shawna took another mouthful of coffee, forgetting to blow on it in her attempt to act casual. It burned her mouth and part of her esophagus. She took a few gulps of cool air before answering. "Medically, really well. His sutures came out. He's eating and walking. Naturally, the surgeons don't want to have anything to do with him anymore."

"Thank God for small favors."

She smiled. The enmity between internists and surgeons was well known and greatly exaggerated. "In fact, only one thing's keeping him on the medical ward. Whoever set off the explosion that injured John didn't bother to sterilize it first. We've got him on a few more days of intravenous antibiotics. Then I have no idea what to do with him."

Tom swallowed his coffee. "Psych will take him."

"I know." She traced the rim of her styrofoam cup. "He still refuses to discuss his case with anyone but me."

"Mmm," Bercelian said thoughtfully. "We might be able to commit him. Usually, you have to prove suicidal or homicidal intent, but they may make an exception in this case."

Nicholson cringed, the idea of commitment unpalatable. "That just seems so mean."

"As opposed to throwing him out on the streets with no money, home, or job. Not to mention no identity." Bercelian studied Nicholson in the dim light from the Pepsi machine. "If you want my opinion, I think you should get him onto Psych by coercion, force, whatever it takes. Eventually, he'll get over his anger and used to us. He'll talk."

Nicholson took a more cautious sip of coffee, haunted by John's words of almost a week ago when they discussed the topic of trust. *I need a doctor whose word is more important than concern for my welfare.* "I don't think he'll talk. He's strong as a horse. Unless you put him on the locked ward, I'm willing to bet he'll run. And he's claustrophobic. He'd go out of his mind on lockup."

Bercelian grinned, and coldness touched features that had always seemed amicable in the past. "All the more reason to talk. Freedom as a reward for information."

His remark sparked anger. Nicholson sputtered wordlessly for several seconds before she could frame words. "I won't have a hand in that! I'm a doctor not a warlord."

He shrugged. "Sometimes you have to get ruthless to help someone. Cruel to be kind, as they say. He'll appreciate it in the end."

Shawna pictured her John Doe, hiding discomfort behind quips and feigned confidence. She, alone, had seen the hollow look of fear on his features and tears in his eyes, watched him struggle against the memories he was trying desperately to escape. More than once, it occurred to her that John might do better to let his unconscious claim the past and start a new life, but she felt certain recollection could not prove any worse than the fight to contain it. *No matter how serious the diagnosis, the patient can conjure something even worse if you leave him in ignorance.* Not wishing to discuss deception any further, Nicholson raised the issue she would rather have kept to herself. "I've been spending as much time with John as I can, trying to stimulate his memory."

"And?" Bercelian prodded.

"I've learned a lot. He plays a great game of cards: poker, hearts, *cribbage,* you name it. Wallops me at pool. Really knows his horses. Did you know he can name the first Kentucky Derby winner?"

Bercelian shook his head, not bothering to verbally address Nicholson's rhetorical question.

"Aristides in 1875." She considered the activities of the last few days. "Let's see what else. He apparently understands at least basic French, Spanish, and German. Can't play the piano worth a damn. Oh, and for a civilian, the guy knows his military trivia. He picked out a bunch of inconsistencies in an old war movie he watched with the nurses."

"How do you know he's not a soldier?"

Nicholson raised a hand and wriggled her fingers. "Prints. If he did serve, it wasn't on our side. And I'd be surprised if John wasn't an American."

Bercelian took another swallow of coffee. "Sounds like you're spending a lot of time with John."

Nicholson shrugged. "I told you, I have the time. And that was your suggestion."

"Indeed," Bercelian conceded. "I take it something untoward happened at today's session?"

Nicholson glanced up, stunned that the psychiatric resident read her edginess that easily. "I . . ." Having started, she forced herself to finish. "He made a pass at me."

If her words surprised her companion, the emotion did not leak through his facade. "Tell me about it."

Bercelian's coolness increased Nicholson's discomfort. "Well." She fidgeted, suddenly feeling as if she were the patient. "I tried to get him to think about family, hoping that would trigger off his memory. The topic came around to past loves."

"And he remembered some?"

"No." Shawna sat straighter in her chair. "Not that he would admit. But he did twist the topic around to my love life."

"That's good."

"Really?" Nicholson felt her sinews uncoil slightly.

"It can be," he clarified. "It shows John feels comfortable around you. You've got a solid relationship, and that's the necessary first step in therapy. Remember transference? If he feels close, he'll react to you as he does to members of his family. Of course, the success depends on your reply."

Nicholson cringed. "I told him about Randy."

Bercelian's lower lip curled inward in annoyance. "So you went on the defensive. That's not so good. Then what?"

Nicholson watched Bercelian's face for clues to his disposition. She knew it could only get worse. "He asked if I wanted to go to The Choice."

"The Choice?"

"You know, that smorgasbord restaurant in Cedar Rapids."

Tom brightened. "Cedar Rapids. So he's a local boy."

She waved the conclusion aside. "Not necessarily. He had just watched a commercial for it on TV."

"Oh." He encouraged her. "And you said?"

"No, of course. I dodged the question like a good little shrink. Give me some credit." Aware of what she would soon have to admit, Nicholson wished she could retract her last sentence.

"And you consider that a pass?"

"No, I consider the kiss he tried to force on me a pass."

Bercelian's eyebrows shot up. "That's a pass all right. What did you do? It's important."

Shawna stared at her shoes and mumbled an incoherent reply.

Bercelian leaned across the table. "Could I have that again, please."

Reluctantly, she met his gaze. "I slapped him."

"You slapped him!" Bercelian repeated. He seemed to have difficulty putting meaning to the words. He sat back, as if to chew it over like a piece of tough meat. "Shawna, you hit a patient? Do you realize the legal ram . . ."

"Don't lecture me," she warned. "I'm mortified. I've never done anything so stupid."

"Why?"

Nicholson misinterpreted the question. "I try not to make a habit of doing stupid things." She channeled her discomfort into humor. "Or, at least, I try to keep each act of stupidity original."

"No." Bercelian redirected his query. "I mean, why did you slap him?"

Nicholson had already considered her motives in the hours since the incident. "Sheer spontaneity? God decreed it my turn to act like an idiot? I don't know, Tom. I really don't."

"I do." Bercelian spoke softly, as if uncertain whether he wanted her to hear him.

"Would you mind enlightening me?"

Now Bercelian stalled. He swished the remaining coffee in his cup before answering. "You're not going to like what I have to say. I cherish our friendship and really don't want to piss you off."

Nicholson sighed, not interested in playing mind games, especially not with a psychiatrist. "I'll deal with it."

Bercelian talked slowly, as if to a child. "I think you're spending too much time with John. You've started seeing him as a friend rather than a patient."

Nicholson tapped a fist on the table, bothered not by the statement but by the insinuation she should handle any case as a disease entity rather than a person. "That's bad? I try to establish a rapport with all my patients."

Bercelian maintained a manner of calm dignity.

"That's fine with a cancer patient. In psych, you have to keep a professional distance. Otherwise, you wind up overlooking flaws. You get unwilling to pin a psychiatric diagnosis on a friend."

"Is that so?" Shawna tried to contain her ire. "I did take a psych rotation. And I don't think I've gotten unprofessionally close."

"For Christ's sake, you hit the guy!" Bercelian had become unprofessional himself. "And I believe you once compared him to a movie star."

She went sullenly silent, aware Tom was making a good argument. "You're right about the hitting. I think bringing up Randy flustered me. But so what if I compared John to Mel Gibson? I was just trying to make a point."

Tom bore in relentlessly. "I sincerely believe no one says or does anything without at least an unconscious reason."

"Don't give me psychology mumbo jumbo!" Shawna was angry now. "What are you trying to say? That I've fallen in love with a total stranger who doesn't even know his own name?"

"Not in love. But you can't deny the excitement of a handsome mystery man."

"As opposed to the dull routine of saving lives?" she shot back. "Cut me a break. You're making me vomit with this romance crap. John is a patient, just like any other . . ."

". . . gorgeous hunk of a patient," the psychiatrist finished. "Shawna, you are, without a doubt, the best medical resident Liberty Hospital has ever had. You're calm and competent. You handle problems well, and you're one of the nicest people I've ever met."

Cheeks still flushed, Nicholson grumbled her thanks and waited for the other shoe to fall.

"But," Bercelian continued, "you do have a flaw."

So much for hesitating to pin a psychiatric diagnosis on a friend. Shawna clamped her fingers to the edge of the table. "I'm certain I have more than one flaw. You've got my attention. Go ahead."

"You're what I like to call a 'collector.' You have a weakness for pretty things."

Bercelian's assessment seemed way off base to Nicholson. "I wouldn't throw away sapphire earrings if that's what you mean."

"That's not what I mean. You can't settle for secondhand furniture like every other struggling resident. You drive a black Porsche 944. I know how much ... correction, how little you make. You're probably in debt up to your eyeballs from that one."

Nicholson's knuckles went white against the formica. Many hours of moonlighting had gone into that car, not to mention an inheritance and a hefty chunk of her salary. "All right, I'm a pretty thing collector. What does that have to do with John?" Understanding hit with jolting force. "You bastard! You're about to say I collect men the same way, aren't you? Who the hell do you think you are?"

He gripped his cup, neither confirming nor denying her accusations.

"That's bullshit, Tom!"

"So, Randy's hideously ugly?" Bercelian said at last.

Shawna revived a picture of her old boyfriend,

tall and lean, his willowy blond features undeniably handsome. "Randy has other qualities."

"Oh?"

The topic made Nicholson irritable. The more her thoughts turned to Randy Oakley, the less controlled her anger became. "Let's just say I made a mistake with Randy. But I don't treat patients differently based on their appearances. And I am not attracted to John."

"Uh-huh." Bercelian continued to press. "And none of the guys in the building are attracted to your roommate. And I'm not attracted to Cheryl Tiegs. And you're not attracted to Mel Gibson. Let's face it. Like it or not, beauty figures heavily in human society. I know you're competent and your treatments don't change based on looks. There's nothing wrong with finding someone attractive. It's only when it interferes with your ability to treat the patient that it becomes a problem."

Shawna ground her teeth, still struggling against rage. She trusted the psychiatrist's abilities too much not to consider his theories viable. *But even the best psychiatrist makes mistakes.* She felt certain she had no romantic attachment to her patient, yet she could not deny a certain feeling of respect, one that might interfere with a psychiatric regimen.

Bercelian's voice turned gentle. "Shawna, we've been friends a long time. I don't want my conjectures to come between us. Like I said before, there's always more than one explanation. If you still want my advice, I'd like to leave you with two thoughts about this case."

"Please." Shawna knew she could not let her annoyance interfere with a patient's therapy.

"First, I suggest you sign off the case. Remember

the part of your Hippocratic oath where it says, 'Do no harm.' "

She said nothing, torn between loyalty to her patient and concern for his welfare.

"Barring that," Tom's features resumed their open friendliness, "try not to hurt him, okay?"

CHAPTER 5

Restless Nights

Carrigan/John Doe came to the conclusion he did not understand women. True, he had only known Doctor Shawna Nicholson ten days and spent three of those unconscious; but she spared him far more attention than their doctor/patient relationship required, including some of her off-hours. The kiss had seemed to follow naturally. Her slap had not. Now, dressed only in the tan pants that had survived the explosion with him, Carrigan settled more comfortably beneath his sheet and blanket and tried to rest.

The incident haunted Carrigan into his sleeping hours. He could still hear Nicholson's angry lament in the tense silence following the blow. "You men and your testosterone! All you ever want to do is have sex and kill people."

Surprised by Nicholson's vehemence, Carrigan recalled how he had resorted to humor. "I haven't killed anyone all morning." His jest had fallen short; not only had it failed to soothe the doctor, but it revived his own fears as well. She had stormed out in a huff, perhaps never to return. *And what will I do without her?* The answer came more easily than Carrigan expected. *I don't need her anymore. Or anyone else. I'm near discharge, and I can make it on my own.* Still, Carrigan could not banish the memory of his last encounter with Nicholson. *I wonder if she'll get called in tonight?* Carrigan considered which of the three second year residents would take call tonight. *Jason Walker.* He remembered what Nicholson had told him about Walker's "black cloud." *Oh, well, maybe I'll see her tomorrow.*

Carrigan rolled to his side, his hand tucked beneath the pillow, oddly comforted by the warm metal of the sharpened butter knife against his fingers. Amidst the conversations of the night shift personnel, calls over the intercom, and groans and snores of other patients, Carrigan finally fell asleep.

An alarm shattered Carrigan's peace, startling him awake. A message blared across the overhead speakers. "Code blue, room 237. Code blue, room 237."

Carrigan blinked in the dim moonlight streaming through his window. The crash cart rumbled past amid running footsteps. He recognized Walker's voice above the ensuing clamor. "What happened?"

Several nurses replied at once, and Carrigan could not make out their words with any clarity. Walker's voice followed. "Smithen is Shawna's patient. Better page her; she'll want to know."

The alarm sounded again, less jarring now that Carrigan was completely awake. "Code blue, room 237. Code blue, room 237."

Carrigan glanced at the wall clock. *Just past 2:00 a.m. Poor Shawna.* At this time of the morning, he doubted she would stop in to see him, even if she happened to come in-house. Carrigan twisted onto his back and let the sounds of hospital routine lull him to sleep.

Later that morning, a less familiar sound pierced Carrigan's slumber, the scrape of a sole on gritty tile. A gentle tug on his IV line followed. Though softer than the accustomed noises of the hospital, a sense of its not belonging caused Carrigan to open his eyes. The scattered glow through the window backlit a stocky male figure, his arms raised as he jabbed a syringe into the injection port on the IV fluid bag. Carrigan's trained eyes detected the unmistakable bulge of a holstered gun beneath the stranger's left armpit.

The realization of danger gripped Carrigan. Attempting to appear casual, he rolled to his opposite side. Using the added distance for momentum, he whipped around toward the stranger. His fist crashed into the man's groin.

The stranger dropped with a groan of pain and surprise. Carrigan pressed his advantage. Seizing the IV line in both hands, he snapped it over the man's head and jerked it tight around a bearded throat. The sudden jolt ruptured the plastic, reversing the flow. Blood and fluid splashed the swarthy stranger as he lurched away, pawing for his gun.

Carrigan wasted a second freeing his knife and ripping out the IV catheter before his life's blood poured out on the floor. The muzzle of the pistol swung toward him. *Shit!* He sprang, catching the man's wrist. The shot went wild, its muffled report no louder than the punch Carrigan slammed against the stranger's jaw Impact knocked the gunman over backward. Carrigan's hand remained locked to the man's wrist, and he lurched awkwardly from his bed. Another bullet struck the ceiling, raining plaster down on Carrigan. As the intruder struggled to his feet, Carrigan drove his knife beneath the stranger's breastbone.

A third shot nearly grazed the side of Carrigan's head as he hammered the handle of the butter knife deeper into the stranger's chest. The man went limp. The gun dropped to the bed, and Carrigan stared in horror as the door to his room inched open to admit the barrel of another handgun.

Carrigan dove across the bed, grabbing the fallen gun as he rolled over the covers. Two shots bit into the mattress. He returned two rounds then ducked as the pistol reappeared in the doorway and its owner squeezed off three more.

Despite the silencers, the hospital staff must have noticed something was wrong. Indecipherable screams and shouts filled the hallway. Peeking over the top of the bed, Carrigan answered with two more shots. *Nine millimeter Smith and Wesson 439.* He identified the weapon in his hand, though it seemed like a heavy dinosaur. *Eight shots in the magazine and one in the chamber. My four and the dead man's three makes seven.* Carrigan remained crouched, not wanting to waste his last two shots, groping for memory of the gun's details and recalling the classic Smith hammer-drop safety. Raising his head to fire, he barely ducked in time to save his face from the stranger's next two shots.

Shifting position, Carrigan glanced up at a different location and squeezed off one of his last two rounds. He flipped down the safety. The hammer fell on the load with a click identical to the sound of triggering an empty chamber; and the safety blocked the firing pin, preventing discharge. Carrigan deliberately swore, completing the illusion of having fired his last shot. Dropping behind the bed, he tried to second-guess the stranger, following movement by sound. *He thinks I'm finished. He'll take his time, aim carefully.* Leaving the hammer down, he eased off the safety.

A harsh voice wafted to Carrigan in a guttural, foreign language he could not identify, though he understood the words. "It's over, Carrigan. Come out slowly, and I might not kill you."

"Carrigan" again. Definitely not a term of endearment. A quick glimpse of the man's feet from under the bed gave Carrigan a reasonable idea of location and distance. He repositioned his finger to the longer, double action trigger stroke the Smith's hammer-drop created. *Got to make this one shot count. If I miss or only wound, I'm dead.* Rising, he aimed and fired. The bullet took the stranger in the forehead. Surprise twisted dark features, and he toppled over backward.

A nurse's scream echoed through the corridors. Carrigan pressed flat to the wall as voices followed. "Oh, my God! Oh, my God!"

"Call security!"

A bass voice boomed in response. "Fuck security. Call the police!"

Police. Carrigan's heart pounded as his mind formed an image of helmeted men with assault rifles.

"What happened?" someone else asked.

In the general hysteria that answered, no one seemed quite certain. Then a frightened voice blared over the intercom: "Code blue, 2 West. Code blue, 2 West." Carrigan sifted through the noise for the more stealthy sounds of approaching enemies. The tracking device in his pocket bumped his hip as he worked his way to the door. Once there, he squeezed his spine against either side of the frame and glanced out. He spotted no more gunmen, but the few night nurses cowered behind their blood-splattered station. Apparently responding to the code call, ignorant of the shooting, Dr. Jason Walker hurried down the hallway toward the fallen man.

Carrigan cursed. *The idiot's going to get himself killed.* Eyes fixed on the hallway, Carrigan fumbled through the first stranger's pockets for a full magazine. Before he could find anything useful, a movement seized his attention. Beyond Walker, a broom closet door edged open a crack. A pistol barrel swung toward the doctor. *Oh, shit, the guy's gunning for Walker.* Jamming the empty Smith and Wesson into his pants, Carrigan raced for the unsuspecting doctor. Walker recoiled as Carrigan slammed against him, driving him into the wall. A bullet tore a burning trail through Carrigan's shoulder. He dropped to one knee, consciousness swimming. Endurance training took over where reflex failed, overcoming the sudden agony of the wound. Surging to his feet, he grasped Walker's arm, spun the doctor, and shoved him down the hallway.

Oblivious to the danger, Walker fought Carrigan every step of the way. "Let go of me! What the hell are you doing?"

Carrigan flung Walker around a corner, calling to a nurse huddled beneath the marbled formica of the nursing station. "Page Nicholson and tell her to meet me at the parking garage." Aware the nurse would hesitate to take an order from a patient, he shouted. "Do it! It's an emergency." To

Carrigan's relief the nurse grabbed for a phone to obey, her gaze locked on the tiny, red hole in his naked shoulder. He hoped Nicholson was still in-house from the code. *If they're after Walker, they'll want her, too.*

Footsteps pursued Carrigan. He gave Walker a wild shove toward the main corridor amid the resident's screamed protests. Walker bolted. Though barefoot, Carrigan caught the sandy-haired doctor before he could disappear around the corner, seized him by the shoulders, and hurled him against the bar that opened the fire exit to the stairs. Walker staggered out onto the landing. Panic colored his cries. "Leave me alone! Damn it, let go!"

Ignoring Walker's complaints, Carrigan pushed him again, sending Walker stumbling down the steps to the first floor. Carrigan's shoulder ached, and the gun chafed his hip. He could not fathom why someone had sent men to murder him. Walker's struggle only added to his desperation. Wrenching open the door at the bottom, he hurled Walker through it with more violence than necessary. "Shut up, damn you! You'll get us both killed."

Walker crashed into the wall and let out a blood-curdling scream that reverberated through the night-empty hall.

Carrigan cringed, aware the shout might bring security as well as reveal his position to his enemies. Jabbing his hand into his pocket, he poked his fist into Walker's back. "This is a gun. Another sound from you and I blow you away. Understand?" Having no intention of actually hurting Walker and not wanting anyone else to see him holding a gun on a doctor, Carrigan did not bother to use the real weapon. Without bullets, it would serve him no better anyway.

Walker stiffened, aware of his peril for the first time. As if in a trance, he allowed Carrigan to steer him toward the main entryway.

As they emerged among the padded chairs, Carrigan caught a glimpse of three men in blue uniforms running toward the elevators. Another slouched in the doorless opening to the outside with the boredom of long routine. Carrigan ducked back around the corner until the footsteps receded. *Security. Probably headed up to 2 West.* Pinning Walker to the wall with his uninjured shoulder, Carrigan examined his wound. It appeared small, hardly worth the pain. The bullet had passed completely through, and the tissues around its path had collapsed and staunched the bleeding. "Give me your coat. We're going out. Don't make a sound or a gesture. If you make me kill anyone, you're dying first."

Walker paled. His body heaved, and Carrigan stepped aside in case the doctor was about to vomit. It occurred to him to abandon Walker here, in the hallway by the main waiting room; but Carrigan guessed the gunmen had come for him and anyone to whom he might have given information. *And I'm not going to let people die for helping me. Not even idiots.* He pulled off Walker's white coat, revealing the familiar hospital scrubs. Carrigan donned the coat, fastening enough buttons to hide his naked chest. "Come on." Grabbing Walker's upper arm, he trotted for the exit.

Regaining control of his stomach, Walker wobbled along in silence. Carrigan wove between the staggered chair rows, keeping the doctor positioned between himself and the security guard to hide his bare feet. Cool, night air funneled through the doorway, its touch soothing. Dusk-to-dawn lights held the shadows at bay around the drive-up and walkway, and a few cars remained parked at the edge between the macadam and the tended grasses and flowers of the hospital grounds. A two-tiered fountain divided the driveway in half. This late, it lay quiescent; its black waters reflected glints of artificial light like jewels. Chirping noises rose and fell in a ceaseless chorus, not quite consistent enough for machinery. Unable to identify the sound, Carrigan concentrated on the parking garage down the driveway to his left.

The security guard studied Carrigan and Walker as they reached the opening. "Nice night," he said conversationally. "Every cricket in the world's out there singing."

Despite not wanting to waste time chatting, Carrigan answered to divert suspicion. He glanced down to make certain the coat hid the pistol in his waistband. "Jason's not feeling too good. I'm taking him home." Carrigan spotted movement beyond the fountain, and he thought he heard a distant crackle of static beneath the sounds the security guard attributed to something called "crickets." *Radios. They're in communication. And they know exactly where we are.* Without waiting for the guard's reply, Carrigan guided Walker toward the parking garage.

The security guard called after them sympathetically. "Hope you're feeling better, Doctor."

Carrigan felt Walker tense. Aware the resident was about to struggle or speak, Carrigan grabbed him around the waist. He slapped his fist against

Walker's abdomen with enough force to drive air from his lungs. "Shut up," he hissed, breaking into a run that forced the doctor along at his side.

The macadam took a sharp right, and Carrigan vaulted a curb to a weathered walkway leading into the parking garage. Dodging the glass doors that opened into an enclosed area for the elevators and stairs, Carrigan half-carried, half-dragged Walker up the ramp. Less than a quarter of the painted spaces held cars at this late hour. Fluorescent lights played over gritty automobiles looking as clunky as antiques to Carrigan. Unable to identify makes and models, he selected a relatively streamlined sports car for its waxed, red paint job. *A person who takes care of his car on the outside is more likely to keep the insides running smoothly.*

The soft scrape of fabric on concrete warned Carrigan of another presence in the garage. He dove beside the car, slamming Walker down with him. The putt of a silenced gun sounded from behind a concrete support post, and a bullet rattled across the ramp. Another shot put a hole in the window of the car behind him.

Shit! Using his knee to hold Walker to the ground, Carrigan tried the door handle of the sports car. It resisted. He groped for the lock. The circle of metal felt cold and unfamiliar to his touch. *What kind of stupid mechanism is this?* Carrigan knew his time was running short. His enemies seemed well trained, and he knew it would not take long for them to notice he was not returning their fire. *Once they figure out I'm unarmed, we're not going to be able to hide.*

Carefully, Carrigan rose to a crouch. A shot whizzed past his ear, from a different direction this time. *At least two enemies left.* Cocking his fist, he slammed it through the driver's window. The glass shattered beneath the blow, forming a cobweb pattern of squares. A touch spilled a high-pitched jangle of shards onto a fur-covered seat. The window broke more cleanly than Carrigan expected. Reaching through the hole, he pawed for a control panel, the metal ledge warm through the linen sleeve of Walker's jacket. Two more shots clattered off the car door as Carrigan found the handle and pulled. The lock clicked, and the door swung open.

The almost imperceptible noises of movement warned Carrigan his enemies were repositioning. A quick glance revealed they had stopped bothering to duck around poles and cars. Three appeared in various positions on the ramp, rapidly closing toward Carrigan.

I'll need a few seconds to get this car going. "Get in!" Carrigan screamed at Walker.

Walker lurched to his knees. Carrigan kicked him toward the door. "Get in," he repeated, incensed by Walker's sluggishness. Desperate, he did not wait, but reached beneath the dash. Nothing felt right. A metal patch with a keyhole replaced the card-activated mechanism he expected. His blood went cold. Wildly, he groped for dials and wires, aware of the passage of every fragmented second.

Above Carrigan, tires screeched and rumbled on the concrete ramp of the second level. *Damn! Now they've got a car. And I had to pick the only vehicle in the lot designed by a crazy man.* Carrigan pawed beneath the steering wheel, wondering if his memory, not the inventor was to blame. *Too slow. Gotta get out of here.* Carrigan backed out. The instinct to run was strong. but he wasted a few seconds grabbing hold of Walker's scrubs. A glance over the doctor's shoulder revealed two swarthy figures raising pistols, and Carrigan knew his attempt to save Walker would cost them both their lives.

A sleek black Porsche whipped around the corner recklessly fast and barreled down on the men on the ramp. The gunmen dove aside, a loosed bullet pinging off the ceiling above Carrigan's head. An instant later, Carrigan recognized Shawna Nicholson in the driver's seat, and his respect for her soared. The car slowed without coming to a full stop. The door swung free.

This time, Walker needed no prodding. He sprinted for the opening and dove over Nicholson. She elbowed him toward the meager rear seats. Carrigan shoved Walker's buttocks hard enough to send him sprawling into the back, then nudged Shawna toward the passenger seat with his hip. "Move over!" Whipping his leg under hers, he floored the gas pedal. The car lurched and sputtered. The stall light flashed red then darkened, and the car leaped forward, its engine revving dangerously high.

Carrigan sensed Nicholson's reluctance as she surrendered control of the car to him and clambered over the gearshift to the passenger side. The mirror gave him a perfect view of the gunmen back on the roadway, their pistols raised and steadied in both hands. "Get down!" Carrigan shouted to Walker, but only Nicholson obeyed. Abruptly, Carrigan swerved, swiping a parked car. The sudden motion sprawled Walker against the side window. From his continued control of the Porsche, Carrigan knew his maneuver had rescued the tires. He looked up to the looming bar of the lowered exit gate.

Carrigan let up the gas pedal and jammed it down again, wondering why the car would not accelerate past a moderate speed. He groped along the gauges for a release button. Twisting a lever sloshed a pair of metal bars tipped with rubber across the windshield with a suddenness that surprised Carrigan. He ducked. The headlights bashed into the exit barrier, snapping it like a twig. "What the hell were those?"

"Wipers." Still low, Nicholson grabbed a lever near Carrigan's knee. "What's wrong with you? You're destroying my car!"

Emerging on the hospital drive, Carrigan made a sharp left toward the main road. "Where's the superaccel button?"

"Shift!" Nicholson hollered, ignoring Carrigan's question. "Damn you, hit the clutch!"

Nicholson's order made no sense to Carrigan. The driveway ended in a T-intersection, and he chose the left turn at random. "Clutch?" he repeated, ignoring Walker's shouted protests from the back seat.

Hysteria tinged Nicholson's voice. "Step on that pedal left of the brake. Don't let it up till I tell you."

Carrigan jammed in the clutch, and immediately felt the car slacken. He watched Nicholson maneuver the gearshift. A glance at its head revealed she had placed it into the third position. "Let the pedal up slowly. When you feel it catch, hold for a second, then remove your foot."

Carrigan obeyed. Uncertain of the catching point, he let the pedal up too quickly. The car bucked, then continued in the higher gear. It accelerated smoothly, and they passed a football stadium and field. A few car lengths ahead, a traffic signal swung over another three-way intersection, its red light casting crimson stripes across the hood.

Seeing no other cars on the road, Carrigan assumed the signal would change for him to go. He ignored it, flicking the wheel to the left. The car whisked around the corner. As the scenery changed from hospital grounds to neighborhoods, Carrigan relaxed, no longer able to tune out Walker's frantic words.

"What's going on? Why are you helping him? He got me here at gunpoint, damn it! We're all going to get killed because of a paranoid schizo—"

Nicholson interrupted. "Jason, pipe down! He's amnesic, not deaf."

Walker's tirade continued, frenzied beyond halting. "Why did you let him in the car? You're just feeding his delusions. He really thinks . . ." Walker broke off with a gasp as Carrigan ran another light.

Nicholson turned her attention back to Carrigan. "Can you handle fifth gear?"

Using the numbering on the floor stick as a guide, Carrigan pressed in the clutch and guided the car into high.

Reaching across Carrigan, Nicholson placed his safety belt around him, then locked on her own. Removing the hospital beeper from her jeans, she clipped it to the sun visor with the mechanicalness that accompanies habit. "I think we lost them, John. You'd better turn on the headlights. Start following traffic signals or you'll get us in even more trouble. And where the hell did you learn to drive?"

"The Reckless Driving Academy." Just as when he had made a similar quip about his endurance, Carrigan found himself immersed in memory. He recalled driving a steel-colored automobile, eyes fixed on a remote control model of a sports car whisking across a deserted, gray parking lot. Beside him, a man steered the toy while Carrigan chased it, his goal to run the smaller car down. A sense of frustration accompanied the recollection. No doubt they had performed the game for hours, the model escaping Carrigan's best maneuvers. Finally, he slammed on the brakes. In response to the passenger's query, Carrigan heard himself grumble, "Just keep playing with your fucking little car." Whipping open the driver's door, the Carrigan of memory flicked a machine pistol from a shoulder holster and blasted the toy to pieces.

Now, as the Porsche rolled to the bottom of a hill, it came upon a four-way intersection. This time, the light blazed green, and Carrigan turned left again. He ignored Nicholson's suggestion to turn on the headlights. In the dark, the Porsche was nearly invisible. "How'd you find us, anyway?"

Nicholson replied above Walker's hysterical complaints. "I was in the garage about to go home when the nurse paged. I used the phone near the elevator. She told me about the guns and that you saved Jason's life. Then I heard breaking glass and the shooting in the garage. I was scared to death."

Carrigan glanced at Nicholson, who was watching a river that paralleled the roadway to his right. Wind chopped its water into waves. "You seemed pretty calm to me." He spoke loudly, hoping the crazed resident in the back seat might take the hint.

Nicholson shrugged, staring at the floor as if embarrassed by his compliment. "I think everyone wonders what they'd do in a situation like that. I always figured I'd panic; but, actually, I was thinking clearly. I guess all those years of codes got me used to emergencies."

Walker had gone silent, but the whisk of fabric against leather warned Carrigan that the resident had slipped directly behind him. Afraid Walker might try something crazy, Carrigan grabbed for his gun. In his haste, he caught the tracking device instead. Undaunted, he jabbed it toward Walker. "Get over behind Dr. Nicholson. Now! And close your mouth or I'll blow your head off just to shut you up."

Walker skittered to the opposite side of the car.

Nicholson was less easily fooled. "That's a gun?"

Carrigan did not want to lie to Nicholson, but he needed to keep Walker in control. "Top of the new line. Walther heat-seeking, laser-controlled automatic. Doesn't even need a sight."

Nicholson looked skeptical; to Carrigan's relief, however, she did not question him. Instead, she twisted toward Walker. "What's the matter with you? For God's sake, John saved your life. Why are you fighting the only person on our side?"

"Saved my life? Our side?" Walker sounded genuinely perplexed. "What are you talking about?"

Carrigan sped through the business district, letting Nicholson explain the situation to Walker. "The nurses told me there was a fight on 2 West and John took a bullet for you."

"A bullet?" Walker leaned forward. "I didn't hear any gunshots."

Walker's denial shocked Carrigan; the danger had seemed all too obvious to him. Still, he guessed someone unused to guns might have missed the muted shots, and he became guiltily aware Walker had spent most of the subsequent time with his face shoved into walls, cars, and concrete. Carrigan noticed no evidence of pursuit, and the lull allowed him the opportunity to wonder why he had risked his life for Walker. *For a heartless killer who sent his girlfriend to die, I seem to have some small slice of morality.* The memory bothered him, so when Nicholson slapped his arm hard enough to sear agony through his injured shoulder, he appreciated the diversion if not the pain. "Take a left here. You'll have to downshift to second."

Carrigan nodded as he winced. "Exactly where am I going?" He spun around the corner, shifting, and the car stalled out. "What the hell?"

Nicholson jerked up the emergency brake to keep the Porsche from rolling back into the main street. "You released the clutch too fast. You can't do that at lower gears. Take it back into first."

Pushing in the clutch, Carrigan complied. Nicholson turned the key. "Give it some gas." The engine roared back to life. "Watch this." Nicholson tapped her knuckles against the tachometer. "Whenever the green triangle comes on, it's time to switch into the next higher gear. Got that?"

Carrigan continued, feeling stupid.

"Next time, I drive. And if there're any dents, you're a dead man."

"What gunshots?" Walker pressed. He took a sharp gasp of a breath as another revelation hit him. "My God! There's no general ward resident in-house."

"Turn right. There, on Woodbridge." Nicholson indicated a road sign. "Then you'll need to take another quick right onto Oakside Lane. Pull up to the last apartment building on the left." She addressed Walker. "Don't worry about coverage, for Pete's sake. They'll find someone. If no residents are free, the staff will just have to do some ward work for a while."

Carrigan followed Nicholson's directions and pulled into a space in the apartment lot near the fire exit between a beat-up sedan and a station wagon. He unclipped his seat belt. "Where did you say we are?"

"My place." Nicholson opened the passenger door, admitting night air.

Carrigan hesitated. "Not a good idea. If they got a look at the car, this may be the first place they come."

Walker climbed out the back. "Who's they?" he screamed, obviously annoyed no one had chosen to answer his previous questions.

Nicholson jumped out and closed the door. Motioning to Walker to wait, she responded to Carrigan. "Before we go anywhere else, we need to make some calls and get you some real clothes."

Reluctantly, Carrigan left the car. Cinders bit into the bare soles of his feet, and his shoulder felt as if a heavy object had rested upon it for hours. He replaced the tracking device in his pocket. Pulling the pistol from his waistband, he slid it under the seat. Without bullets, it could only frighten people or draw unwanted attention. "All right, but quickly." He left his door unlocked. Eyeing Walker, he found the resident tense and restless. Aware panic would make Walker unpredictable, Carrigan tried to include the younger doctor in the conversation. "I don't know who they were. I was too busy dodging bullets to check ID."

Nicholson led the way toward the main entrance at the opposite end of the cinder block building. "If it helps, they looked like Arabs to me."

Carrigan shook his head, no closer to recalling the truth. Now that Nicholson pointed it out, he had noticed that the gunmen all seemed swarthy, much like the soldiers in his memory of the explosion. The term "Arab" seemed unfamiliar. Keeping one step behind Walker, he studied the apartment. It stood in a line with three nearly identical buildings, each seven stories tall. Aside from the main entrance, he recognized the heavy steel fire door and suspected another like it graced the opposite side of the stairwell. Windows lined up in stately rows, their sills painted brown and their screens supporting filmy curtains or shades. The first pink streaks of the false dawn glimmered off chips of pyrite in the walkway.

Nicholson yanked the glass-paned door wide to reveal a dimly lit lobby containing two elevators, restrooms labeled with international symbols, and rows of metal postal boxes. To the right, a hallway stretched into darkness. From the layout of the building, Carrigan guessed it led past apartments or utility rooms to the stairs at the far end. The trio stepped inside. Nicholson let the door swing closed. She hit the elevator button, and the whirring sound of movement emerged from the shaft. "I've still got a couple of Randy's T-shirts. They should fit you. I've got a pair of his running shoes, too. What size are you?"

"You're kidding." Flattened to the outer wall, Carrigan peered through the glass of the door. He watched a silver BMW pull into the lot, though, from this distance, he could not identify the passengers.

Nicholson laughed. "I guess if you don't know your name, you're not likely to know your shoe size."

The elevator doors rumbled apart to reveal a well-lit but small interior. The sight of it ran a chill through Carrigan, and he felt certain he would rather face more gunfire than the prospect of squeezing himself into it. He seized Walker's shoulder, not wanting to lose the doctor until he sorted the situation out in his mind. "We're taking the stairs." Without further explanation, he started down the hallway. "And I think I may know half my name. One of the gunmen called me something that didn't sound like a swear word." He did not mention that a remembered girlfriend had referred to him the same way, though the repetition seemed to clinch his identity.

"Fifth floor." Nicholson followed Carrigan and Walker past the coffee shop. "What's your name? We may be able to get some real information now."

"Quite pushing," Walker protested. He opened the door to a concrete stairway with metal handrails.

As Carrigan had suspected, the fire doors stood on either side, and the one to the right would open near Nicholson's car. "I'd rather not say. The name didn't sound familiar enough for me to feel certain it's mine. And I don't want to get you too deeply involved in something this dangerous." *The less they know, the safer they are.* Carrigan suddenly wished he had never mentioned the incident.

"Fine." Nicholson's voice echoed through the stairwell as they climbed. "But I'm curious. Just tell me first or last name."

Carrigan considered. When he recalled Katry using it, he had believed it his given name. Now that seemed less likely. "I can't be sure, but I'd bet on last. I'd like to hope I'm not on a first-name basis with hired killers." As so many times before, the joke failed to ease his apprehension. Carrigan recalled that the pants he wore matched the uniforms of the men he had murdered, raising the possibility of treason.

Rounding the fourth floor landing, Walker stopped at the door numbered five. Panting, he reached for the handle.

"Wait." Carrigan pushed Walker aside, nudged the panel open a crack, and peeked out. The single hallway appeared deserted. Toward the end, the corridor faded into obscurity; but the red, white, and blue lights of a Pepsi machine revealed no shadowy forms near the elevators. A mottled gray-black carpet spanned the hallway between yellow walls interrupted by numbered apartments. "Which one?"

"Five-twelve." Nicholson indicated the third door on the right, across from a fire alarm mounted on the wall. She retrieved her keys. "And, by the way, we're sure to wake up my roommate. Don't mind anything she says. She takes a bit of getting used to." Nicholson slapped her left hip. "Darn it, I did it again. I left my beeper in the car." She flung up a hand. "I guess it doesn't really matter now."

Still alert, Carrigan slipped from the stairs and waited by the door until Nicholson used her key to open it. Nicholson entered first, followed by Carrigan and Walker. The door clicked shut behind them.

Nicholson flicked on the overhead light, and Carrigan took in the apartment at a glance. To his left, the kitchen looked clean except for a few dishes in the sink. A countertop separated it from a living room containing a single couch, two antique end tables with lamps, a glass-topped coffee table, a television, and a stereo system. A squat, push-button telephone occupied a corner of the coffee table, a bowl of nuts the center. Just beyond the counter, a doorway opened into the bedroom with a bathroom parallel to the kitchen. A sleepy voice wafted from the other chamber. "Shawna?"

"Sorry to wake you, Tracy." Nicholson gestured at Carrigan and Walker to sit. "Emergency. I've got people with me," she warned.

Walker paced. Carrigan took a seat on the couch, watching Walker suspiciously, still not trusting the doctor. He worried that Walker's confusion might compel him to attempt escape or, worse, try to overpower Carrigan. *Deep down, he still thinks I'm the enemy, and I can't blame him.* He recalled how his own bewilderment and fear had caused him to attack Walker in the hospital. *He may even be right.*

The scrape of drawers sounded from the bedroom, and Tracy Harlowe emerged wearing sweatpants and a polo shirt labeled "Liberty Fitness Center" in a circle above her left breast. Her blonde locks were swept back in disarray, making her appear as if she had just stepped off a practice field. From the firmness of her muscles, Carrigan guessed it was not an unusual look for Harlowe. And he liked what he saw.

Harlowe returned Carrigan's stare with the same

interest. "Wow," she gibed. "This is the kind of stuff I'm supposed to bring home from work, not you."

Nicholson seemed more annoyed than amused. "Tracy, this is John, and you already know Jason. See if you can't find some of Randy's old stuff to fit him. Jason, we've got alcohol by the sink and gauze four-by-fours in the medicine cabinet. Why don't you clean up his wound?" As the others went to obey, Nicholson picked up the telephone receiver.

Suddenly alarmed, Carrigan questioned. "Who are you calling?"

"The police." She punched out a "9."

"No." Springing forward, Carrigan snatched the receiver from her hand and slammed it into the cradle. "No police."

Nicholson back-stepped, as startled by his manner as his words. "Are you crazy? You're injured. There're guys with guns trying to kill us. We need help."

The bathroom door swung closed. Attracted by the movement, Carrigan shouted. "Walker, you leave that door open!"

"I have to pee," Walker returned. "Do you mind?"

"No." From the corner of his vision, Carrigan saw Nicholson reaching for the phone. "Go ahead and pee. Just leave the door open." He grabbed Nicholson's hand, gripping more tightly than he intended. "I said no police."

Nicholson ripped her fingers from Carrigan's hold, shaking her hand in pain and anger.

Walker whined, but he did not try to shut the door again. "There're women in the room."

"One's a doctor. The other's a gymmie. Just do it!" The need to keep tabs on his companions wore on Carrigan, and his inability to make sense of his situation only added to his frustration.

"Gym-mie?" Nicholson repeated softly but did not demand explanation.

"I don't have to go anymore." Walker grumbled and came back to the main room with a bottle of alcohol and a fistful of paper packets. He patted a couch cushion, then sat on the one beside it.

Harlowe shouted from the back room. "You have a choice. 'Save the Whales' or 'Virginia is for Lovers.' " She emerged with an armload of T-shirts and a clean pair of running shoes. "Neither one suits you. And what's this crap about guys with guns. If this is your idea of a practical joke, it's not going to work." She looked at Nicholson as she spoke.

"I wish it were a joke." Nicholson explained her half of the preceding events.

While Nicholson talked, Carrigan shed Walker's coat and allowed the doctor to wash and dress the wound in his shoulder. With no idea of self or direction, Carrigan did not know how to evade his enemies. One thing seemed clear. *The gunmen want me. I've got to get the others safely away from the shooting.*

Nicholson seized on Carrigan's moment of introspection to make another attempt at the telephone. Infuriated by her deception, he tore free of Walker, grabbed the base of the phone, and ripped it from the wall. The plastic clip remained in the jack, and the cord came free, trailing wires. "I said no police!"

"Why?" Nicholson screamed, equally angry.

"Don't you understand?" It seemed obvious to Carrigan. "Back at the hospital, I killed people."

"Don't be stupid." Nicholson's tone mingled fading anger with sympathy. "It was self-defense."

"Shawna." Not wanting to discuss his concerns in front of Walker and Harlowe, Carrigan drew Nicholson into the bedroom and whispered. "Self-defense or not, it was easy. I've killed before. No doubt. And I was trained."

It took Nicholson several seconds to grasp a concept that seemed painfully obvious to Carrigan. "What are you saying? You think you're a murderer?"

That being self-evident, Carrigan did not bother to reply.

"How about a cop? A soldier?"

"Fingerprints," Carrigan reminded her. "I'm neither."

Nicholson considered, her explanation becoming more bizarre. "Maybe you're an American James Bond."

"James who?"

"A spy," Nicholson clarified. "One so secret even our government doesn't keep your prints on file."

Carrigan dismissed the idea. "If so, there's no way it would have taken them ten days to find me. Besides, that's all the more reason not to call the police. Depending on what I know or say, my own people might have as much cause to kill me as the enemy does." He met her eyes and thought he found sincere concern in their depths. "And we're avoiding the much more likely explanation. I'm a hired gun. Dirty as it seems, that theory doesn't require nearly as much whimsy."

"No," Nicholson kept her voice low. "It requires more because it defies what we've seen."

"I don't understand."

Nicholson explained. "A hitman wouldn't have risked himself for Jason. Your personality's all wrong for a criminal."

"My personality?" Through the doorway between the rooms, Carrigan watched Walker rise casually. "How do you know it's my real personality? I don't even know who I am."

Nicholson took Carrigan's hand. "Amnesia may make you forget, but it's not going to change your basic disposition. You're not . . ."

Walker made a break for the door. Concerned about the possibility of danger lurking in the hallway, Carrigan brushed Nicholson aside and whipped the tracking device from his pocket. "Freeze or you're dead."

Loosing a cry of despair, Walker went still.

Harlowe gasped, then, studying the device in Carrigan's hand, began to laugh. "What are going to do? Shoot him with an ergometer?" She pulled open a drawer in the end table and produced an object that looked reasonably similar to the one in Carrigan's hand except for the brand name, Elekü-ben, emblazoned beneath the display. "This sucker measures distance run, calories expended, and work performed. Aunt Aggie brought it back from Europe. Where'd you get yours?"

Walker groaned. "I can't believe this. First, there's a gunfight going on around me, and I don't even notice it. Then I start listening to this lunatic because he threatens my life with a fitness device. Would anyone object if I just crawled back to the hospital and stopped looking like a horse's ass?"

Feeling a bit sorry for the doctor, Carrigan put the tracking device back in his pocket. "Wait. Let me make sure it's safe first." Waving his companions into the other room, Carrigan pressed his back to the wall and fiddled with the doorknob.

In response, a round of automatic gunfire tore through the door, this time without a silencer. Glad of his caution, Carrigan returned to his companions. Their mood had changed. All three stood near the bed, eyes wide in shocked disbelief.

Carrigan's voice sounded loud in the hush. "They're after me, not you. Once I leave, they'll chase me. By the time you get the phone working, I'll have enough of a head start."

Nicholson broke out of her trance first. "You can't go alone. You've got no car, no money, no directions. You don't even know who you are."

Carrigan shrugged. "Who'd go with me?"

"You're my patient." Nicholson met his gaze, and there could be no doubt she was serious.

"No." Carrigan denied the possibility. "You'd be more hindrance than help."

Obviously insulted, Nicholson leaped to her feet. "Fuck you, dickface! I got you out of the garage, didn't I? Without me, you would have gotten your stupid head blown off."

Carrigan grinned sweetly. "You care." Nicholson's motivations sounded flimsy to him, and he suspected even she did not understand the real reason why she wanted to accompany a man pursued by assassins.

"No. But I took an oath to protect my patients. And, God damn you, that's what I'm going to do."

"Fine. Then you go through the door first." Carrigan had no intention of letting Nicholson get hurt, but his kidding did seem to dissolve some of the tension. *Maybe it's best she goes with me, at least until I can find a safer place to leave her.*

Jason Walker echoed Carrigan's thought. "Count me in. The only reason those killers haven't broken in here yet is because you're crazy. They're afraid of you. I'm not staying so they can slaughter me after you're gone."

Harlowe nodded in agreement, plucking nervously at the ergometer through her sweatpants' pocket. "We'll get killed without Rambo, here."

Assuming Harlowe addressed him, Carrigan considered, suspecting the killers' patience had more to do with good strategy and uncertainty about his arsenal than any concern over his sanity. Every professional knew accuracy took precedence over speed. He recalled the layout of the hallway in picture-perfect detail: the elevators far to the right, the fire stairs three doors down, the location of Nicholson's car, and the only three exits from the building. "I'll take those clothes. Then I need to borrow a hammer."

CHAPTER 6
Shattered Mornings

The images of an old monster movie flickered across the television in Shawna Nicholson's apartment, splashing light over the couch, chairs, and tables. Carrigan found the camera cuts so jolting, the technique would have distracted him from the story if he had had the opportunity to watch it. But he was using the screams of the beach party only to cover his own clamor, a crude technique designed to do little more than add to the confusion. Mostly, he trusted the unconventionality of his plan to keep his enemies from making sense of any noises they might hear. Though they had, thus far, shown little regard for the lives of bystanders, they had not acted with amateurish haste nor had they wasted ammunition. They believed they had him cornered, his resources limited. His life, and those of his companions, depended on proving them wrong.

Nicholson, Harlowe, and Walker watched Carrigan from the bedroom doorway. A black, Liberty College T-shirt stretched taut across his chest and shoulders, and Randy's running shoes fit more comfortably over a thick pair of Tracy's white gym socks with gold and blue stripes around the calves. In addition to the hammer, Carrigan clutched a

Pepsi bottle filled with the rubbing alcohol Walker had used to clean his bullet wound. Capped with a tampon wick, the soda bottle would serve as an imperfect incendiary device once lit with matches Nicholson had supplied.

Choosing a stretch of wall between studs and toward the fire stairs, Carrigan swung the hammer. Its head easily smashed a hole through the painted plasterboard. Propping the claws in the opening, he quietly tore off chunks amid a spray of powdered mortar.

Harlowe cringed. "There goes our security deposit." The comment sounded more hysterical than humorous.

"Who lives next door?" Carrigan asked as he knocked out a cross timber with the hammer, enlarging the space to human size. The idea of adding more people to those he needed to protect seemed nearly as abhorrent as facing the enemy guns, and three passengers would already strain the confines of the Porsche.

Nicholson answered with the same calm courage she had displayed at the parking garage. "Dr. Stanford and his wife. They're off in Churchill Downs for the Derby. They go every year."

Relieved by the news, Carrigan stepped into the cavity between the layers of the plasterboard, brushed aside the electrical wire, and tapped an opening into the neighboring apartment.

A brass headboard blocked Carrigan's exit. Catching it, he shoved a queen-sized bed, gray with dislodged plaster, into the center of the room. Emerging into a sleeping chamber similar to the one in Nicholson's apartment, Carrigan motioned at the others to follow. *One more wall and we'll be in 516, the apartment nearest the fire door.* Ignoring magnificent furnishings, he jogged into the main room, silently pushed aside a couch, and started on the wall with his hammer.

Soon, Nicholson, Harlowe, and Walker joined Carrigan. Harlowe fidgeted, glancing repeatedly over her shoulder. Walker rubbed his hands as if washing them. "Who lives in the next place?" Carrigan asked amid the hiss of falling shards of plasterboard.

"Surgery resident," Nicholson told him simply. "Whether he's in or not depends on how dead those guys you fought in the hospital are."

Carrigan widened the gap rapidly, then hooked outlet wires over the nails jutting from wooden supports. "You mean there are degrees of death?"

Nicholson explained. "No. But Rob's on surgical emergency call. If you left those men even a little bit alive, Rob got called in to tend them."

Carrigan doubted either of the strangers he fought could have survived long. Still, he recalled the hospital security officers heading toward 2 West and the gunman remaining in the broom closet. *A hired gun against rent-a-cops.* Carrigan shook his head, aware of the likelihood that other people had been wounded or killed in the subsequent scuffle. Clutching the Molotov cocktail in one hand, the hammer in the other, Carrigan broke through the final layer of plasterboard into a private chamber. Clothing lay strewn across a sheetless mattress and chest of drawers. No one occupied the bed, and the absence of apartment 516's tenant pleased Carrigan. He stepped through the hole, mapping the probable locations of the gunmen by formulating the strategy he would use in his adversaries' stead.

*From the shots, at least one is waiting by the door
to Nicholson's apartment. Probably, there's another
at the elevator and one near the fire stairs. They
didn't try to break into Nicholson's apartment, so
they're cautious. That suggests their numbers are
limited.* He rattled off commands. "When I go out,
keep the door open, but stay out of the direct line
of fire. When I tell you, make a break for the
stairs." Recalling he was dealing with frightened
civilians, he warned, "Don't hesitate, no matter
how bad it seems. You're going to have to trust
me to know when it's safest. Sorry," he added for
Walker's benefit. "If we make it to the car, smash
in as best you can and leave mc the driver's seat.
Understand?"

Walker, Harlowe, and Nicholson exchanged uncomfortable glances, but no one questioned or challenged. Drawing the matches from his pocket,
Carrigan lit the cotton of the tampon. The homemade incendiary could do little more than delay,
but the extra seconds might spell the difference between life and death. If his enemies had stationed
a man at the stairs, Carrigan guessed that man
would need to peek around the fire door for a shot
at the hallway. *They're afraid I might have armed
myself in Nicholson's apartment. Otherwise, they
would have broken in. Therefore, the guy'll hide
behind the door. Fire exits always open toward the
stairs.*

Carrigan whipped open the apartment door and
hurled the bottle toward Nicholson's door. Without
waiting to see it hit, he whirled, slamming against
the fire door. His shoulder met resistance. Then the
door gave, staggering the man stationed behind it.
Bullets rattled against the frame, louder than the

more distant clatter of breaking glass. The fire door sprang closed, and Carrigan found himself on the landing, facing a reeling Arab clutching an AK-47.

Catching the gun, Carrigan smashed his fist into the stranger's face. The blow sent the man lurching toward the steps. Carrigan tore the assault rifle free and turned it on its owner. The blast tore through the stranger, toppling him down the steps.

A shout of pain wafted through the thick, metal door as someone tried to wade through the nearly invisible alcohol flames. Carrigan toed the fire door ajar. His maneuver was met by a spattering of bullets that tore through the layered steel as if it were paper. Carrigan returned fire down the hallway, assessing the layout in the instant before he pulled the trigger. Two men stood near the entrance to Nicholson's apartment, one flattened to the wall, the other slapping at alcohol flames that burned his pants leg. Carrigan's shots took the second man out. Another stranger ducked behind the Pepsi machine, confirming Carrigan's strategic guess. "Run for the stairs!" he shouted, spraying bullets through the hallway to cover his companions' race for the door. One wild slug tore through the glass of the fire alarm. Sound blared through the building, and Carrigan hoped the system was rigged to shut down the elevators. It would buy time.

Carrigan waited only until his three companions darted through the door before springing it closed behind them. "Go!" They raced down the steps. Carrigan doubted the enemy would follow. They would know as well as he how easy his lead would make it for him to whirl on any landing and gun them down as they gave chase. *Whatever kind of murderer I am, I must be good at it. So far they haven't dared to underestimate me.*

Pounding footsteps began to fill the stairwell as pajama-clad tenants responded to the fire alarm. As Carrigan rounded the third floor landing, the door whisked open. A woman in a bathrobe and curlers got one glimpse of the AK-47 in his hands and screamed. Attention redirected to this new threat, the people echoed her fear. Shrieks reverberated through the stairwell, and the footfalls became frenzied.

"It's okay!" Carrigan shouted over the chaos. "I'm a cop," he lied. "Out of my way!" Elbowing past his three companions, he shoved through the crowd.

Some people pressed aside to let Carrigan through. Others ran, panicked, before him. A young boy tumbled down half a flight of stairs, and it was all Carrigan could do to grab the child's arm and pull him from the path of a frantic man. Carrigan carried the boy to the safety of the lowest landing as the crowd streamed through the two exits. Pushing the youngster toward the left door, Carrigan followed the group funneling through the right-hand door to the parking lot.

Carrigan heard the click of a car door beneath the noises of the crowd. He glanced over to a metallic silver Cadillac in time to see two men with AK-47s hurtle out of the front seat to hide behind the open automobile doors.

"To the car!" Carrigan commanded. He ducked between the Porsche and its neighboring station wagon. The gunmen fired blindly into the crowd. Two men and a woman fell. Others scattered, screaming as they ran through the parking lot. Harlowe, Nicholson, and Walker made a dash for the car as Carrigan covered them with a rain of gunfire aimed at the Cadillac, trying desperately not to catch anyone in the cross fire.

A blue compact car zipped into the parking lot, its driver wearing rumpled scrubs, apparently a resident returning from a late night call. Clumsy and slowed by lack of sleep, he seemed not to notice the panicked crowd. Suddenly, his attention riveted on a screaming woman clutching a toddler. He veered from her path and toward the line of fire, gaze locked on the child, oblivious to the flying bullets.

Nicholson whirled, gasping at the sight. "Jim! Jim, no!" The pause nearly cost Nicholson her life. Harlowe grabbed her roommate's shirt, jerking her toward the Porsche. Nicholson stumbled to her knees; and shots flew over her head, chewing divots in the asphalt that peppered Walker. Harlowe shoved Nicholson toward the car, then assisted Walker into the back.

The compact barreled toward the cross fire. Concerned for the driver, Carrigan swiveled his weapon to the car, careful to avoid the windshield. Bullets rattled across the hood in warning, then he targeted the tires.

Seizing Carrigan's moment of distraction, the enemy launched a barrage of AK fire. He dropped back to a crouch behind the station wagon. *Six thousand misses to every hit.* The rampant inaccuracy of automatic weapons came to Carrigan's mind unbidden. Then a slug tore through the station wagon and crashed into his left forehead, flattening him, sick and dizzied, to the pavement. Three more followed, drilling holes through the door and whizzing above his chest and face; at least one of the enemy was using a handgun. Carrigan did not know whether to bless or curse his luck. An AK hit there would have killed him; but, without the single shot's precision, the gunman probably would have missed altogether. Battling unconsciousness with superlative training, Carrigan low-rolled across the macadam and scrambled for the Porsche.

The driver of the compact jammed on his brakes. The car skidded to a screeching halt, then spun clear of the gunfire.

Head down, Carrigan lurched into the Porsche's driver's seat. Nicholson thrust the key in the ignition as Carrigan pressed the gas. The Porsche roared to life. He pulled the door closed, slammed into reverse, and swerved the car from its space amid a shower of cinders. Jabbing in the clutch again, he shifted into first and whisked forward, dodging running tenants. A volley of gunfire shattered the rear window, spraying glass over Walker and Harlowe curled in the back seats. Then the gunmen stopped shooting to climb back in their car and give chase.

Unlike Carrigan, the strangers did not bother to avoid pedestrians. Anyone who did not throw themselves out of the path of the Cadillac was cut down by its wheels. Even as he raced from the lot, a sense of outrage welled in Carrigan, and the naturalness of the emotion comforted him. *What do you know. I do have scruples.* As he tore out of the parking lot and reversed the directions he had taken to arrive at the apartment building, guilt touched him even through the agony that threatened to shatter his head. *If I hadn't triggered the fire alarm, none of those civilians would have died.*

He dispelled the thought. *I didn't kill those people; my enemies did. I'm not responsible for their cruelty.* Still, Carrigan knew he needed to find a safe place to leave his companions before anyone else got killed.

Carrigan's throbbing head made him forget his injured shoulder. Blood trickled in a winding line along his temple.

Walker shifted position with a muttered grunt of pain. Carrigan realigned the rearview to find Walker rolling up his pants leg to examine his right leg. "Is he all right?" Carrigan asked.

Harlowe answered. "I'm no doctor, but it looks like bruises and scrapes."

Walker elaborated. "Just debris. Got a chunk of driveway in my calf that hurts like a son of a bitch."

Harlowe looked up, catching Carrigan's gaze in the mirror. She gasped. "You're hurt."

Startled by Harlowe's words, Nicholson craned to see the left side of Carrigan's forehead while he readjusted the mirror. Her lids widened. "Christ. We've got to get you to a hospital." Her expression became frantic, dark eyes nearly bugging from their sockets. "Shot in the head? How the hell are you driving?"

Carrigan dismissed Nicholson's concern. Despite the pain, he had no difficulty concentrating and his thoughts remained vividly clear. "That bullet went through layers of steel and plastic first. It looks worse than it is. I'm fine." It seemed a necessary lie.

Walker abandoned his own wound to check on Carrigan's, obviously chagrined that attention to his smaller injury allowed him to miss a more critical one. "You'll need to see a doctor."

"I've already seen two." Carrigan pitched his voice to indicate that the discussion had ended. "And one hospital shoot-out was enough. No more."

"But—" Nicholson started.

"No more!" Carrigan roared, voice startling in the closed confines of the car, and the shout stabbing pain through his head. He softened his tone, feeling deserving of the pain. "I'll be fine."

The others fell silent. The clock on the dash read 5:36 a.m. The false dawn had disappeared into the wee hours before sunrise. The scattered illumination provided by street lamps scarcely penetrated the darkness. Carrigan kept the Porsche's headlights off as he rounded the corners of Oakside and Woodbridge Lanes and whipped onto the main road paralleling the river. He cut the last turn short. The Porsche skidded across the gravel shoulder, kicking dust onto the road behind them. The powder deflected the Cadillac's lights into a cloud of glare, spurring an idea.

Flipping the car into high gear, Carrigan whisked down the roadway, weaving from macadam to shoulder. Dirt flew, forming a gray wake behind the Porsche. "Seat belts on," he instructed his passengers and heard the answering clicks as Harlowe and Walker complied. Nicholson yanked Carrigan's shoulder harness on before placing her own.

Carrigan sped through a yellow light, then a red one, the tires chewing ruts into the gravel of the shoulder. At first, billowing dust channeled through the shattered back window. But, as the speedometer eased upward to flutter around 120 mph, the powder hovered like smokestack exhaust; and the Cadillac disappeared in the fog.

Harlowe's fingers gouged the leather of Carrigan's headrest.

"Slow down. Slow down." Walker's admonishments became a plea as serious as Carrigan's fear of elevators.

This time, when Carrigan veered onto the shoulder, he continued past it onto the grass of the riverbank. He stomped on the brake pedal. Momentum tossed him against the seat belt. The brakes locked, and the car skated to a halt on the grass. Anticipating a smoother stop, it took Carrigan a second to cram the shift into reverse and back silently into the stirring dust. "What the hell's wrong with this car?"

Nicholson's reply mixed agitation with offense. "You slammed the brakes at 120, for Christ's sake! What did you expect to happen? I've got anti-lock brakes. Any normal car would have skidded to China."

Gravel crunched as the Cadillac sped past, invisible in the floating dust. Gently, Carrigan guided the Porsche back onto the road. Aware it would not take the men in the Cadillac long to realize he had tricked them, he knew he would need to act fast. The most logical evasion required him to turn 180 degrees. *But they'll expect me to do that. Therefore, I'll have to try something different.* "Headlights?"

"Button near your left hand," Nicholson replied. "But why would you want to . . ." She trailed off, leaving the rest of her question unspoken as Carrigan flipped the switch. The halogen lights swiveled up like giant eyes, and the settling dust allowed less than a foot of visibility. He drove in the same direction as before, slowly, simulating a cautious driver.

As he expected, within moments, a larger car passed them on the opposite side of the road. Darkness and roiling dirt made it impossible to identify for certain, but that would serve for the Porsche as well. Carrigan guessed the Arabs expected him to act rationally; they would assume he'd keep the Porsche's lights off, turn around, and put as much distance between them as possible. "I think we lost them. For now, at least."

Harlowe settled back as far as the tiny rear seats allowed. "I can't believe this is happening. I feel like an extra in a Steve McQueen movie."

Carrigan shrugged in ignorance. "Steve who?"

"Steve McQueen." Harlowe leaned forward. "You know. He did a lot of old action-adventure movies."

Carrigan glanced at Harlowe over his shoulder before turning his attention back to the road. "You mean like Arnold Schwarzenegger?"

Harlowe, Walker, and Nicholson shared a laugh at Carrigan's expense. "Not exactly," Harlowe said.

The Porsche came to a four-way intersection, the light green in Carrigan's direction. "Take a right," Walker said, his words clipped with pain.

Carrigan complied and found himself in Liberty's business district. He passed an all-night grocery, two gas stations, and a Taco John's. "Where are you steering me, Walker? I need to find somewhere safe to leave you three."

Shawna opened her mouth to protest, but Carrigan cut her short. "You have an oath to protect your patients, I know. But I have an oath of my own. This John Doe does not drag untrained soldiers into war. I can evade these guys easier alone, and I'd venture to guess you three would do better without the gunfire."

She sagged in her seat. She seemed relieved, and Carrigan guessed she appreciated the excuse to escape the action, despite her insistence to the contrary. Sadness touched him. He hated to admit dependence on anyone, but he knew he would miss Shawna Nicholson.

Distant sirens screamed over the normal pound and zoom of traffic, drawing nearer.

Walker addressed Carrigan's original question. "I think we should go to my place."

"Your place?" Carrigan gingerly shook his head as he drove by a video rental store and a fluorescent blue liquor store, both closed for the night. "No way. You saw how quickly they found Shawna's apartment."

"This is different." Walker put a hand on each of the front seats, his face between them. "I live twenty minutes from town on a rural route. I just moved there and haven't had time to send out change of address forms yet. It's in the middle of twelve acres of timber with a long gravel drive. If anyone comes up, we'll hear them. There're two exits, and I take a three mile walk by the lake every morning. I know the woods."

The sirens wailed louder. A police car whipped past, an ambulance close behind. Their shrill alarms, and more approaching, seemed to enfold the Porsche with sound.

Carrigan recalled from watching television that "woods" was the term for large tracts of trees. He felt torn between his concern that the gunmen might obtain Walker's address and the realization that he could hardly dump his companions in some random location. *If Walker knows his woods, it should give him an advantage; and I suspect the gunmen will chase me, not them.* "Okay," Carrigan conceded. The car whisked past a fruit stand, and he rocketed through another red light without thinking.

A car horn howled through the darkness, accompanied by the screech of brakes. A pea green sedan smashed into the rear of the Porsche on the driver's side. Jolted, the seat belts locked. Walker gasped. The collision spun the Porsche, and its forward momentum crashed the front bumper into a telephone pole. The engine stalled. The sedan fishtailed around behind them, blocking the road.

A speeding police car slammed to a halt, brakes squealing as it rotated in a full circle. It skidded to a stop parallel to the sedan, its red and blue lights flashing across both cars and the intersection. "Shit!" Carrigan poked around the dash for a starter button. He pressed levers at random. The radio blared rock music. Water sloshed across the windshield, followed by a stroke of the wipers. The sough of the defroster sounded softly beneath the melody. Through the rearview mirror, Carrigan watched two policemen exit the car, leaving it to block traffic. They headed for the sedan.

Nicholson snapped off the radio, heater, and rear defrost. "What are you trying to do?"

"Get us out of here." Carrigan's search became more frantic as the policemen reached the other car.

"Are you crazy?" Nicholson jerked her keys from the ignition. Sliding the AK-47 from Carrigan's lap, she forced it beneath her seat, strategically placing her feet to hide the jutting barrel. "He's seen our plate. You're the one who doesn't want any cops. Leaving the scene of an accident will get every one in the state out chasing us." She seemed more distraught than Carrigan had ever seen her, though whether from aftershock or the damage inflicted on her expensive car, he could not guess.

Walker loosed a tense sigh. "Finally police, thank God. A blessing in disguise." He added hastily, "So long as the guy in the other car's not hurt."

Carrigan stabbed at the gauges; but, without the keys, nothing in the car functioned. He watched as one officer returned to the black and white car and the other headed toward the driver's window of the Porsche. Carrigan knew reason would work better, but desperation left him time only for intimidation. "Not a word, Walker, or I'll gun you down right here and now. And the police with you." The threat was not wholly idle. He had no intention of injuring the doctor, but hazy memories told him the police might force him to violence.

As the officer came to the window, Carrigan lowered the glass and tried to appear casual. The policeman poked a pudgy face up to the Porsche, studying its interior. "Everyone okay?"

"Yes, sir," Carrigan replied stiffly. He covered his head wound with a cupped hand.

"What happened?"

The question seemed stupid to Carrigan. He craned his neck through the open window to stare at the huge crater in the Porsche's side. "He hit me." He pointed toward the sedan.

The intensity of the policeman's stare annoyed Carrigan. "She says *you* hit *her*."

Carrigan could no longer contain his sarcasm. "That's right, sir. I sideways-ed into her."

The policeman was unamused. "Show me your license and registration."

Harlowe and Walker seemed to stop breathing. Carrigan hesitated, uncertain of the policeman's request but quite sure asking him to clarify would be unwise. He could see the policeman carried a pistol at his belt, and it occurred to him to grab the AK-47. But the sight of Shawna Nicholson reaching casually to the sun visor for her beeper stopped him. He heard the almost imperceptible click as she thumbed the switch off and back on, then sound shrilled through the Porsche with a suddenness that startled everyone.

"There it goes again." Nicholson punched the button, instantly silencing the beeper. Shielding the blank display with a cupped hand, she pretended to watch for a number, then addressed the officer. "Sir, that's Dr. Jason Walker." She gestured at Carrigan. "And I'm Dr. Nicholson. We were showing off my car to my friends," she waved vaguely at the back seat, "when the beeper went off. There's an emergency at Liberty Hospital. Jason was rushing to get there and wasn't paying attention. I'm really sorry. He's not usually like this. He must have hit his head on the dash. Concussion. For his sake and the patient's, we need to get to the hospital fast." She jabbed open the glove compartment and handed the policeman a packet of papers. "It's registered to me. The insurance is in there, too. I know it's illegal to leave the scene, but this is urgent."

The policeman hesitated, obviously uncertain.

Taking Nicholson's cue, Carrigan rubbed his hand down the side of his head, smearing the trickle of blood and revealing the wound.

Nicholson clipped her beeper back on the visor. "Could I at least use a phone?"

The officer stared at Carrigan's forehead, features etched with concern. He glanced toward his own car, face alternately tinged red and blue by the lights. "That's not necessary. We're aware of the emergency. There's two, in fact. We're still sorting details, but they'll need all the doctors they can get at Liberty. There's been shooting and other violence. We're on our way to the second scene now."

"Shooting?" Nicholson clambered out the passenger side, expression appropriately concerned. "My God!" Then, as if seeing Carrigan's wound for the first time, she winced, then motioned for him to slid into her seat. "Scoot over, Jason, you're in no condition to drive."

Glad for Nicholson's quick thinking, Carrigan fumbled awkwardly into the passenger's seat, feigning disorientation.

The fresh, deep bruise and Nicholson's act obviously impressed the policeman. "I'll radio ahead and let them know Dr. Walker's coming. I'd give you an escort, but we're on our way to a major emergency. Can you make it safely on your own?"

"We're fine," she insisted convincingly. "You go."

Seizing a pad of paper, the policeman jotted down some information from the packet she gave him. Returning it to Nicholson, he waved her away. "Go on, Doctor. We'll take care of this later." He inclined his head toward the sedan.

"Thank you," Shawna said, taking the driver's seat. The policeman waited until she restarted the

Porsche and it rumbled off in the general direction of Liberty Hospital.

Awed by Nicholson's maneuvering, Carrigan clapped a hand to her leg in a gesture of respect. "Nice job, for an amateur."

Nicholson stiffened at his touch. She knocked his grip aside, suddenly angry. "Nice job. Nice job? My credibility as a doctor is shot to hell. I lied to a cop! Me, goody-goody Shawna Nicholson, lied to a cop when I should have begged for his help—"

Walker interrupted. "That's right. That's right! I said get help. Why didn't you?"

Curious, Carrigan encouraged an answer. "Yes, why didn't you?"

Nicholson turned on Carrigan. "You mean other than your gentle promise to 'gun us down'? For some stupid, inexplicable reason, I felt we owed you. You told us to stay in my apartment. Maybe if we had, we'd have police protection, you'd be halfway to wherever, and no one would have died. We forced ourselves on you, and I would have felt like an ass if I got you thrown in jail for giving us a break. You saved Jason's hide. You rescued Jim Mason in the parking lot, though you had to shoot at him to do it. You said no police. I have to believe you have a good reason."

"His reason is he's nuts!" Walker shouted from the back. "We put our lives in the hands of a f—"

Tracy interrupted. "Stay out of this, Jason." She pounced on Nicholson's thought. "Driving without ID, let alone a license. Not to mention gunning down strangers, never mind that they shot first. Shawna's right. The truth wouldn't matter. They'd pitch him right in the slammer until things got sorted out, if ever. I heard he's real claustrophobic. It'd drive him insane in the first half minute."

"Short trip." Walker muttered but did change the subject. "We really ought to get to the hospital. The cop was right about Liberty needing every doctor."

Harlowe snorted. "Jason, there'll be nine thousand surgeons and trauma specialists. Do you really think they'll miss two internal medicine residents?"

Nicholson continued yelling at Carrigan over the conversation in the back seat. "You destroyed my apartment and my $35,000 car! And, by the way, even if the insurance company believes my story, which they won't, my premiums will go up to a million. I can't believe the cop didn't notice the missing back window and the bullet holes and . . ." Rage garbled words that already seemed partially nonsensical to Carrigan. " . . . *Mr. John Doe,* I'm not falling for a maniac, even if he is pretty!"

Now even Shawna's gone over the deep end. Carrigan clasped his hands and blinked through a stunned silence that included Harlowe and Walker.

The Porsche glided toward North Liberty, a wounded shadow streaking through the dawn.

CHAPTER 7
End Game

In the past, the spring forest had always seemed serene to Jason Walker, a quiet place where he could observe wildflowers, blooming trees, and mayapples and forget the cares of the day. But in the silence that followed the roar of the vanishing Porsche, the night-dark woods seemed to crush in on the circular illumination of the single, county-owned security light in the base of his driveway. Dawn played over his rented A-frame, sheening off cedar walls painted gray-blue. Walker suspected his landlord had built the structure himself, with little knowledge of an architect's craft. Cracks in the woodwork left the house drafty and bug-infested year-round. The upper, triangular tier had never been connected to the remainder of the house; it served only as a storage area. A jutting sun porch kept the front door in shadow.

The events of the last few hours seemed surreal to Walker, an unusually vivid nightmare. Yet the nervousness of Shawna Nicholson and Tracy Harlowe, their presence at his home, and the bruises that riddled his limbs and chest confirmed the reality of car chases and gunfire. Thinking back, Walker realized fatigue and denial had caused him to miss clues that might otherwise have seemed obvious: the nurses' fear, the rattle of bullets on concrete in the parking garage, the John Doe's urgency. Now, everything came together except for the who and the why. And, comparing his own reactions to Nicholson's quiet dignity and composure, Jason Walker felt like a raving idiot.

"This way." Walker fished his keys from his pants pocket and led his companions past the cockeyed, sagging garage that held his Dodge Omni. "Watch the stairs. They're crooked." Cautiously, favoring his left leg and feeling the way with his toes, he descended a set of steps constructed from railroad ties to his front door. Opening it, he ushered his friends into a long, dark hallway leading into the kitchen and living room. Once there, he snapped on the switch.

Overhead lights bathed a desk covered with multi-shaped, smoke-colored office organizers in a neat array. A wall shelf above it held reference books and novels placed in alphabetical order. A wooden bar with a gold-flecked, red formica top served as a kitchen table surrounded by stools with broken supports between the legs. Dust filmed every stick of furniture, and bits of paper clung to the carpet. Walker flushed, aware of the oddity of his housekeeping. There was no clutter; every item stood in its assigned spot, yet he was less compulsive about cleaning. Worn, wooden steps led into a recessed family room with a television, two stuffed chairs, and a couch discarded by his parents. Two sets of glass doors covered by curtains opened to the backyard. Through the cracks between the drapes, Jason caught a glimpse of the woods and the lake cove he loved. A hallway off the living room led to the bath and bedchambers.

Tracy trotted into the family room and sprawled across one of the chairs. "I'm glad that's over."

Shawna sat on the steps, legs dangling. "Good riddance," she mumbled with an atypical irritability Jason attributed to the stress of the last few hours.

Walker stopped in the bathroom, opened the medicine chest, and gathered a handful of cotton balls. He grabbed the brown bottle of peroxide and followed the women. Limping past Shawna, he took a seat on the chair opposite Tracy. "Did you see the way John handled that gun? Matching fingerprints or not, he's combat trained."

"Can't be," Shawna snapped.

"Maybe the fingerprint people made a mistake." Tracy swiveled her chair in a jerky, rocking motion trying to soothe her frazzled nerves.

"Not likely." Walker set down the supplies then glanced at his watch. *6:21, two minutes since John left. We promised him ten before calling the police.* "The way I see it, he's either secret service, a foreign soldier, or both. And if he's a spy, someone would have come in and shipped him off to Botswana for therapy."

Shawna glanced sharply at Jason Walker as if personally affronted. "John has to be American. He speaks English. Without an accent."

Walker shrugged, glad of conversation that distracted him from the possibility they all understood tacitly. *This may not be over yet.* "A Russian spy would speak English without an accent, too. From what you and the nurses said, John's speech gets awkward at times. His being a foreigner would explain why he has trouble with common objects and concepts, like cornfields, slang, and land owning."

"I don't buy that." Harlowe's chair squeaked softly with each movement. "Russian, German, American. A car's a car. Shawna had to teach that guy how to turn the ignition key."

Jason rolled up his torn pants leg, discovering bruises and scrapes. The worst of his injuries seemed to be the ragged abrasion in his calf from which he had pulled a fragment of blacktop while in the car. He soaked the cotton balls and washed the wound methodically. "Did you know the nurses found some currency on him? It looked like foreign money, though I have to admit I couldn't find any of it listed in the guide." He gestured vaguely toward the bookshelf.

Shawna scuffed her shoe on a stair. "Do you mind talking about something else? John's an American. I just know, okay? He just feels American to me."

Tracy stopped shifting and leaned forward mischievously. "Oh, so you admit you've been feeling him."

Shawna glared. "Don't give me shit. I got enough of that from Shrink Bercelian. I'm as glad to see John go as anyone. Gladder."

Having achieved the intended reaction, Tracy Harlowe pressed. "Oh, come on. Tall, dark, handsome and . . ." Raising her fingers like claws, she adopted a cheap monster movie accent, ". . . mysterious." She returned to her normal voice. "Isn't that what every woman desires?" Resting her chin on steepled fingers, Harlowe sighed, batted her eyes, and stared distantly.

Shawna frowned. "I've got news for you, Tracy. My daydream prince doesn't carry a machine gun.

And why do you keep harping on it? You know I hardly know the guy."

Jason smiled as he restored his pants leg, enjoying the game. "She's doing it because it's fun watching cool as a cucumber Nicholson get hot and bothered. If you'd stop reacting to it, she'd quit teasing."

Shawna rose. "Well, the razzing stops here. I don't like John. End of discussion." She looked around as if searching for something. "I need a phone. I promised John a head start, and he's got it. Now, I'm calling the police. We need protection, and I've got to report my car stolen. I can't exactly write it off on my taxes."

The image made Walker chuckle. "Charitable donations: one 1985 Porsche 944 given to Russian agent as getaway car."

Harlowe consulted a clock over the desk. "Lighten up, Shawna. At last give him the full ten minutes we promised."

Nicholson hunched to sit back down.

Tracy gave Jason a devilish look, then whispered musically. "John and Shawna sittin' in a tree ..."

"That does it!" Shawna leaped to her feet. "Where's the phone?"

Walker pointed out the dial telephone on the kitchen wall, and she started toward it.

Tracy Harlowe's sudden gasp stopped Nicholson in mid-stride. Walker followed Harlowe's shaking finger to the glass doors. A human figure was silhouetted against the flimsy curtains.

"Quick!" Shawna hissed. "Away from the glass."

Recalling how easily the AK-47 bullets had penetrated the metal fire door, Jason raced up the steps with Tracy close behind. "This way." He led the women into the bedroom. Waving them to the bed, he stepped around it and peeked out the bedroom window. The sunrise backlit a shadowy form moving toward the glass doors, clutching an assault rifle. Walker stepped away from the window. Fear gripped him, and his mind blanked.

"Gotta call 911." Nicholson sprang toward the door.

A sound galvanized Walker, the familiar, hollow slap of a hand banging against the post supporting the sun deck that shadowed the front door. He recalled how many times he had slipped on the loose railroad ties and staggered into that same pillar. "No! Shawna, the phone's too near the door. We have to get out fast." Sacrificing silence for speed, Walker slid up the window screen. His heart hammered, and tears of panic blurred his vision. *My God, I can't believe this is happening. What are we going to do?* Feet first, Walker wriggled through the opening, swiveled, and dropped to the ground. His injured leg buckled, sprawling him. Scrambling to his feet amid a chorus of stinging bruises, he pressed tightly to the wall, as much for comfort as caution. He did not dare look around for enemies, as if the magic of not seeing them would make them not exist. Still, the skin on his back crawled from imagined bullet wounds, and the women's exits seemed to span an eternity.

When Tracy's feet touched earth, Jason Walker bolted into the forest, the women close behind him. A harsh, foreign shout pursued them. Bullets rattled and thunked through the greenery at their backs, desperate shots at impossible range. Walker bolted in terror, breathless and aching within a dozen strides. Harlowe kept pace easily, but Nicholson panted, too, the penalty for a sedentary doctor's life. Desperation lent them speed, and Walker's knowledge of the terrain gave him a slight advantage. He dodged between familiar trunks, vaulted downed trees he knew from his walks, and straggled through a ribbon of stream. He twisted his ankle on a jutting stone, tearing a line of pain along his leg; but even that barely slackened his reckless pace.

The gunmen must have had little experience with running in woodlands. They fell behind, their pursuit loudly announcing their location. This did not reassure Walker. *Slower perhaps, but better trained to run. Got to hide. I can't keep up this pace much longer.*

The pathway veered at a rocky cliff that dropped sheerly into the lake. At the corner, nearly all of the oaks, birch, and locusts bore evidence of a beaver's teeth. Many saplings lay on the ground, their bases and stumps whittled to points. Walker gasped in a lungful of air. "Down," he whispered. Confused, the women ground to a halt. To demonstrate, he slithered down the rock face, not bothering to test his handholds. A stone broke free, tumbling into the lake with a splash. Jason winced but continued until his feet touched the familiar slick, narrow ledge along the water. Hugging the cliff face, he worked his way sideways, dodging a stone dislodged by Harlowe above him.

The path to the beaver's den seemed longer than he remembered. He heard a gruff, vocal exchange above him and held his breath. Then his toe met empty air, and he ducked around the corner into the cave. Several inches of cold water sloshed into his running shoes as he eased deeper into the recess. Soon, the women joined him. They waited in a frightened silence, the cave muffling even the lapping of water against the cliff and the rasping of air through overtaxed lungs.

Ten minutes dragged by before Shawna risked speech. "How did you know about this place?"

Jason recalled the weeks spent trying to track down the beaver. "I did a lot of exploring whenever I had free time during the day."

Harlowe shivered in the damp darkness. "Think they're gone?"

In an attempt to comfort, Walker put an arm around her, but he was shaking as much as she was. "I don't know. Let's give it some more time."

Nicholson moved close to the others. "Much as I hate to admit it, I wish John was here."

Her statement seemed the sort that requires no answer. Had Walker felt any less scared, the implication might have mangled his ego. But under the circumstances, he shared her wish. "We'll be fine." He spoke the necessary platitude though it failed to soothe even himself.

The next hour passed like six, in clumsy silence. Walker's muscles knotted from standing with his weight unbalanced, his twisted ankle felt massive, and the urge to urinate became unbearable. "I'm going out to check if it's safe."

Tracy gripped his shoulder. "No. I appreciate the gallantry and all, but let's face it. You're hurt. I'm in a lot better shape for running and climbing."

He accepted the insult grudgingly but refused to concede the point. "It's dangerous." He could have kicked himself for the understatement. "I'm not hurt bad. I know the woods, and I am the—"

"Man?" Tracy interrupted. "That better not be what you were about to say."

That being exactly the case, Jason wisely said nothing. This did not seem the time to delve into the relative merits of males and females.

"No," Shawna Nicholson said, her tone uncertain for the first time since Jason Walker had met her. For people who dealt with issues of life and death daily, they both seemed to be easily stymied when their own survival lay on the line. "We all need to stay here till those killers are gone. And we stick together."

Harlowe glared at Walker one final time before placing an arm around Nicholson's shoulder. "The bastards followed us here, despite John's trick driving. The cops haven't even managed to connect the Porsche with the shoot-out yet. We're halfway to nowhere, outside Liberty's jurisdiction. Who do *you* think'll find us first?"

Walker shivered, nearly losing his urine, even though he realized Tracy was trying to shake them up to get her point across. He could see strengths and weaknesses about both strategies. If they stayed quietly in place, Carrigan's enemies might give up and leave. Yet the gunmen had so far seemed unreasonably tenacious. It made some sense to slip away before the sun came up fully, while the Arabs combed other parts of the forest. Anxiety made him fretful and impatient, and he felt drawn toward Harlowe's strategy. For all he feared what he might find outside the cave, the anticipation that accompanied remaining in place was quickly driving him to madness.

Releasing Nicholson, Harlowe stared out over

the wind-ruffled waters. "Now, are there any other ways out of here?"

Shawna shook her head. "I think we should stay put."

Jason chewed his lower lip. "I could swim. There's a cove to the right that extends into my backyard. It's only about a quarter mile, but the water's pretty cold."

Harlowe glanced up the cliff face, unclipping the ergometer from her waistband and kicking off her shoes. "Here," she handed the ergometer to Nicholson. "The way you were gasping from our stroll through the woods, you need to learn how to use this. And then use it." She smiled at her clumsy attempt to diffuse the tension, then reached out and stirred the water with a finger. "I think I'd rather chance the cold."

"Tracy, wait!" Shawna lunged for her roommate.

Harlowe pushed off from the lip of the cave and glided into the lake.

Nicholson's grasp fell short. "Damn you, Tracy. Get back here."

Walker resisted an almost overpowering urge to dive after Tracy, seize her legs, and haul her to safety. As if reading his mind, Shawna blocked him from following. He balled his fingers into fists and watched Tracy Harlowe swim a modified breaststroke. Despite her clothes, she moved with athletic grace. Her limbs flashed white through murky, green waters. Her head remained above the water, and instead of splashes, her strokes made only soft swishes.

Walker's knuckles blanched, and it required a premeditated effort to pry his fingers open. Sixty yards of swimming brought Harlowe to the mouth of the cove. She paused, treading water, then spun to the right, toward Walker's house. *Once she turns that corner, we won't be able to see her.* Jason leaned forward, hoping to watch Harlowe as long as possible. Something moved at the corner of his vision.

Sudden terror stiffened Walker, an instinctive grab for the cave mouth all that saved him from tumbling into the lake. He swung his gaze to three gun-toting figures who materialized from the woods across the cove, less than twenty feet from Tracy Harlowe.

Apparently Nicholson saw them, too. Her lips splayed open for a scream.

"No." Jason made a clumsy dive to cover Shawna's mouth, and they pitched over backward. He landed beneath Nicholson in shallow water, the splash muffled by the cave. Stone flayed his elbow and jarred agony through his already aching calf and ankle. He moaned, forcing speech around pain. "It's too late to warn Tracy. Don't give us away, too."

Shawna scrambled to her feet, her T-shirt and jeans darkened in patches from the water. Soaked, Jason staggered up beside her as a voice cut across the lake, its syllables crisp but uninterpretable.

Harlowe whirled toward the men on the bank. Walker's position accorded him only a view of the back of her head, but her words wafted clearly, her tone high-pitched with fear. "I don't understand you. Please, I don't understand."

"My God." Shawna latched onto Jason's arm and repeated the blasphemy a dozen times.

One of the gunmen spoke in heavily-accented English. "Come here."

Harlowe hesitated.

A single gunshot exploded through the hush. Walker bit his tongue. Nicholson's choked-off scream was lost in the after-echoes.

"I said, 'come here.' "

This time, Harlowe obeyed. Her sleek stroke became a frenzied chop that hampered shoreward movement. She hauled her dripping body to the bank. Immediately, the men came forward. Two pinned her arms behind her while the third, the one who had spoken, stood directly in front of her.

Walker stared in horror. Distance blurred the commander's face to swarthy obscurity, but the thin, tan fabric of his uniform revealed well-muscled shoulders. He spoke again. "Where are your friends?"

Walker could not make out Tracy's reply, but the commander slapped her face with enough force to jar her head backward. Her pained gasp was clearly audible.

"We've got to do something." Shawna's head jerked in every direction as she assessed the possibilities. "They'll kill Tracy."

Jason licked his lips, trying to concentrate, but panic scattered his wits leaving only one thought. *Why did I pick now to stop listening to my chief resident? I should have stopped Tracy. I could have talked her out of it.* Guilt hammered him, a grim echo that rose above the fear. *It should have been me.*

A garbled discussion ensued between the gunmen in their guttural language, then the commander addressed Harlowe again. "Fine. Your friends don't matter. We'll let them live, and you, too. Just tell us where Carrigan is."

"Who?" Harlowe managed, her voice cracking in mid-word.

The commander's fist slammed into Harlowe's face. The blow shocked loose a sob, and her body sagged between her captors.

Walker hugged the cave wall, teeth clenched and eyes closed. "We've got to do something," he whispered, repeating Nicholson's words in an attempt to mobilize his thoughts. He wrenched his lids apart.

The commander gripped his AK-47 in both hands. "Where ... is ... Carrigan!"

Harlowe whimpered, her voice tremulous. "Please. I don't know who you're talking about. I really don't ..."

The answer was obvious to Walker, but he realized it might not seem so easy with an assault rifle shoved in his face.

"The crazy man driving your car. The murderer." The commander drove the gun butt into Harlowe's abdomen.

Breath hissed from Tracy's lungs. She doubled over. Her captors released her, and she sprawled, face first, to the ground. The commander pinned a booted foot between Harlowe's shoulder blades and pressed the gun barrel to the back of her head. "Where is Carrigan?"

Shawna shook Jason. "Give me your keys."

It took Walker a second to comprehend her words. "My keys?"

"Give them to me!" Nicholson forced a hand into his pants pocket, closed her grip over the keys, and wrenched them free with a violence that tore the lining. She stepped out onto the ledge.

Shocked, Jason glanced across at the gunmen, but they seemed preoccupied with Tracy Harlowe.

By the time he looked back, Nicholson had started the climb up the cliff face. "Wait," Walker whispered frantically, but Nicholson ignored him. Dirt pattered down on him, gritty in his mouth. He slid to the ledge and scrambled after Nicholson, every movement painful. "What are you doing?" He cringed as she crested the rise, but no cries of discovery greeted her. She clawed to level ground, and Walker quickened his ascent to follow. "Wait." He threw himself over the rise, glad to discover Shawna had waited for him.

"Come on." Shawna grabbed Jason's arm, helping him to his feet. Together, they skittered into the woods. "We have to get back to your place. Fast."

"There's a neighbor just a half mile up the street. We can call the cops from there."

"Too far. Tracy doesn't have that long."

A gunshot snapped. Harlowe's scream shrilled, echoing through the cliffs, chilling Walker to his core.

Shawna's urgency disappeared, and her grip fell from Jason's forearm. She stood, rooted to the ground. "Not Tracy. Oh, please, God, not Tracy."

"Keep going." Walker wrapped an arm around Nicholson's waist and yanked her forward. *The shot came first. The scream after. Tracy's alive.* "They're just trying to scare her. We can still help."

Nicholson stumbled, then regained her balance. She bolted toward the house. Walker barely kept pace with her, trying to shut out the sounds behind him. By the time they reached the edge of his backyard, he heard another bang and a howl of pain. He bit his tongue again, this time hard enough to draw blood. *No denying it anymore. He's shooting AT Tracy.* He dashed toward the glass doors, but

Nicholson darted past, around the front to the garage.

"Where are you going?" Jason screamed. "We need to call the police."

Nicholson panted, sorting through his keys. "By the time they get here, it'll be too late." She ducked into the garage.

Torn, Walker chose to stay with Nicholson. He ran up just as the Omni rumbled to life and jerked onto the gravel of the driveway. The passenger door swung open.

Walker jumped in as another gunshot sounded in the distance. He reached to close the door as the car lurched forward. Off balance, he tumbled out the door and rolled, the stones gouging his back. "Shit." He clambered painfully to his feet.

The Omni skidded to a stop. "I'm sorry," Shawna said, sounding more frustrated than apologetic. "Get in. Hurry!"

Walker leaped into the passenger's seat, this time grabbing a tight hold on the dash before whipping his door closed. Nicholson twisted the steering wheel to the right. The tires chewed into the grass of Walker's yard, hurling divots. "Where are you going?" Jason yelled.

Shawna gave no verbal reply, but the Omni whisked around the house and toward the forest.

"Are you crazy?" A tree loomed in the windshield, and Walker threw up a protective arm. The car swerved. The trunk cracked against the side mirror, then scraped a gash along Walker's door. "You can't drive through woods!"

"I'm not letting my best friend die." Shawna zigzagged around a blackberry copse, then veered onto a familiar footpath.

Jason tried to recall whether any large obstacles lay across the route, forcing himself to ignore the press of trees to his right. A sapling cracked and ruffled beneath the carriage. A branch smacked the side mirror, this time tearing it free.

Nicholson swiveled left, bringing the Omni dangerously close to the bank of the cove. The car plowed through a mound of weeds. Walker's vision filled with torn greenery. Then, suddenly, they came within sight of the clearing by the water where the strangers had tortured Harlowe. Walker saw no sign of the men. A single figure remained, still and silent in the dirt.

Shawna slammed on the brakes. The Omni skidded, spinning through dew-damp moss. It sheered toward the water. The bumper bounced from a tree, jarring Walker to the floor. The engine stalled.

Before Walker could catch his balance, Nicholson was out and running. He opened his door and watched her kneel in front of the body. As he placed a foot on the ground, Shawna's howl of grief told him more than words could. He approached more cautiously. His gaze swept the surrounding forest for evidence of movement. Finding none, he trotted to Nicholson's side, braced for the worst.

Jason had seen death before, from the corpse he and his partners had dissected in anatomy lab to stubble-faced, old men fighting their last battles against heart disease or cancer. But nothing in his career prepared him to view the body of a beautiful young woman who was also a friend. It took an effort of will to look; but, once he did, he was unable to glance away. Tracy Harlowe's glazed, green eyes glared at the rising sun. Bruises mottled her cheeks, and a single bullet entry hole mangled her nose. Walker could see where previous shots had cut through a hand and a thigh.

Tears clouded Jason's vision, dulling Tracy's corpse to a splash of white against the foliage. Then, distant rustling reached his ears, growing closer, the thrash and stomp of men unused to forest. He caught Nicholson's shoulders and felt her shivering beneath his touch. "We've got to get out of here," he heard himself say. "Now!"

The world seemed slowed. Shawna rose, mechanical as a robot, and the doctors raced back toward the Omni in a hush vibrant with horror.

A man shouted something, then gunfire swept the clearing, too distant to strike the car but nearing swiftly. Walker stiffened. Nicholson loosed a terrified scream. Then both scrambled for the driver's seat at once. Walker's shoulder hammered Nicholson's side. Her shoe scraped along his calf, then came down hard on his ankle. Pain only fueled his desperation. Walker dove into the Omni as Nicholson tumbled to the dirt, hand banging the lower door ledge. Though he would have preferred to drive, he scooted to the passenger side to give her room. She scurried into place, slamming the door on a heavily accented entreaty:

"We want Carrigan. Tell us where he is, and we won't hurt you."

"Go! Go! Go!" Jason shouted.

Shawna hit the ignition and hammered the shift into reverse. "That's what you promised Tracy, you bastards!" she shrieked through hysterical tears, though only Walker could hear her in the closed car.

"Go!" Jason cringed beneath the dash. "Damn it, just go!"

The car hurtled backward with a suddenness that slammed Walker's head against the glove compartment. Stunned, he slid to the floor as the car jounced and rattled backward over the uneven pathway. Jason gasped, twisting and clawing for a steadying hold on the passenger seat. "What the hell are you doing?"

Halfway around in her seat, Shawna did not bother to answer. She fought the wheel as the tires thumped over branches and stones, her attention on a pathway never intended for vehicles. "Damn this Smurfmobile! Jason, are you going to get power steering before or after indoor plumbing?"

Leaves shrouded the back window, completely obscuring vision. Walker gasped, whirling to grab for the wheel. "Shit! Left! Left!"

Nicholson whipped the wheel counterclockwise. The Omni's rear parted branches, tree limbs scratching high-pitched lines along the trunk, then the path reappeared. The tires clomped over a boulder and bounced to the ground, jarring Walker back to floor. He clawed for the seat.

The trees thinned, then divided; and the house came into sight. At the boundary between woodlands and yard, Nicholson whipped the Omni's back end around. The unexpected maneuver flung Walker against the passenger door. Becoming used to the abrupt shifts and bumps, he managed to shield his head, but the impact spasmed pain through his injured leg and ankle. "Ow! Damn it!" He snatched the seat belt, braced himself and sat. The Omni surged forward as he clipped the metal end into the buckle with a satisfying snap.

"Where is this neighbor of yours?" Shawna

shouted, anger an obvious facade for fear, guilt, and grief.

"North. Next driveway." Shaken past the point of breaking, Jason Walker slumped in his seat and sobbed.

The red and blue lights of a patrol car slashed through the North Liberty forest, shattering the last remnants of peace the woods could ever hold for Jason Walker. Huddled with Nicholson in the back seat of Deputy Harry Schreiber's car, he pressed his clasped fingers to the early stubble growing on his chin. His thoughts felt thick, clotted by lack of sleep and the aftermath of too much adrenaline. Nothing made sense. The best course of action eluded him as it never had in medicine, and he appreciated Nicholson's presence and her ability to concentrate even from the depths of her sorrow. She had rushed them to the neighbors' house, only to find it empty; apparently the Beckners had left for work. A lower level window had proved easy to jimmy. Once inside, Nicholson had called the sheriff, and the thirty-minute wait for the arrival of three deputies had seemed the longest in Walker's life.

Static blasted through the car, followed by a voice Jason recognized as that of a short, stocky deputy who had introduced himself as Schooley. "We've checked out the house. No signs of forced entry or struggle. All's quiet."

Walker had been awake for more than twenty-four hours now. His head felt lead-weighted and buzzed from the effort to remain awake and civil. He clenched his fingers more tightly, seized with the sudden compulsion to wash his hands.

Schreiber looked at Walker, graying hair framing large, blue eyes and a rugged face. "You're sure it's number 219, Mr. Walker?" He used a gentle tone devoid of judgment, but Jason could not help feeling patronized.

"That's *Dr.* Walker," he corrected. He glanced at Shawna sitting quietly beside him. He knew her best friend's death had hit her hard, and this was the first chance she had to consider the long-term implications. "And I know my own house. I didn't say they actually broke in. They were getting ready to, but we didn't stick around to get killed."

"Mmmm." Schreiber hefted the radio mike but did not speak into it. "But someone was killed there?"

"Not in the house." Jason felt certain he had explained this at least twice. "On the trail through the woods." He amended. "Well, not actually on the trail. In a clearing near the lake."

Schreiber spoke directly into the handset. "Ten-four. Walker says the body's in a clearing near the lake." He replaced the mike.

A high-pitched noise obscured the reply, but Schreiber apparently understood because he did not request a repeat. Instead, he twisted for a better view of his passengers, taking a clipboard and pen in his meaty hands. "Okay, let me see if I've got this right. "You and her ..." He indicated Nicholson, "... and your missing friend saw these guys trying to break into your house. You ran and hid in a cave. Then your friend went for help and you saw her get shot."

"We didn't see her—" Shawna started.

"We heard it," Jason said, nearly simultaneously.

Schreiber raised his hands for silence. "One at a time, please. You first, Dr. Walker."

Walker sighed, beginning to wonder if he had dreamed already having given the information to Schreiber and his two associates. For what seemed like the fourth time, he told the story of Harlowe's slaying.

Schreiber listened patiently, scribbling notes as he went. "Machine guns, you say."

"Yes, sir."

"How do you know that?"

"We saw them."

Schreiber chewed the end of his pen. "But not the shooting."

"No," Jason confirmed. "Not the actual shooting. But we saw the guns here and at the apartment."

"Apartment?" Schreiber's brows rose, and he swiveled further in his seat. "Which apartment was that, Dr. Walker?"

Walker cast a nervous glance at Nicholson. It made sense that the deputy would find mention of the Liberty gunfight interesting, though only five hours had passed since the hospital incident and less since the shoot-out. But he and Shawna had not yet worked out details of what to tell the police about Carrigan. The truth seemed mandatory, but he felt a strange need to protect the patient he had rescued from death and who had returned the favor twice over. "Shawna's apartment. In Liberty. We ran scared from there, then hid here—"

Schreiber stopped Jason. "Whoa! Wait. Let me—"

He was, in turn, interrupted by the radio. "We're about twenty-five yards down the trail. Nothing here. Can we get some more details?" Again, Schooley spoke. He carried the only belt radio.

Reluctantly, Schreiber set down the pen and turned his attention to the handset. "Yeah. I'll let you talk to Walker. There may be some connection to the Liberty incident here, too."

"One corpse at a time. You there, Walker?"

Jason leaned over the seat and Schreiber's shoulder. "I'm here."

"We're about twenty-five yards down the trail behind the house. Where do we go from here?"

Walker considered, hating to admit a weakness usually ascribed to women. "I'm not real good with distances. Can you give me landmarks?"

The contact disappeared for several seconds, then Schooley came back on, a hint of humor in his tone despite the situation. "There's trees. How do you describe trees?"

Walker chewed his lower lip, further annoyed by the flippancy. "That's not much help. How about this. The trail makes a sort of a bend to the right, then quickly left. There's a moss-covered stump. Are you there, yet?"

Again, time passed in silence, then the radio flickered back to life. "There's been a lot of stumps. The path curves from the start."

Irritated, Jason turned his head to study Shawna Nicholson. "Do you think you could talk them to the right place?"

Nicholson shook her head. "I'm sure I could take them there. It's pretty much impossible to describe woods in any coherent fashion."

Nevertheless, Walker attempted to do so, with little success. Landmarks, even as transient as mushrooms and wildflowers, helped him find his way by sight. Mentally remapping the area in anything more than vague detail seemed impossible, and putting memory into words even more so. Frustration gripped Walker, and the deputies became equally impatient.

Schooley's partner, McPherson, finally ended the charade, "We'll keep looking. Now, this alleged body. Are you sure it was a human body? And definitely dead?"

Walker could contain his irritation no longer. "Of course, it was a fucking human body. Her name was Tracy! Tracy, damn it! And I'm a doctor. I know death when I see it. I hardly think we needed a second opinion."

Schreiber jerked the radio away. "You can't cuss over the air. It's against FCC regulations. Are you trying to get me fired?"

Jason slipped over the boundary from annoyance to rage. "What I'm trying to get is help. We need protection."

"And you may just get it." Schreiber raised the radio mike but continued to address Walker. "But first we need to know what's going on. And we need to find that . . . Tracy."

Shawna took Jason's hand and gave it a reassuring squeeze. She said nothing aloud; anything soothing could not help but sound patronizing. As usual, Walker appreciated her calming presence that gave him a moment to reassess his words and actions. From this point, he decided to let her do most of the talking.

Schreiber slammed the partition between himself and his passengers. Jason could still hear the crackle of the radio, though he could make out only pieces of the conversation, not enough to fit together as a coherent whole. After a few moments, Schreiber turned. "They're going to look some more, and they'll secure the area. If they don't find her, would you be willing to guide?" He added before Walker had time to consider the implications, "We'll be there with you, of course. We can't force you to go, but we may be a long time finding her without you."

"We'll go," Shawna said. Her voice, though subdued, seemed all the more powerful for her long period of contemplative silence.

The grim certainty of her statement shocked Walker speechless. Given one second longer, he would have refused for them both just as glibly as she had affirmed. Jason realized with sudden horror: for them both.

Schreiber nodded, running a hand through his military buzz cut. "Killers generally leave the scene as soon as possible, especially when we show up. It's pretty unlikely they'll stick around." He added carefully, "Unless you've got something they want?"

Nicholson shook her head without elaborating.

Walker could not contain the explanation any longer. North Liberty's sheriff and deputies had the right and need to know as much as possible. "They want a someone, a patient of Shawna's suffering from amnesia."

Nicholson took over. "I'm sure Tracy already told them everything we know. They've no reason to want us anymore. They've almost certainly gone after him, and I'm not leaving Tracy lying on the ground any longer than I have to."

Schreiber studied his passengers. "I don't know enough to guess what's going on here. Why don't you tell me as much as you can, understanding we will get interrupted. And you'll have to repeat it all for Liberty P.D."

This time, Walker deferred to Nicholson, but she said nothing. As Jason gathered the phrases to tell the story without making it sound any more bizarre than it was, an awkward hush ensued. Weariness hampered his powers of speech, and the flare of irritation, though brief, had drained him to numbness. In the last hour, he believed, he had exhausted his emotional repertoire.

The radio rescued Jason from the explanation. Schooley's voice sounded deep beneath the static. "We're not finding anything here. We'll need backup. Maybe the Lassie patrol ..." He paused emphatically. "Unless your civilians can help."

Schreiber threw the question to his passengers.

"Let's go," Shawna Nicholson said.

Walker nodded, forsaking his own best judgment for one he trusted more.

"We're on our way," Schreiber confirmed. He hung up the handset and started the engine, both hands on the steering wheel.

"Car's in the driveway near the house. Meet you there."

Schreiber reached over to key the mike. "Ten-four." He pulled onto the road and headed toward Walker's house.

Despite its familiarity, the house seemed dark and sinister. Jason's aversion trickled toward hysteria as they rounded the short stretch of road and turned onto the gravel driveway. Morning light displayed the other car, its lights off and its motor quiet. Even from a distance, Walker could discern Schooley's short, burly frame and McPherson's long-legged stride as they headed toward the vehicle from beyond the house. Their presences pacified him only slightly.

Schreiber pulled up the second cruiser behind the first. He climbed out of the car, then opened Walker's door. "We'll keep the two of you safely between—"

A round of gunfire from the side woods cut off his explanation. McPherson collapsed. Schooley dove behind the first patrol car. Schreiber dropped to the ground, low-crawling to use his door as a shield and pawing for his revolver. "Stay in. Stay down."

Walker's wits exploded in terror. Gunshot peppered the bullet-resistant rear window, leaving opaque blotches where it hit. Apparently, a second terrorist had come up behind them, near the street end of the driveway. A third opened up on Schooley, muzzle flashes in the forest gloom revealing his position near the house.

Six more shots pounded the window before Walker thought to duck. *We're dead. Oh, God, we're all dead.* No other ideas penetrated Walker's mind. Even Nicholson's screams failed to register.

"Down in back!" Schreiber shouted. He raised his head, firing two return shots at the gunman by the house. Another barrage pounded the cruiser's rear window, knocking fragments of the weakened glass down Jason's neck. Seized by a sudden, desperate need to run, he shifted. Schreiber lunged for the radio, the gesture answered by a round from the house. Blood splashed Walker's forehead. Schreiber jerked back, swearing with a vehemence that put Walker's indiscretion on the radio to shame.

Schooley's voice emerged thready beneath a roar

of static. Walker caught only the phrases "backup" and "officer down." A moment later, a solid reply came over the radio. "Ten-nine, 816."

No answer followed.

"Ten-nine. I need a ten-nine.

Silence.

"Respond 816. 817, are you in your cruiser? What's your twenty?"

Walker dared not raise his head to determine whether pinning fire or something worse kept Schooley from repeating his request. Tears blurred his vision, and he could not help focusing on the single decision, this time Shawna's, that would cost them all their lives.

"I heard gunfire. What the hell's going on out there!"

Schreiber reloaded swiftly, then fired several shots at the gunman near the driveway. A triumphantly whispered "yes" told Walker he had hit his target. Then he whirled, concentrating wholly on the enemy near the house. Bullets rang from reinforced steel and glass, riddling the cruiser. Even as the barrage from behind ceased, the urge to flee became inescapable madness. Jason straggled from the car, plunging to the gravel on hands and knees, stones grinding into flesh. Oblivious, Schreiber half-rose to take careful aim. He and the gunman fired as one. The deputy's body sagged forward, wedged between the door and the frame. He hung there, eyes wide and unblinking. The gunfire from the house ceased, leaving only the terrorist in the side woods, the one who had fired the first shots.

Walker bolted for the woods on the opposite side, mind empty, driven only by fear. Shawna plunged after him. "No, Jason! Wait! The car. It's faster. More protected."

Walker continued running. Nothing short of a physical barrier could stop his headlong flight.

Nicholson scurried after Walker. "Jason, stop! Stop!"

The last gunman pelted the cars, his view of Nicholson and Walker obscured by the vehicles. Common sense dictated the two remain in the cruiser where they could drive away or at least call for help. But good judgment had long left Walker's repertoire; and, this once, blind panic seemed to work in his favor. Nicholson tackled him, and they both rolled into the woods between his house and the road. An explosion rocked the driveway behind them. Impact knocked them into a flailing spiral, and fire engulfed the area where the car, and they, had once sat.

Nicholson gained her feet first. "Go!" She prodded him up.

Walker needed no further urging. He fled through the trees in panic, charging recklessly between trunks. Limbs clawed his face. He fell more times than he cared to count, broken branches and deadfalls stamping bruises the length of his body. His lungs spasmed, and his throat felt raw, assailed by a mixture like fire and blood. The minutes it took to charge into the neighbor's clearing dragged like days, and the Omni parked on their gravel driveway seemed a sanctuary more blessed than any church. He raced for it.

Nicholson shouted a warning. "Careful." She described her concern in a single word. "Ambush."

Jason was beyond caring. If someone hiding in the Omni blew off his head, at least the desperate, gasping agony would end. He wrenched open the driver's door and climbed inside, instinctive caution operating beyond his control. His gaze swept every seat and found nothing disturbed. Twisting the key, he slammed into reverse as Nicholson reached the passenger door. Hesitating only long enough for her to climb inside, Jason gunned the engine and headed for the rural route amid the crackle of gravel, trailing a white wake of powder.

The instant the tires hit the dusty roadway, his panic eased, admitting a trickle of sense and relief.

"Slow down," Shawna cautioned, staring at a road kill Walker mentally identified as a possum. "If we crash, we're just as dead as if we were shot."

This time, Walker complied. He had learned the danger of braking on gravel weeks ago when he tapped the pedal to avoid a deer and skidded a quarter mile. "Did you see . . . him?" An image of Schreiber's still face and glazing eyes filled Walker's mind, and he started to shake.

"He was dead, Jason. There's nothing we could have done for him."

Stones popped and crunched beneath the tires. "What do you think happened? I mean to the other two."

"If the hoods didn't get them first, the explosion probably did." Through her own fear and sorrow, Shawna anticipated the conscience burden they would suffer once terror unleashed them. "Hundreds of soldiers have died trying to haul corpses out of a battle zone. I was just as guilty of that. All I could think of was Tracy's body lying out there . . ." She trailed off. "Jason, I got three men killed trying to retrieve a corpse that was beyond help."

Jason winced, certain Nicholson spoke from regret, not to belittle a friend's death. It was his turn to comfort, but the words came only with difficulty. "You didn't get them killed. They chose to go. It's their job to investigate murders. We couldn't just forget Tracy and not tell anyone, leaving her killers on the loose. And we needed protection." Dread forced him to add, "We still do." The car whipped by the familiar houses, cornfields, and pastures with milling horses.

"I wasn't talking about the initial call. Those deputies poked around for half an hour or longer. The shooting didn't start until we arrived. If I hadn't agreed to take them to Tracy, they would have found her eventually. The killers attacked because we were there. They wanted us."

Walker shivered, his worst fears confirmed. "You think they'll keep after us." The rural route ended at a stop sign before an intersection. Walker pressed in the brake, waited for a pickup truck to rumble past, then automatically pulled out onto the road toward Liberty. "We need to get to a phone. Call 911 again."

"Jason, wake up. You're not in Philadelphia anymore. Half or more of North Liberty's law enforcement just died assisting us."

"We'll drive to Liberty, then call. Get under their jurisdiction."

Nicholson brushed invisible crumbs from her bucket seat. "Liberty's not much bigger. It's got what? A dozen cops, at least one of whom believes John, not you, is Jason Walker. What are the chances we'll get them to believe anything from me after my bald-faced lie this morning?"

Walker slowed as he entered downtown North Liberty. "I think the bodies will prove self-explanatory. We'll tell them the rest."

"No."

"No?"

"No." Nicholson squeezed Walker's leg. "I don't know if that explosion took one car or both. Those killers could have gotten hold of a police radio. They'll know our every move. Going to more cops is the first thing they'll expect us to do."

"Of course. It's the only logical thing to do."

Shawna threw up her hands to indicate he had made her point for her. "Going against the obvious course of action is the only thing that's ever worked for us against these killers. If you hadn't fooled them by running when staying with the car made more sense, we'd have died with the deputies. I think it's time to call in a professional, someone who knows how to deal with Arab terrorists."

"Who?" North Liberty disappeared behind the Omni, and Walker returned to normal highway speed. "The National Guard? The CIA?" He grew sarcastic. "The Equalizer? Face it, Shawna. I don't know the Feds' number. That's what the police are for."

"No, you face it, Jason. The cops aren't going to turn off their radios or call the army's Delta Force based only on our word. I won't be responsible for any more deaths. We're going to have to take this into our own hands."

Walker stopped at a red light. "What are you saying? We need to purchase a few automatic weapons of our own? I'm no vigilante. I'm scared witless. When the shit hit the fan, I couldn't even tell the good guy from the bad guys."

"You did fine. That ruse of yours, running from

the patrol car, that saved our lives. And the killers might think we died in the explosion." Nicholson leaned across Walker and pointed through his window at a convenience store. "Stop at this gas station."

Jason knew he had acted out of panic, not clever strategy. Luck seemed unlikely to take them far. *Not if we depend on Jason Walker and his black cloud.* "What's your plan?" He cut the motor but made no move to leave the car.

"The only person who's shown he can handle those Arabs is John."

Jason blinked, wondering why Shawna insisted on calling Carrigan "John" even after she had learned his name. *As if the man she treated in the hospital is somehow different from the one the Arabs killed Tracy to find.* "Are you out of your mind? They're after us because they think we know where he is. They said they just wanted Carrigan."

"And you believed them?" Nicholson's tone went so heavy with derision that Walker flushed. "Don't you understand? You know Tracy must have told them everything she knew about John, yet they shot her anyway. At the house, they weren't trying to capture us. They were trying to kill us. They think we know too much, and they're not going to let us live." She glanced around the pumps, apparently seeking something. "John's the only one I've seen successfully face off with those killers. If he can't protect us, no one can."

Jason traced the smooth line of the steering wheel, missing his usual clarity of thought. Superficial logic propelled him toward the police, but he had trusted Shawna in a crisis for too long to ignore her wisdom. "John's probably halfway across the continent by now. And even if he isn't, how do you propose we find him?"

Nicholson's smile looked grim as a Halloween jack-o'-lantern. "I don't think he's gone far. He doesn't remember his purpose, but he does know it must have brought him to Liberty for some reason. And for the first time in my life, my own carelessness may work to my advantage." She reached out her hand. "Jason, lend me change for the phone."

CHAPTER 8

Recall

While Jason Walker and Shawna Nicholson dodged enemies in the North Liberty woods, Carrigan switched license plates with a battered Pinto abandoned in a park's lot. He knew the maneuver would not fool the gunmen, but he hoped it might buy time against the police once Nicholson reported her Porsche stolen. In the early darkness, miles passed swiftly. The town of Liberty disappeared behind him, replaced by ancient houses with wooden porches, crumbling outbuildings, and muddy, pig-filled pastures. Where there were pigs, the air lay thick with their pungent excrement; but where cornfields and patches of forest replaced them, it smelled clean and damp from dew. Carrigan reveled in his open freedom; even the odor of the pigs seemed welcome.

An edge of sun arched over the western horizon. A band of copper-pink colored the world behind straight, knee-high stalks of corn; and where the gold touched, the sky seemed torn to strips of baby blue. Without a destination, Carrigan pulled onto the gravel shoulder, cut the Porsche's engine, and watched the parade of hues the sunrise tumbled across the sky. The blue expanse seemed too bright, the yellows artificial as a mechanical canary in a cage, the pinks and oranges vivid as children's candy.

Within twenty minutes, the sun came fully over the horizon, a glowing ball blinding in the absence of mountains and buildings to dilute its glory. Awed, but no closer to understanding his purpose, Carrigan flipped down the sun visor and twisted the ignition key as Nicholson had taught him. The engine sputtered but would not turn over. *What now?* Carrigan turned the key back to its resting position and tried again. The starter kicked in with its machinery growl, but the engine still refused to start.

Carrigan released the key, slid it from the switch, and sat back in annoyance. *Oh, well. Let's see how much I know.* Whoever had trained him must have taught patience as well, because Carrigan accepted the challenge gracefully. With the efficiency of routine, he explored the car. The other key Nicholson had provided opened the rear hatch, uncovering a blanket, a balled up, grease-stained sweater, booster cables, and a set of ratchets. He discovered the buttons on the dash functioned with the key in place. He found the sequence that opened the sun roof, but it took time before he located the switch that exposed the workings beneath the hood.

Carrigan stared in bewilderment at the twisted metal tubes, plastic hoses, belts, and coils that looked more like a madman's art than functioning apparatus. *I ought to know how to fix this.* Carrigan slammed down the hood, feeling helpless as a child. *Damn this memory thing! Now what?* He glanced down the road. At the far edge of his vision, he saw a cluster of lights winking off as the sun crept into the sky. *A town? Maybe I can get some help.*

He leaned against the driver's door, considering. The barrel of the AK-47 gleamed back at him, crammed beneath a seat too low to hide it effectively. He considered taking the weapon but discarded the idea instantly. *It'll just scare people, and the police will shoot me before they arrest me.* Instead, he carefully secreted the barrel beneath the blanket he had found in the trunk. Giving in to frustration, he kicked the tire and started the walk toward town.

As Carrigan trudged beside the roadside ditches, reality seeped back into his memory. The revelations no longer came with the sharp, vivid rush of his recollections of murder. It occurred to him he needed to get ammunition for the assault rifle and the 9mm Smith and Wesson tucked beneath the seats, the thought accompanied by the realization that guns and bullets were illegal. *Black market.* And suddenly the bills he had found in his pocket gained meaning. *Paper with value. Underground currency for illegal purchases.* Plagued by partial understanding, he shook his head.

First, Carrigan came upon a granary, dark and padlocked. Four-wheel drive trucks and stock trailers lined the roads beside cracked sidewalks. Glass-fronted stores faced the main street, and Carrigan identified an appliance shop, a post office, and the distant placard of a grocery before he discovered the only open business in the village. A cheap, plastic sign proclaimed it as Bob's Tavern. *A bar.* Carrigan breathed a sigh that mixed excitement with relief. This, at least, seemed familiar, and he knew he could find help if he handled things well.

Glare obscured Carrigan's view through the window. Rather than press his nose to the glass, an action which could only amuse the gang inside, Carrigan pulled open the door and entered. Despite the hour, a dozen patrons sat around the counter on wooden bar stools. As one, they turned to stare at the newcomer. Then they returned to their drinks, their mumbled comments blending into an incoherent hum.

There was only one bartender, flanked by shelves of bottles of varying size and shape. The conversations made it obvious the patrons all knew one another and Carrigan did not fit in with them. He was the youngest by at least ten years. The black T-shirt hugging his lean, athletic frame seemed out of place amid a sea of comfortably loose jeans and bib coveralls over white undershirts or cutoff flannel button-downs. An inch under six feet tall and less than two hundred pounds, Carrigan found himself one of the smallest men in the bar, and he lacked the obligatory beer gut the older men shared. His shaggy, black hair, feathered by the hospital barber, also jarred. The tavern's other patrons wore caps with sports emblems or lettered with strange names such as "John Deere," their faces as tanned as old leather.

Carrigan slammed the door hard enough to rattle the glass. Silence fell over the patrons, and they whirled back to face him. "Excuse me," Carrigan said politely, careful to keep uncertainty or weakness from his voice. "My car's broke, and I wondered if someone could help me get it started."

No one responded. Every man turned back to his drink, and the conversations resumed. The burning odor Carrigan now knew as cigarettes and cigars revolted him, but the aroma of beer beneath it reminded him he had neither eaten nor taken a drink since the previous evening. Carrigan smiled. True, no one had volunteered to help, but he noticed no active hostility either. He guessed if he could gain the farmers' trust by seeming to belong, it would not take long before he mustered the volunteers he needed. Encouraged despite his failure, Carrigan took a seat beside a heavily-whiskered stranger, hooked a pretzel from a bowl, and chewed it idly.

Several minutes passed before the bartender wandered over. "What'll you have?" His bright, dark eyes probed Carrigan through roiling smoke, and he wiped his fingers on a stained apron.

For the first time since awakening in the hospital, Carrigan felt at home. "A beer?" he tried tentatively, hoping he had chosen the correct name for the brew he smelled. In the past, the nurses had laughed at his strange names for food and beverages.

But the bartender accepted the order without blinking. He trotted off, returning shortly with a foaming glass of tan liquid.

Carrigan took a gulp. It tasted bitter and dirty, like water from a rain gutter, but he forced himself to swallow without making a face. It occurred to him the bartender might have passed him sewage as a joke, but the man's placid features convinced him otherwise. No creases of amusement appeared on the bartender's face, and the crowd did not stare with the rapt attention cheating a stranger ordinarily inspired.

"That's a buck," the bartender said.

"Huh?" The words made no sense, and Carrigan spoke before he could think. He returned his gaze to the man behind the counter.

"A buck," the bartender repeated.

Feeling foolish, Carrigan asked the inevitable question. "What's a buck?"

Impatience crinkled the bartender's features. "The beer. That." He pointed. "It's a buck."

Carrigan stared. "I thought it was a beer."

The bartender was shouting now. The background noise died to a buzz. "But it's a buck!"

"Okay." Carrigan tried to understand. "Whenever I'm done with this one, give me another buck."

The bartender's cheeks turned red, and a pulse hammered at the side of his jaw. "You gotta pay for the damn drink."

Suddenly the situation became all too clear to Carrigan. The idea of cash, which had eluded him on his walk into town, became real. Though uncertain of the reason, he knew the strange bills in his pocket would not satisfy the bartender, and he felt equally sure he had not needed "bucks" to order drinks in the past. "Shit," Carrigan berated himself honestly, trying to make amends. "I'm sorry. I don't have any bucks."

"You what?" The bartender wiped his hands on his apron with quick, nervous strokes. "You don't have any money?"

The buzz died to silence.

Carrigan realized his chance to make a good impression had disappeared, and he harbored no wish to turn a difficult situation into a fight. "No, sir. I'm sorry."

The bartender seemed as confused as Carrigan. "You come in here, and you don't have any fucking money? You order a beer and you can't pay for it? Now what the hell am I supposed to do?" His tone conveyed controlled anger. "I can't let you get out of here like this. Everyone—"

The bartender was interrupted by a portly giant of a man who shoved between Carrigan and the man beside him. "We don't need your kind." He glared down at Carrigan, dark, hay-speckled hair poking from beneath a "Kile's Feed and Grain" cap. "We don't need no pretty boy, muscle-bound, city fellows coming in here from out of town cheating us out of money. We're people. We work for a living. You go right the hell back where you came from. Right now. After you pay the man for that drink."

Now every eye in the tavern turned toward them expectantly. Carrigan kept his movements unhurried, confident of his diplomacy skills and, if those failed, of his martial training. He rolled his eyes toward the stranger. "Excuse me, sir. I really feel this is between me and him." He inclined his head toward the bartender. "Why don't you just go back and have a seat. We'll work this out to our ... mutual satisfaction."

"I don't think you heard me, boy." The large stranger raised meaty hands and latched his thumbs onto the suspenders of his bib overalls.

The position struck Carrigan as particularly stupid. *Idiot. I could punch your face in before you pulled your hands from your pockets.* He watched the other man, keeping his expression unconcerned. He had come for help with his car. Violence was neither attractive nor desirable. *He's got no idea what he's up against. But he's local. I'm not. If I hurt him, I may have to deal with every man in the bar.* Carrigan trusted his abilities as a fighter, but it would only take one gun to kill him.

If a fight becomes necessary, there are ways to win without injuring anyone.

"Ralph." The bartender spoke soothingly, patting the farmer's forearm. "Ralph. Go back to your seat. Don't worry about it. Everything's under control. The kid, here, is right. We'll work it out."

Ralph turned his aggression against the bartender, but his gaze never left Carrigan. "I know you. You're going to be too soft on that city punk. Well, I'm just sick of it. We're going to settle this up. Right now." The farmer jabbed for Carrigan's face.

Without bothering to rise, Carrigan caught the punch on an outside block. Seizing Ralph's forearm, he yanked the farmer off-balance, then wrapped his free arm around Ralph's throat in a stranglehold that trapped the farmer against him. It happened fast, but it seemed like all the time in the world to Carrigan. It would have been easy to break Ralph's neck. Instead, Carrigan gave Ralph a humiliating, cocksure kiss on the cheek. Then he hurled the man away.

Dead silence surrounded Ralph as he staggered awkwardly backward, tripped over a bar stool, and crashed to the wooden floor. Then every man in the barroom howled with laughter. Even from Carrigan's angle, the image of a man seven inches and a hundred twenty pounds lighter than Ralph twirling the farmer like a ballerina seemed hilarious. It was all Carrigan could do to hold back his own laughter when he turned back to the bartender. As he moved, he saw Ralph's features turning a deep shade of red-purple. *It's not over yet.*

Ralph lurched to his feet, potbelly quivering beneath his overalls. "You little son of a bitch! Nobody does that to me." The men between Ralph and Carrigan scampered out of the way as Ralph sprang for Carrigan, furious and unyielding as a charging bull. He led with a powerful, right-handed punch that, to Carrigan, seemed as pathetic as one launched by a brawling child.

This time, Carrigan intercepted the blow with an inside block. He snapped the farmer's arm downward, drawing him unsteadily forward. With his opposite hand, he caught the cartilage at Ralph's windpipe and drove his thumb against the carotid. He kept Ralph too overbalanced for another attack and jerked the farmer lower with every word. "You don't want to do this. I'm not in the mood. It's been a long, trying day; and I'm getting very annoyed." Carrigan released Ralph, planted a hand on the farmer's thick chest, and shoved him, flailing, against the door.

Ralph regained his feet, chest heaving. Carrigan watched his expression and his hands and read mixed intentions. Ralph's fingers curled like claws, tensed for another round. Yet his features betrayed uncertainty. The casual precision of Carrigan's defense seemed more machinelike than human, and Ralph obviously debated whether to rescue his dignity or his life.

One of the other patrons made the decision for Ralph. A smaller, younger man draped a jacket over Ralph's shoulders like a cape and steered him toward the door. "Come on, Ralph. Becky's waiting for you. Let's get out of here."

To Carrigan's relief, Ralph went. The door banged shut behind him.

More careful now, Carrigan slid sideways on his stool in order to keep watch on the door. *It wouldn't be the first time some bully decided to defend his honor with a contraband gun and hang the penalties.* Carrigan waited for the more immediate consequences of besting a local.

Ripples of conversation passed through the crowd. A lean man stepped to Carrigan's side, his square-cut face supporting a flat nose beneath a wide-brimmed, leather hat. He slapped a dollar bill to the counter. "My name's Ben Hascol. I've been waiting for someone to put Ralph in his place for the last five years. It's been a pleasure." He clapped a hand to Carrigan's shoulder. "Where's your car?"

"John." Suspecting it would prove safer not to give the surname "Doe," Carrigan chose the first one that came to his mind. "John Nicholson." He smiled, glad to have gotten off so easily.

"Come on, guys!" Hascol roused his neighbors. "Let's help this fella get back on the road."

This time, several men rose. They tossed bills to the bar, presumably to cover their own tabs. But more than one had the same idea as Hascol because the bartender pressed a few into Carrigan's hand. "Your drink's paid several times over, and I don't want the money anyway. Ralph's broke up enough furniture in here. It's just nice to see him walk out red-faced for a change."

Half a dozen men funneled through the exit. Unsure of the proper amenities, Carrigan pocketed the cash and followed the others onto the country road. Hascol opened the passenger door of a battered, green pickup, and Carrigan stepped in. Several of the others clambered onto the bed and knelt in crusted mud dotted with spilled herbicides and curled, brown stems. Descriptions of the conflict they had all witnessed wafted clearly through the window.

Hascol smiled. "Which way?"

Carrigan pointed.

The truck sputtered. The engine turned over, and the ancient vehicle rattled and creaked from town. Hascol ignored the bawdy conversation behind him. "John, I got a little place about a mile out of town the other way. If you take a right down the gravel road, I'm box 56. You ever in the area again, stop by."

Hascol continued, telling some story about Ralph's indiscretions with a female cousin, but Carrigan's mind sped off on its own track. The incident sparked the memory of another bar, far bigger, more crowded, and louder. Synthetic metals and plastic replaced beer-stained wood, and colored lights slashed and sparked from the polished surfaces. Tightly-packed patrons jerked across the floor space, their movements cutting and sudden, more like a war game than a dance. In contrast, the loud music glided from acoustically rounded walls, as smooth as the dancers were sharp.

Carrigan saw himself in a different light than the previous recollections. He carried no weapon. He leaned casually against the rapidly-changing colored patterns on the countertop discussing the game of laser darts with a burly bartender dressed in red. Beside him, Katry sipped a drink, staring out over the dance floor, honey-blonde hair wound high into a braid.

A narrow-faced stranger approached. He wore his hair in a semi-long, modern style, sun-yellow and professionally streaked. His features appeared perfectly symmetrical, unlined, and handsomely chiseled; he was the type accustomed to getting anything he wanted. Resting a foot on the rail around the bar, he leaned toward Katry. "I had a dream about you last night. We were making wild, passionate love beneath a waterfall in Bahanis Bay."

Aware Katry could handle herself, Carrigan turned only half an ear toward the man's rusty line.

"We're not in Bahanis," the stranger continued. "But dreams do have a way of coming true. What do you say? Let's have some drinks, spin around the floor a few times, and go around to my place?"

Katry lowered her drink to the bar. Slowly, her head swiveled toward the stranger. She loosed a sound, half-snicker, half-snort, then returned to her beer.

Stunned, the man lost all his suave pretenses. "Hey, come on—"

Katry interrupted. "Look, pal. I'm here with someone, all right? Go annoy someone else."

The stranger glared, slamming a fist on the countertop. "Oh, just 'cause you're here with some guy gives you the right to be obnoxious?"

The anger in the stranger's voice rang clear despite the surrounding noise. Excusing himself from his conversation with the bartender, Carrigan rested his elbow on the bar, his chin in his hand, and watched the proceedings with interest.

Katry touched Carrigan's knee beneath the counter, but she spoke directly to the stranger. "I don't need a license to be obnoxious when some jerk uses an antique line on me. Now just go home, little boy." She waved him toward the door. "Your mom wants you."

Katry spoke loudly enough to draw attention,

and soon several patrons stopped to watch the altercation. Apparently accustomed to respect, the stranger measured Katry, then Carrigan with his gaze. He made a grab for Katry's wrist.

Katry rose, catching the stranger easily. Fast as thought, she blocked his arm, whipped him in a circle, and hurled him into her empty seat. "Me and my date are leaving. Why don't you stay here, seeing as you like it so much?" She stomped toward the exit, leaving the stranger openmouthed and sputtering in her chair.

Carrigan studied the man. A cruel smile twitched across his features and he shook his head in judgment. Turning on his heel, Carrigan followed his girlfriend from the bar. Only then did he remember that Katry called everyone worthy of respect by his or her last name.

Engrossed in his memory, Carrigan allowed Hascol to drive past the Porsche. The sun gleaming from glossy, black paint revived him. "We just passed it."

Hascol pressed the brake. The truck came to a stop then U-turned back around and pulled up behind the Porsche. The dent in its side looked like a cavern. A few shards of glass still clung to the back window, and bullet holes marred the body.

One of the farmers spat. "What the hell did you do to this thing?"

Carrigan handed Hascol the keys and opened the driver's door, not caring to explain the damage. "Oh, nothing. Little bit of loose gravel." Lame as it was, the explanation could not have fooled the farmers. Whether from politeness or disinterest, they did not press.

Hascol climbed into the contour seat and twisted

the ignition. As before, the starter choked to life, but the engine did not respond. Hascol looked up at Carrigan. "John, where exactly are you from?"

Carrigan became defensive. "Why? What's your point?"

Hascol tossed back the keys, and Carrigan caught them with a flick of his fingers. "Know what 'E' means?"

Carrigan closed his fist around the keys. "No," he admitted. "What?"

"On this here gauge." Hascol tapped a broken, filthy nail against the fuel indicator. "This thing here with the picture of a pump and numbers. You know what 'E' means. It's opposite of 'F'." He climbed out of the Porsche. "Son, you ain't got no gas in your car."

So far, the men seemed to accept Carrigan's ignorance easily. "What's gas?"

"Right." Hascol's voice went gritty with sarcasm, and he laughed. "That's a good one. What's gas?"

The other men chuckled along with him. Some peeked in the windows, apparently impressed by the Porsche.

Hascol wandered back to his truck. "Come on In my truck, I've got a couple few gallons I use for my lawn tractor." He hauled a dimpled, red and yellow gas can from the bed. "Let's put some in and get you on the road here." He flicked open the gas plate, unscrewed the cap, and dumped in a foul-smelling liquid from the can. "Just make sure you stop and get more before too long. Next place, there may not be any big, fat, ugly guy for you to beat hell out of to get help for your car." Hascol tossed the empty can back into his trunk.

"Thanks, Ben." Carrigan crawled into the

Porsche's driver's seat recalling how, scarcely an hour past, these same men would not talk to him. One simple act, a minor maneuver that left their bully looking sheepish, and suddenly they could not do enough for Carrigan. He did not delude himself. *It ended well because I was careful. Bully or not, they could never have tolerated a stranger hurting or killing one of them.* Carrigan twisted the key and tapped the gas pedal. This time, the engine roared to life, and Carrigan tried to think of a tactful way to ask his new friends to stand away from the car. Slamming the door, he opened the window. "Been nice talking to you guys. See you later." He slapped the shift into gear, turned the Porsche 180 degrees, and headed back the way he had come.

In daylight, the road seemed more interesting than it had at night. Tractor trailers, truck-drawn wagons of farm implements, and an occasional car rumbled past; and the patchwork of field, timber, and pasture seemed endless. Yet, soon, the sense of freedom its openness inspired became tainted by a loneliness radio D.J.s could not pierce. Carrigan's thoughts turned to Shawna Nicholson. He tried to picture her in the bar of his memory, in Katry's place. No question, the doctor would have brushed off the forward stranger equally as quickly, though perhaps with more finesse and less insult. Instead of a derisive snicker, Nicholson would have answered with a polite "I'm not interested." When pressed, Carrigan guessed, Nicholson would have cooled the stranger's ardor with words; but there the comparison ended. Where Katry had resorted to violence, he doubted Nicholson would.

The incongruity of this thought struck Carrigan instantly. *Right. Like she wasted any time hitting me when I tried to kiss her at the hospital.* Carrigan recognized the difference. Katry's passionless precision had achieved its goal, to rid herself of a troublesome stranger, while Carrigan had read anger, surprise, and fear in Nicholson's blow. The shock, at least, had come as much from her own actions as his.

Suddenly, a high-pitched sound shrilled through the car, startling Carrigan from his thoughts. He cast about for its source and discovered Nicholson's beeper still clipped to the passenger's sun visor. A second whistle reverberated through the Porsche. One hand on the wheel, he reached for the beeper. As he brushed it, the clip slid free, snapping closed; and the beeper tumbled to the passenger's seat. It shrieked again.

Carrigan scooped up the beeper. He touched the button with a finger, and it quieted in mid-tone. Numbers flashed across the display: 2706. *Great. She forgot this thing again.* He tossed it back to the passenger's seat and continued driving. It occurred to him the caller might be facing an emergency, and he ought to at least let him or her know Nicholson was unavailable. *That's stupid, there must be other doctors they can call besides Shawna.* He sat back, trying to enjoy the ride. But something bothered him, some fragment of information that went against his training. A lesson rose, the words of a man he could not remember but knew he had learned to respect. *If something normal seems out of place, investigate.*

Before Carrigan could contemplate further, the beeper went off again. He cut it off on the first tone, and the same number flashed on the display.

Several seconds passed in silence, then the beeper sang out again.

Give up already. Carrigan grabbed the beeper, preparing to twirl the dial that would shut it off permanently, but a thought stopped him, and he thumbed the button instead. *The hospital knows Shawna needs time to get to a telephone. From what I've seen, it's customary to wait at least ten minutes before repeating a page.* Before he could drop the beeper back to the seat, it sounded again.

There's something wrong. Carrigan dialed off the beeper, now committed to pursuing the peculiarity. He had seen Nicholson answer pages from his hospital room telephone often enough to know how it was done. His drive had taken him most of the way back toward Liberty, and he knew he would soon reach the city limits. *The worst that'll happen is I'll waste a little time. I have no idea what I'm supposed to be doing or where I'm going, so it doesn't make a damn bit of difference. Maybe I can calm down some raving surgeon and save Shawna a little grief.*

Soon signs changed the street name from X66 to Sand Road. Another sign welcomed Carrigan to Liberty. He pulled up to a four-way intersection with several other cars, careful to stop at the overhanging red light. Ahead, houses dotted the roadside while, to the right and left, he saw billboards and electric signs, most still dark in these hours before the start of morning business.

When the light shifted to green, Carrigan turned right. He passed a discount department store and a mall of clustered shops to his right. Ahead and to the left, a brilliantly lit gold and white sign with red print said "Burger King." A smaller, blue and white sign in its parking lot attracted Carrigan's attention. Perched on a glass booth, it held a picture of a telephone receiver and the word "Phone" on every side.

Watching for a gap in the traffic, Carrigan whisked into the left lane, then turned into the restaurant lot. He braked between painted lines, leaped from the car, and walked to the booth. The door folded open. Carrigan kept his foot wedged against it so it could not spring closed. Removing the receiver, he cradled it between his chin and shoulder. He punched out the hospital prefix followed by the four numbers from the display.

A nasal, female voice addressed him with the unmistakable whir that accompanies computer generations or recordings. "Deposit ten cents, please."

Ten sense? Carrigan shook his head, but he knew it would do no good to argue with a machine. Slamming down the receiver, he trotted across the parking lot and inside the restaurant.

Rows of plastic-coated tables lined the aisles. A couple occupied one, eating from styrofoam containers. Behind a cash register on a counter, a teenager dressed in a burgundy and blue uniform, twisted a pliable microphone stem in bored circles. When Carrigan approached, she snapped to attention. "Can I help you, sir?"

"I need to use your phone. It's an emergency."

"Pay phone's outside." She pointed through the window at the booth Carrigan had just vacated. "Lots of places have gone to a quarter, but ours is still just a dime."

Her explanation only confused Carrigan, but the word "pay" caught his notice. Thrusting a hand in his pocket, he pushed aside the tracking device and removed the dollar bills the bartender had given him. Dropping them on the counter, he pushed them toward the girl. "Please. I can pay. I just need to use your phone."

The girl stared at the four dollars and back at Carrigan. "Where are you calling, Africa? I said it only costs a dime." She pinned one bill beneath her finger, flicked it toward the cash register, and brushed the others at Carrigan with her knuckles. Ringing up a no sale, she gathered change and slapped it to the counter.

Carrigan stared. A lot of facts had seeped back into his memory, but this concept of money still seemed strange. There was a feeling of vulgarity about it, as if it was the kind of thing discussed in privacy rather than out loud in a public place. He fidgeted, deciding he had no recourse but honesty. "I don't know how to use the pay phone."

The teen gawked, her features frozen in a mask of incredulity. She recovered quickly, flushing as if embarrassed for him. "Oh, I get it. Don't worry, sir. Lots of people don't know how to read. It's no big deal." The more she spoke, the more flustered she got.

Carrigan waited, aware he was the one who should feel humiliated, but too ignorant to understand why. "Is one of these a ten sense?"

"This one." She poked one of the two dimes she had given in change. "Pick up the receiver, push one in the slot, and dial your number."

"Dial?"

She considered. "Well . . . tap out, I guess. It's a push-button."

Carrigan returned the extra bills to his pocket and scooped up the change. "Thanks." He headed for the parking lot.

As Carrigan pushed out the door, the girl called after him. "Thank *you.*"

From her tone, Carrigan knew she spoke more out of habit than courtesy, and he did not bother to turn and acknowledge her words. Instead, he jogged back to the telephone. He found the slot easily, inserted a dime, and again poked out the number. This time, he heard a ring, and then a voice saying, "2 West."

Carrigan hesitated, so involved in working the telephone he had not thought out what to say. "Um, I ... This is ... I mean, Dr. Nicholson's beeper ..."

"John?"

Carrigan made a noncommittal grunt, not yet ready to reveal his identity.

The person on the other end apparently took it as a positive response. "John, this is Karen. Remember? I took care of you on 2 West."

Karen had been Carrigan's nurse many times since she gave him his first glimpse of Liberty, Iowa after his accident. "I remember. Were you trying to page Dr. Nicholson?"

"No, you. Dr. Nicholson said to keep trying until you either answered or my dialing finger broke. An emergency, she said. Told me to tell you to call her." Karen rattled off a seven digit number.

Having nothing to write on or with, Carrigan memorized the digits. *Whatever my difficulty recalling the past, I seem to have a damned good memory.* "Thanks."

"Wait, John!" Karen called, though Carrigan had not yet reached to hang up the receiver. "Those two men you killed in the hospital. No identification, but the police think they might have been

Libyan terrorists. They're calling in the feds and everything! And they want to talk to you."

Carrigan bit his lip. It made sense for them to come looking to question him, yet the thought of turning himself over to an antiterrorist squad chilled him. *I have to know who I am first and which side I'm on.* He kept his voice steady. "Karen, did Shawna tell you her location?"

"No. Just a phone number. She seemed scared."

"Okay. I've been driving straight since the shooting," Carrigan lied. "I need to turn around. Tell the police I'll meet them at the hospital in four to five hours." He tapped the cradle with his finger, cutting the connection. Unless they had already identified him, the "feds" would have no reason not to trust him; and Carrigan guessed a five hour head start could get him reasonably far. Releasing the metal bar, Carrigan inserted his other dime and dialed the number Karen had given him.

The phone was answered on the first ring, and Shawna Nicholson's voice sounded distant beneath the sound of rushing cars. "Hello?"

"Shawna?"

"Oh, thank God."

Carrigan appreciated her gratitude, but her voice trembled, weaker than he remembered and uncharacteristic. "What's wrong?"

"They killed Tracy. I don't know what to do. I . . . could you?"

Carrigan interrupted, trying to make things easier for Nicholson. "Where are you?"

"Harvey's Kwik Stoppe between North Liberty and Liberty. It's a gas station."

A gas station. Perfect. Hascol said I'd need more

gas, and Shawna will know how to get it. "Stay put. I'll be right there."

Nicholson's voice gained volume, and she seemed relieved, more like the strong, confident woman Carrigan knew. "Be careful. They may have followed us, hoping we'd contact you."

Before he could reply, Carrigan heard a click, and the line went dead. He hung up the receiver and hurried back to the car.

CHAPTER 9

Rendezvous

A half hour after his conversation with Shawna Nicholson, Carrigan peered out through the lobby window of a brick and wood motel next door to Harvey's Kwik Stoppe. Concealed behind a floor-length curtain, he kept his hand resting on the wall-mounted pay telephone and ignored the curious stare of the receptionist behind an oak desk at the opposite side of the room. Across a lawn of oaks and crabgrass, the gas station consisted of a simple, white cinder block convenience store and a stretch of concrete with two rows of pumps. Behind it, a field of foxtails, ragweed, and daisies extended to a patch of forest. Nicholson and Walker waited near a telephone booth at the side of the store. Nicholson paced, head low, shoulders sagging. Still dressed in his hospital scrubs, Walker kept his back pressed to the wall of the convenience store, face buried in his palms. Walker's gold Dodge Omni was parked nearby.

Beside the gasoline pumps, two compact cars idled. A middle-aged man in a suit filled one's tank while a woman waited in the passenger seat. The other sat empty while its driver paid inside the store. A young man dressed in a dark blue jumpsuit fussed around the other set of pumps, his frizzled hair tied into a ponytail. Carrigan saw no sign of the gunmen's Cadillac but was not reassured by its absence. *They know I'd recognize it, so they'd exchange it. If I could remember how to steal a car, I'd have abandoned Nicholson's Porsche, too.* Carrigan lifted the receiver and placed it to his ear.

The placard on the phone instructed Carrigan to wait for the dial tone and deposit twenty-five cents. He pulled change from his pocket: a nickel and three quarters. Randomly selecting one of the larger coins, he dropped it in the slot and again tapped out the number the nurse had given him.

Carrigan heard the blunted rings through the receiver, accompanied by the more distant but sharper jangle of the gas station telephone. Nicholson stopped pacing and raised her head. Obviously startled, Walker jumped. Carrigan waited while the doctors exchanged words, apparently deciding whether they should answer the call. Finally, Nicholson edged into the booth and picked up the receiver. "Hello?" she asked tentatively.

Carrigan's gaze swept the area around the gas station. "Shawna, I'm calling from a restaurant on the other side of the woods. You and Jason go across the field behind Harvey's. I'll meet you in the trees." He awaited a reply.

"All right," Nicholson said. "Be careful."

Carrigan hung up, studying the convenience store, the station, and the roads and fields around it for any evidence of movement. As Nicholson and Walker headed for the field, he listened for the sound of a car starting, watched for someone to emerge from a restroom or for the teenager to nonchalantly abandon his post. Satisfied no one was tailing the doctors, Carrigan exited the motel lobby and followed the line of its brick wall. The parking lot contained thirteen cars besides the Porsche, the same as when he had entered the motel. No one came through the lobby door behind him.

Still tense, Carrigan returned to the Porsche, pleased but not surprised he and the doctors had lost the gunmen. He knew it was not uncommon for people trained to pursue professionals to fall prey to the unpredictability of panicked civilians. *They put themselves in their quarry's place, forgetting frightened people unused to being hunted don't act rationally. So far, they've assumed I would run logically, like a professional, and driving off to a little, no-name farm town couldn't have been something they expected.* Carrigan climbed into the car, started the engine, and pulled out of the motel lot, eyes still trained on the tract around the gas station. *Apparently, they have no idea I've lost my memory. So far, that's served me well, but I'm about due to make a mistake.*

The AK-47 lay beneath the seat, fully hidden by the blanket Carrigan had found in the rear hatch. He pulled into Harvey's parking lot, seeking a place to leave the Porsche while he chased down Walker and Nicholson, *As long as I'm here, I might as well get that gas.* A glance at the dash revealed the needle of the fuel gauge flush with the red line. Uncertain how to fill his tank, he pulled alongside the pumps tended by the man in the jumpsuit and eased down his window.

The youth trotted over. An oval patch sewn onto his uniform identified him as Ed. He leaned toward the opening, his uniform reeking of gasoline. "Morning, sir. Fill it up unleaded regular?"

The question seemed ludicrous. *As opposed to*

filling it up unleaded unusual? Carrigan stared. *Does the kid think I want him to spill it all over the ground?* Suspecting there was a logical explanation behind the query, Carrigan resisted the urge to become sarcastic. "Just put gas in it. However much it needs."

Ed's brow creased, and he gave Carrigan an odd look. Saying nothing more, he trotted toward the pumps.

Carrigan opened the car door, exited, and slammed it behind him. Leaving the car in Ed's care, he circled the convenience store until he got a full view of the field. Wind ruffled the taller weeds in waves. Toward the center, Nicholson and Walker shuffled gingerly through sand burrs, keeping their naked forearms clear of swaying plants. Carrigan gave a low, sharp whistle.

Nicholson whirled, shielding her eyes from the sun's glare with a cupped hand. Walker winced then turned more slowly. They ran toward Carrigan.

Alert for enemies, Carrigan waited until the doctors drew up, panting, beside him. Walker fidgeted, eager as a child. "Never thought I'd say it, John, but I'm glad to see you."

"Jack," Carrigan corrected before he could think.

Dark circles underscored Nicholson's eyes, and they appeared swollen. She stepped forward, as if to catch Carrigan in an embrace. He reached for her, but she shied from him.

"Jack?" Walker watched Nicholson's odd behavior without comment. "Why Jack?"

"It's my name," Carrigan admitted, wondering why that particular memory had surfaced now.

Walker's voice quickened with excitement. "Jack, huh? Jack Carrigan. Are you sure?"

"Are you kidding?" Confused and offended by Nicholson's rejection, Carrigan belittled Walker's question. "Let's get out of here."

"Wait." Walker gave Nicholson a knowing look; obviously the doctors had already discussed the matter he was about to raise. "I don't mean to hold things up. But you wouldn't let me pee back at Nicholson's apartment, and she made me wait for you so I wouldn't leave her by herself. If I don't go soon, I'm going to pop."

The reference naturally turned Carrigan's thoughts to his own bladder. He could stand to use the restroom also. "I'll go with you."

Nicholson looked stricken. No doubt, the reality of Harlowe's death had hit her hard, and the thought of being alone, even for a moment, distressed her.

Walker removed a leather wallet from the back pocket of his scrubs. He whisked out a ten dollar bill and handed it to Nicholson. "I, for one, am starved. Why don't you go in the store and buy some food? Sandwiches, pop, chips, whatever." He looked at Carrigan. "Where's the Porsche?"

"Out front getting filled with gas." Carrigan watched Nicholson, alarmed by the change in her take-charge manner. He had seen it before, people jolted by an abrupt and unexpected killing, struck by the sudden realization that they are involved in something more lethal than a game. From experiences he could not quite recall, he expected her to either flee from company or cling to it. Yet, though Nicholson had gone to great effort to call Carrigan back, she avoided contact as surely as if he carried a contagious disease. The incongruity confused him. *It's almost as if she fears a touch will commit her to something awful. Like me, perhaps?* The thought made him smile, and it occurred to him that she became uncomfortable under very predictable circumstances. *Like whenever I try to touch her.*

"Full serve, I take it." Walker emptied his wallet and handed all the bills to Nicholson. "Coming?"

Walker led the way around the opposite side of the convenience store where the cinder block was interrupted by two wooden doors labeled "Women" and "Men" respectively. Walker twisted the knob of the men's room and shoved the spring-loaded door open with his elbow.

Carrigan watched Nicholson disappear around the front of the store, then turned to follow Walker. Through the open door, he saw a tiny, white-washed cubicle with a single stall and a urinal. Walker released the panel, and it slapped against Carrigan's hip, held ajar by his body. As Carrigan's view of the outside world disappeared, the walls seemed to crush in on him. Terrified, he stood in awkward confusion, and memory struck, hard as a physical blow. His mind replaced the graffiti-scrawled walls of the gas station restroom with the plush carpet and chrome of a high-rise elevator. And special forces commando, Jack Carrigan, stood in the doorway, paralyzed with fear and very much aware of who he was.

Carrigan embraced the recollection and the flood of knowledge that accompanied it. Anchored in the past, he heard an impatient voice waft from behind him. "Yo, buddy. You getting in or not?"

Carrigan recalled how many times he had made this same decision in this same high-rise, and every time the same. For the sake of the only job he knew, he always masked his fear behind a grim smile and hid the claustrophobia inspired by nine months in enemy hands. *Nine months crushed like a flower in a paperweight, torn out, questioned, beaten and crushed again. Nine months waiting for the government who decorated me to buy my freedom with money or blood. Nine months before I gave up on my superiors and slaughtered my own path home.* "Not," Carrigan replied, stepping away from the elevator door. "I'm not getting in." *It doesn't matter anymore. After this briefing, I'm going to die.*

Several people elbowed past, glaring or whispering half-interpretable comments about the rudeness of the young man blocking the elevator. Resolved, Carrigan ignored them; their concerns were too petty to consider, their insults too mumbled and diffuse to sting. He shoved through the doorway beside it and into a little-used stairwell. Ignoring a painted, red handrail, he took the reinforced concrete steps two at a time, undaunted by his impending twenty-five floor climb. Whatever his current emotional classification, he was still in the Americas' highest rated ranking for physical fitness.

The padded soles of Carrigan's shoes made no sound on the concrete, and the stairwell funneled every tiny noise into an echo: the occasional whisk of fabric against concrete, the tinny touch of a hand on the rail, the rare and distant clatter of other footfalls in the stairwell. In the tomblike silence, thoughts of death came unbidden, and Carrigan relived the single incident that had haunted him even after all other memory abandoned him. He could not stop himself from thinking of Katry.

Carrigan had known from the start he should never share a mission with Katry; but wiser, higher-ranking government heads prevailed. Carrigan had sworn to himself he would not let his love for Katry interfere with his vows to his country. He had hardened his heart, forced himself to treat her as any other government agent, and his efforts had worked too well. He had taken his impartiality one step too far. He had condemned her to death, knowing the consequences of that action would chase and torment him through eternity.

After Katry's death, four sessions of drinking and doping himself to oblivion had only impressed her image in Carrigan's dreams, and he awakened sick, alone, and crying. His efforts to forget inspired him to drive his car at reckless speeds, to pick fights with the largest, toughest men he could find, and earned him the agency designation "SDB" for self-destructive behavior. Defeated by his own intensive training, he steered the car and won the brawls and never let himself believe he had wanted it any other way.

A paid vacation followed. With nothing to take his thoughts from Katry, he had contemplated suicide. But a single gunshot seemed too bland, too easy for Jack Carrigan. He needed a wild blaze of glory, bright and golden as the sun, and he needed to die for the cause of the same country for which he had sacrificed Katry. He had thrown himself boldly into his work, fighting the underground war against the country that had imprisoned him: the United Middle Eastern Powers, the "Abduls" as the commandos vulgarly called U.M.E.P. soldiers, in the patronizing, stereotyped way all soldiers name their enemies. The combat triumphs and the honors his country bestowed upon him lost all meaning. He mechanically fought the private, guerrilla battles that kept the Americas free, allowing its citizens to enjoy their holovisions, telecommunications systems, and computer-operated cars and to deny the existence of the wars.

As Carrigan rounded the twenty-fourth floor landing and opened the heavy, steel door to the twenty-fifth floor, he knew the suicide mission he had accepted was exactly what he wanted: a blow to the U.M.E.P., a triumph for the free world, and certain death for Jack Carrigan. Now, only the details remained.

Carrigan trotted through the long, empty hallway from habit and stopped before the door to the Washington Travel Bureau. The climb had barely taxed him, but he waited until his heart rate decreased back to normal and his breaths came with complete ease before pulling open the door and entering the room.

Green walls held framed posters of all the glamorous vacation resorts anyone would want to visit, but Carrigan had seen the pictures too many times to even cast them a glance. Low tables held magazines, and chairs lined three of the walls. A counter spanned the fourth. There, a paunchy, middle-aged man discussed his vacation plans with a wide-eyed brunette behind the counter.

Carrigan took a seat, seized a glamour journal at random and pretended to read. He had no interest in the Washington Travel Bureau; though functional, it was merely a front for briefing headquarters. He waited until the man turned, trotted from the room, and slammed the door, then he rose casually and walked behind the counter.

Tiny computer consoles dotted the area behind the desk, and file cabinets held printed, colored brochures. Three women agents tended the area, two familiar to Carrigan. He slipped around a row of files to the door marked "Employees Only" and placed his fingers on the knob. Before he could open it, a friendly, sandy-haired woman he knew as Frieda clapped him on the shoulder. "Finally. Big man's about chewed off his own nose waiting."

Carrigan knew she referred to Colonel Harper, a top-ranking official involved in situations of the gravest importance to national security. Under ordinary circumstances, Carrigan would pay dearly for his tardiness, monetarily or with extra duties. But, this time, he knew he was beyond reproach. "It's a fucking suicide mission. What's he going to do? Dock my pay?" Without listening for a response, he wrenched open the door, revealing the routine, mirrored chamber, the armored door on its opposite side, and its surveillance equipment. This was the part Carrigan hated most. Once inside, the doors would lock while the scanners and computers assessed him, identifying him by a long list of parameters. The process did not bother him, he had become accustomed to it. He just hated the thought of being shut into a tiny room, helpless to open the door and leave until the computers deemed him worthy.

Closing his eyes, Carrigan forced himself inside and pulled the panel shut. He focused his thoughts, trying to block out the click of the locks and the soft whir of the cameras. In his youth, the world had always seemed so large; but, since his imprisonment, it appeared to have shrunk, outgrown like a child's favorite pair of shoes. Rows of high-rises pressed up against one another, families packed into one- or two-room apartments, and nothing in the cities was accessible without smashing into an elevator, a tubelike elevated crosswalk, or one of a million crowded public transport systems.

The humming stopped. Carrigan opened his lids and swiveled his gaze to the display. Bold, red letters proudly identified him, as if he were some splendid scientific discovery: JACK R. CARRIGAN, SFC. SECURITY RANK: 1-A. Then, the locks clicked, and the door swung open to usher him into the briefing room.

Three chairs faced a hologram projection area beside a podium, one of the seats conspicuously unoccupied. Carrigan recognized the other two men: Moritz Taylor, a stubble-haired, veteran artilleryman and De Witt Diamant, a powerfully built, black agent known for courage, loyalty and a willingness to take cases other men refused to touch. The presence of Diamant reinforced the seriousness of this mission. *If the government is willing to sacrifice one of their best men, it has to be important.*

At the podium, Colonel Harper glared, brows squinted over dark eyes hard as diamonds. "Carrigan, you're late."

That being self-evident, Carrigan did not bother to reply. He accepted the chair beside Diamant and met Harper's stare without flinching.

"I said you're late, Carrigan," Harper pressed. His expression did not change, as if painted on his round, red-tinged face.

Carrigan still saw no need to answer but knew better than to antagonize a superior. "Yes, sir. You're quite right. I am late."

"And?" Harper squinted.

And? And what? I deserve to be whipped, shot, hanged, bludgeoned, and thrown out the window so I can plunge to my deserved death? Carrigan checked his sarcasm. "And, I'm sorry, sir. I needed to work out some tension, so I took the stairs."

"You needed to work out some tension," Harper repeated stiffly, as if he found the words painful. "This isn't a game, Carrigan. If you can't handle it, we'll find someone else."

Carrigan knew he had a reputation as a trouble-maker, but his allegiance and composure under pressure had never come into question. Even after Katry's death, he had done nothing to jeopardize a colleague or mission. Carrigan tossed back black hair several inches past regulation length. "Oh, I can handle it." He paused just long enough to make the delay noticeable, "Sir."

Diamant came to Carrigan's rescue. "With all due respect, sir. Even late, I'd rather have Jack backing me than anyone else."

The colonel met the testimonial with a grunt, but he let the matter rest and began the briefing

Now, standing in a gas station restroom doorway, Carrigan recalled how Colonel Harper had told his operatives a tale that would have seemed prepos-terous if not for his hard-won knowledge of Middle Eastern politics and religion. In truth, Carrigan knew the two concepts could not be separated. First hand, he had endured and witnessed the crazed boldness of U.M.E.P. citizens not just willing to die but obsessed with military murder-suicide for their religious ruler and their country. For the U.M.E.P. soldiers, death was not a thing to be feared, but an honor won, a chance to find heaven and send as many enemies as possible to hell.

Their leader, the Caliph Nabil Abd'El-Rahman was a madman worshiped by his people as the savior's third coming. Carrigan recalled listening and watching in awed silence as Colonel Harper unraveled the tale of the familiar ultra-religious, Sunni, elitist regime of the United Middle Eastern Powers. He told the trio of special forces commandos how, in the current year, 2058, Abd'El-Rahman planned to break treaties held sacred for nearly a century and launch worldwide nuclear strikes, leaving their imaginations to trace the mad chaos of attack and counterattack that would destroy every man, woman, and child in every country of the world. As if from an ancient comic book, Harper described a time travel device attempted, failed, and abandoned by more scientists than Carrigan could count and now perfected by the U.M.E.P.

From Abd'El-Rahman, Carrigan expected plans as demented as brilliant, the familiar, twisted logic of a schizophrenic who would dare to believe himself a god. Armed with understanding, Carrigan accepted what other men might deem impossible, believed without question the Caliph's warped plans and the explanations detailed by Harper. Intelligence men as committed to uncovering information as Carrigan was to acting on it had uncovered an odd story. From the colonel, Carrigan learned the U.M.E.P. had channeled all its wealth into building three of the time travel devices. They used one to send another to an unspecifiable, underground site in the year 1985. This same machine would be used to send several of the most gifted U.M.E.P. citizens, male and female, to the same time, there to locate the device transported earlier and retrieve Nabil Abd'El-Rahman at the age of ten. This done, the U.M.E.P. would take their young leader to a far future, after the radiation effects of the nuclear holocaust they caused had dispersed, and create a society of homogeneous and perfect people.

The idea seemed utter madness, as difficult to accept as the inane soap operas Carrigan had watched from his hospital bed. Yet, history had produced leaders equally insane and followers as fanatical, mass murder committed in the name of racial purity, politics, or religion: the Christian crusades, Rome's destruction of the Greeks, Hitler's Reich, and Stalin's purges in the U.S.S.R.

Luckily, the U.M.E.P. government had left a crack in their plan, a basic limitation in the engineering of the time travel devices. Though the units could accurately target a time and safely place their cargo above or below ground, the traveler could arrive anyplace in the world. With no way to set where their transported machine would arrive, the U.M.E.P. commissioned a device capable of locating it. Here, Abd'El-Rahman's luck ran short. One of his physicists was an American double agent who convinced some of her coworkers to turn against the regime. Those who remained loyal died mysteriously, with the aid of Carrigan's colleagues, and the principles of the tracking device belonged only to the Americans.

Now, Carrigan clapped a hand to his pocket and massaged the tracking device through the fabric. He recalled how Colonel Harper had entrusted one to each of his commandos, keeping the last for the government's files. And Harper's warning rang more clearly than anything else he had said in the briefing: "If a tracking device falls into enemy hands, it's all over. In an emergency, destroy the devices first, yourselves second."

Now, suddenly, the explosion Carrigan had remembered in Liberty's Intensive Care Unit became vividly logical. He recalled how Taylor had created the diversions with mortars and flares, directing enemy resources and firepower while Carrigan and Diamant sneaked into the compound dressed in U.M.E.P. uniforms. *I obliterated one of the machines. My presence in the hospital and the fragments in my chest are proof of that. But, either Diamant failed or the U.M.E.P. government sent an advance squad. In any case, Diamant had to have destroyed his tracking device. Otherwise, the U.M.E.P. soldiers would be searching for their time travel machine instead of bothering with me. I've got what they need.* He tapped the device in his pocket, reassured by its presence. *And I can't let them have it.*

Though complex, the memory and realizations came to Carrigan in seconds. Awed by his discovery, he stood in silence, still holding the gas station restroom door ajar. A tug at his arm and Walker's protestations shook Carrigan from his remembrances. "Aw, come on. You're not going to make me leave the door open here, too, are you?"

"No, of course not." Though uncomfortable with the enclosed space, the need to urinate overcame fear. Carrigan stepped inside and let the door swing shut. After using the facilities, both men rejoined Nicholson at the Omni.

Shawna Nicholson clutched a brown paper bag. Leaning against the driver's door, she stared out over the highway. Her posture combined the feigned nonchalance of a posed model with the grim edginess of a hunted deer. Her wind-tangled hair, grimy, water-spotted tee shirt and comfortable jeans with the cuffs speckled with clinging sand burrs seemed out of place, like a car advertisement onto which somebody had drawn a beard and mustache. Still, Carrigan knew Nicholson well enough to see through the fatigue, grief, and fear to the beauty and confidence he remembered. "I told the attendant we'd need to leave one of the cars for a while," she said. "Which one are we taking?"

Carrigan glanced from the Omni to Nicholson's dirt-coated, bullet-riddled Porsche beside the full-serve station. "Doesn't matter. The enemy knows both. Whichever would draw less attention."

Nicholson loosed a single derisive snort, not unlike Katry's reply to the man in the bar of Carrigan's memory. She opened the driver's door of the Omni and started to slide inside. "Jason would you please move my car from the pumps. If I look too closely at what he's done to it, I'll lose my mind. And, if you don't care, I'd like to drive."

At a nod from Walker, she traded keys, and he trotted toward the Porsche.

Carrigan sprang forward and caught the handle before Nicholson could pull it closed. "Let me drive."

Nicholson looked up, one foot on the gas station driveway, the other on the Omni's floor. She jabbed a finger toward the Porsche and addressed him stiffly. "That was a gorgeous, state of the art, $35,000 wonder car, not a matchbox. Haven't you done enough damage, Mr. Carrigan?" She offered him the paper bag.

Carrigan stared, glad to see Nicholson had regained some of her assurance, but floored by her
hostility. A number of thoughts converged on him
at once. No matter his ignorance of 1985 automobile design, he was still trained to escape pursuit.
He also wanted to remind Nicholson that she had
called him in a flustered panic. Then, he realized
she had courage if not training; letting her drive
would free his hands for exchanging gunfire. He
accepted the bag and reverted to humor. "Oh, I
see. So now that we're friends instead of doctor
and patient, we're no longer on a first name basis?"

Walker parked the Porsche out of the way of the
pumps then crawled into the back of his own car.
As unobtrusively as possible, Carrigan collected
Nicholson's beeper, the AK-47, and the Smith and
Wesson from the Porsche. Placing the guns under
the seat, he took the passenger's position in the
Omni, balancing the bag of food on his knees.

Nicholson methodically pulled a rectangular object from her waistband and clipped it to the sun
visor.

Amused by the habitual gesture, Carrigan tossed
the beeper into her lap.

Nicholson stared at the beeper, expression mu-
tating from startled to confused. She glanced momentarily at Carrigan then at the ergometer she
had reflexively placed in the beeper's usual location. "Oh." Her eyes went moist, and she stared
out the window. Uncharacteristically, she pocketed
the beeper, as if she could not stand to even glance
at the exercise measuring device she had handled
so casually moments before.

Mercifully, Carrigan plucked the ergometer from
the visor, out of Nicholson's constant sight, and

passed it to Walker in the back seat. Walker accepted the object without comment.

Regaining control, Nicholson started the engine. "Okay," she said as if the lapse never occurred. "Where to, *Jack*?"

Carrigan fastened his seat belt. "I don't believe those soldiers followed us. I think we lost them, and they got your addresses from some place or other. There's no question anymore that they're after me, and nothing you know can hurt them—"

Walker interrupted. "Whoa. Back up, Jack." He leaned across the seat back. "You may think nothing we know can hurt them, but they apparently don't concur."

Carrigan furrowed his brow, puzzled. Once the U.M.E.P. obtained the tracking device, nothing, not even Jack Carrigan, could stand in their way. "Why do you say that?"

Nicholson gave a brief description of the events of the last two hours, and Carrigan considered.

"Did you see the gunmen's car?"

"No," Walker said, then mulled his own response. "No, I didn't see the Cadillac anywhere."

Carrigan twisted to meet Walker's gaze directly. "Probably wouldn't have been the Cadillac. They'd had time to switch cars. Did you see any vehicles at all?"

"Not at my house." Walker looked at Nicholson, as if she might furnish the answer for him. "I didn't think about it elsewhere. My neighbors had a car in their driveway, but I don't know if it was theirs." He grimaced, obviously abashed. "We work such long hours in the hospital, I never had much time to get to know my neighbors. And the woods hide most of them anyway. There's a million places to stash a car."

Carrigan believed they had found the answer. "They probably got boxed in by the deputies. Or maybe they thought the shooting would draw me out." He dismissed the need to know the reason. Following an enemy's line of thought too closely resulted in false assurances of their next course of action. "In any case, the best thing I can do for you is get you somewhere safe. Really safe, this time. Some place unassociated with either of you where the Abduls would never, *ever* think to look." Recalling Ben Hascol's offer of help in the farm town, Carrigan smiled. "And I think I know just the place. Shawna, get back on the main road. Head south."

Nicholson pulled out of the gas station. "Abduls? You know something you're not telling us, don't you?"

Carrigan considered. *No question, the U.M.E.P.s already think I've told everything. Shawna and Jason deserve to know the details.* Still, Carrigan realized his experiences with the U.M.E.P. government gave him insight the others would not have. Without it, he doubted even he would accept the truth. It occurred to him, briefly, the safest place to leave the doctors was probably the hospital with its federal agents and anti-terrorist squads. *But it wouldn't surprise me if the U.M.E.P.s are watching the hospital. Besides, if I go to the hospital, whatever federal agencies 1985 has will question me, and there's not a snowball's chance they'll buy a word of my explanation.* "Yeah, I got my memory back. My name *is* Jack Carrigan. I'm an American special forces commando, and I've got a story you ain't going to believe."

CHAPTER 10

Jack Carrigan, SFC

J ack Carrigan appreciated his companions' silence while he told a tale that sounded ludicrous even to his own ears. As the Omni sped past the Liberty city limits, his story came to an end, its conclusion met by Nicholson's continued hush and Walker's raucous laughter. Walker leaned forward. "Look, Jack, if that really is your name. A simple 'none of your business' would have sufficed. Now pass out the food."

Carrigan reached into the paper bag, not caring whether Walker believed him or not. *Soon enough, this'll be over, one way or another.* Either Carrigan would locate the time travel device and prevent the deaths of billions of innocent people or not. In any case, Walker's support or derision could not change the consequences.

Carrigan's fingers touched plastic, and he pulled three wrapped sandwiches, three cold, moist cans of Coke, and a three-quarter pound bag of M & M's from the bag. Passing a sandwich and soda to each of his companions, he left the remainder of the food in his lap. The empty bag rattled to the floor.

Nicholson trapped a can between her thighs and rested her sandwich on her leg. "So let me get this straight. You come from the year 2058? And, if the guys with guns, these United Middle Eastern people, get that device thing from you, there's going to be a nuclear holocaust?"

"That's right." Carrigan took a bite of his sandwich. The meat and bread tasted unfamiliar but tolerable; the plastic balled up in his mouth, its consistency chewy and unpleasant. Screwing up his features in disgust, Carrigan worked the plastic to the front of his mouth with his tongue and fished it out with his fingers.

Nicholson glanced at the remainder of the sandwich in Carrigan's lap. "Gross, Jack. You forgot to take the wrapper off."

"Forgot, hell." Carrigan tore off the cling wrap, damp with condensation from the sodas. "Where I come from, they use the digestible stuff."

Nicholson made a high-pitched noise of revulsion. "You eat wrappers? After some dirty gas station attendant handled them?"

Carrigan balanced the Coke sideways on his lap. "First of all, we don't have gas stations. Second, like your mouth is sterile? And third, it's made of some wonder bioplast that doesn't hold dirt and germs well."

"Nice touch." Walker spoke around a mouthful of food. "But I'm not taking the bait. A united Middle Eastern alliance is an oxymoron; the Arab countries have been at war with each other forever. And what about Israel?"

Walker's point defied Carrigan. "What does Israel have to do with the Middle East?"

"What does Israel have to do with the Middle East?" Walker snorted. "What you trying to say?

Israel moved? After years of defending itself? Jewish history begins and ends in the Middle East."

Carrigan took another bite of his sandwich. "There comes a point where survival of the race outweighs geography. If my understanding of history serves, lots of countries offered to take Israel's people when they moved. The Americas were lucky to get them. The Israelis were brilliant military strategists. Still are."

Nicholson pulled up in front of a stop sign.

Walker clasped his soda in both hands, protecting it from spilling as Nicholson accelerated again. "Wait a second. If these Arab guys are from 2058, how come they're using Russian weapons we've had since before Vietnam? Why not lasers or phasers or whatever future weapons you've got?"

The answer seemed obvious to Carrigan. "Where would they get ammunition? Besides, lasers went out with mirror-armor. They cost a fortune to operate, caused a lot of accidents, and were useless against vehicles or uniforms with reflective shielding." Carrigan had always held a fascination for weapons and eagerly seized the opportunity to elaborate. "Everyone thought masers were going to be the great answer—that's amplified matter instead of light—because their beams punched through what lasers bounced right off. The basic concept worked fine, but when a magnetic field hit the power packs, they immediately heated to a state indistinguishable from an explosion. Hell, the really neat stuff was the water guns in the twenties. They shot a jet with enough velocity to cut through steel. Ammo was easy enough to come by but a pain to carry. It needed so much—"

Shawna interrupted. "Could we talk about something else besides great ways to kill people? Please?''

Walker pressed. "So what are you saying, Jack? We'll be at war the next 73 years?''

Carrigan considered, wishing he had paid closer attention in his history classes. "Not hardly. We've got a world economy to consider. After the magnetic dust bomb hit Silicon Valley in 2035, I don't think anyone could deny that. That was when the treaties released the bans on chemical warfare and placed them on the dust bomb. Wars went underground. Shit, it's the twenty-first century, Jason. We're not fighting for land and slaves any more. Can't hardly afford to wipe out another country's industry and resources, so people like me fight the battles.''

"Dust bomb?" Walker sneered. "Big deal. Twenty-five extra cases of Pledge.''

Walker's belittling of a holocaust annoyed Carrigan. "Jason that 'dust bomb' you so cheerfully dismiss will screw up electronics manufacturing in the area for the next hundred and fifty years.''

"Cut it out!" Nicholson shouted. "I don't want to hear it.''

Walker slapped a palm to his forehead. "Oh, come on, Shawna. You don't really buy this line of shit he's feeding us, do you?''

"I don't know," Nicholson admitted. "I'm not sure it's any more bizarre than some of the other explanations we came up with. And it does fit with what we've seen. Besides, if John ...'' She corrected herself. "... I mean, Jack was going to make up some weird story, don't you think he could have come up with something more believable than 2058?''

Walker shoved the last piece of sandwich in his mouth and flung up his arms in annoyance. "This is stupid. A time machine? How would one of those things work?"

Carrigan chewed the last bite of his sandwich and picked up his Coke. The mechanism for opening the can looked unfamiliar. *It's one thing for Walker to think I'm deluded, but I'm not going to let him convince Shawna I'm being intentionally deceitful.* "Damn it, Walker, do I look like a physicist to you? I didn't invent the fucking thing. I just pushed the button. It worked. Have you ever flown in an airplane?"

"Of course."

"Could you build one?"

"No," Walker admitted. "But I have a general idea how it works."

Nicholson stopped at a three way intersection. "How about a microwave, Jason?" She looked at Carrigan. "Which way?"

"Left." Carrigan steered her in the direction of the farm town. When Walker said nothing in defense, Carrigan tried a different tactic. "Wait a minute!" he shouted, pretending to be hit with a sudden inspiration. "Jason Walker. Didn't click till now. *The* Dr. Jason Walker . . ." He trailed off.

Nicholson turned the car and continued down the street.

"What?" Walker sounded genuinely interested now.

Carrigan traced the edge of his soda can without meeting Walker's gaze. "Never mind."

Walker sat back. "Crap. You're just playing with me."

Carrigan shrugged. He mumbled, "*The* Jason

Walker. Who would have known?" He smiled, as if at a private joke.

Walker went sullenly silent. This time, Nicholson pressed. "What about Jason? Is he going to be famous?"

"Never mind." Carrigan shook condensation from his finger. "Jason doesn't believe me anyway."

Walker leaned forward again, his hand heavy on Carrigan's headrest. "Come on. Just tell me."

"All right." Carrigan watched Walker's expression in the rearview mirror. "Think universal vaccine."

An innocent wonder stole the creases from the doctor's features, and his jaw sagged. "Really?" He sounded excited despite himself. "I create a vaccine that wipes out all illnesses?"

Carrigan delivered the coup de grace, trying to keep a straight face as he lied. "No, you get eight to fifteen years for fraud." He reached for the pull tab.

"Very funny." Walker's expression lapsed back to normal. He added casually, "You have to shake that well before opening."

"Hmmm?" Carrigan glanced at the can, shrugged his ignorance, and started rotating it vigorously from side to side.

"No." Nicholson caught Carrigan's wrist, but she aimed her comment at Walker. "Jason, you dipshit! Do you really want pop all over your car?" Keeping one hand on the wheel, she wrestled the can from Carrigan's grip. "Here, take mine. And please don't shake it."

Carrigan seized Nicholson's Coke by the top and pulled it free. Setting it between his own legs, he reached for the M & M's. "Okay, before I do anything stupid, tell me how I'm supposed to open this."

Walker answered first. "Grab it by the front and back and pull the sealed apart at the top open."

At Nicholson's confirmatory nod, Carrigan pinched both sides of the bag and pulled gently. Nothing happened. He yanked harder, and the bag tore, flinging M & M's through the Omni. They bounced from the windshield, sprayed over Nicholson and Carrigan, and rattled from the gauges.

Nicholson and Walker lapsed into a wild fit of laughter. Carrigan stared at the tattered, half-empty wrapper still clutched in his hands. Then, the ridiculousness of the situation hit him, and he laughed along with them. "Oh, funny. Let's make an idiot out of the guy with the assault rifle." He tapped the blanket-wrapped barrel with his heel.

As they entered the town where Carrigan had found help for the gasless Porsche, Nicholson slowed to the posted 25 mph. She spoke between snickers. "It . . . wasn't on purpose. You . . . just . . . pulled too . . . hard. Everyone does it sometimes."

The trio broke into another wave of laughter.

Nicholson's easy mirth pleased Carrigan. It felt good to see her snapped from her horrified trance, even if it was at his expense. He tried to remember Hascol's directions. "A mile past town, we should come upon a gravel road. Take a right and go to box 56."

"Wait a second." Walker's voice contained a note of triumph, as though he had finally located the loophole in Carrigan's story. "You've been in 1985 for ten days, all without leaving Liberty Hospital. You've been out all of six, maybe seven hours." He glanced at his watch. "And you're telling me you already know people out in this God-forsaken wilderness."

Nicholson accelerated back to the 55 miles per hour speed limit, then braked smoothly as the Omni came upon a gravel road. She turned right. Stones skittered from beneath the tires making raspy, hollow noises.

Carrigan smiled. "I make friends fast. Right, Jason?"

"Uh, sure. Must be that kind, gentle way you entwine your fingers in their windpipes. Got my attention real quick."

The three laughed again.

The roadway twisted and wound between corn fields. Tractor-drawn cultivators chugged in straight lines along the rows. New, glossy-painted outbuildings stood beside collapsing farrows and corn cribs. Scattered houses whisked by; the first box number read 51. Another mile passed before they rounded a forested corner and came upon a white, prefabricated house with a cinder block base. A silver mailbox big as a man's head stood at the mouth of the driveway, mounted on a stick of firewood branched into a Y-shape. It read: "Rt. 1, Box 56. Benjamin Hascol." Nicholson pulled into the dirt driveway.

The driveway swung around the side of the house, and Carrigan inspected the building from habit. Curtained casement windows interrupted the cinder block, indicating a full- or half-finished story in the basement. The upper level stood far enough above ground level to require elevated porches at the front and back doors. A yard full of mowed grass and oak trees surrounded the house. Beyond it, an aging barn towered, its red paint peeling. A barbed wire fence met its rear wall, leading out back and as far as Carrigan could see. A Chevy Blazer parked alongside the pasture. Carrigan stared, not daring to believe only one family occupied this huge dwelling nor the waste of surrounding lands.

Nicholson parked behind an old Dodge Dart and the familiar, green pickup Hascol had used to drive Carrigan to the Porsche. She cut the Omni's engine. "Now what?"

"Honk the horn," Walker suggested. "From the fences, I'd guess he's a stock farmer, probably cows. He might be in the barn rather than out with a tractor somewhere."

Nicholson obeyed, then craned her neck to study Walker. "How do you know about farmers? You're from Philadelphia."

"Hey, there're tons of great hospitals on the east coast. Liberty has a good reputation, but you don't think I came all the way to Iowa because I couldn't get into Johns Hopkins." Walker looked up suddenly. "Do you?"

Staring out the window, Carrigan watched the Blazer bounce across the grass toward them.

Nicholson tapped the balls of her hands against the steering wheel. "I never thought about it. Why did you come to Iowa?"

"Country setting," Walker admitted. "I got sick of fearing for my life, having to track down friends every time I wanted to go out at night. I was tired of hearing about shootings, counting how many blocks away they occurred, and discovering I could do it on one hand. I like the open spaces."

Carrigan felt his first moment of camaraderie with Jason Walker. *Beneath that selfless dedication to his work, he's human.* He watched the truck rumble closer, a burgundy and white Blazer with rusted quarter panels. Coated with grime, it certainly never left the farm; it did not even have a front license plate.

The doctors went silent as the Blazer rumbled and quivered to a stop. Ben Hascol jumped out. The farmer wore threadbare overalls over a sleeveless, flannel shirt. Sweat sheened his square-cut face. Matted, dark hair poked from beneath a blue cap that read "Dillon Precision Products" in white letters, the D and first P intertwined.

As Carrigan, Nicholson, and Walker exited the Omni, Hascol wiped his brow with the back of his left hand and extended his right. Carrigan accepted the gesture. The farmer's meaty hand engulfed his, rougher and more callused than any he had encountered. "Well, I'll be. John. Didn't expect to see you back. Certainly not so soon." Hascol's voice was booming and sincere, but Carrigan sensed reluctance.

"Ben Hascol, Shawna Nicholson and Jason Walker." Carrigan indicated his companions. "They're doctors at Liberty Hospital. They need a place to stay, and I thought I'd take you up on your offer."

Hascol removed his cap, revealing wavy hair plastered to his head. "John, I'm a man of my word. If you need a bit of help, a place to stay, that's fine. But I saw the bullet holes, and I ain't doing anything that's going to get me arrested. My boys are off at college. If I go to jail, there won't be anyone left to tend the farm. This place has been in my family a hundred and fifty years. I'm not going to lose it for somebody I don't know."

Carrigan went appropriately serious. "Ben, it's not illegal, I promise you that. I wouldn't do *anything* to hurt the country." Carrigan forced aside the memories of Katry, the realization of murders he had committed for the nation he loved and chose to serve with a devotion every bit as fanatical as Walker's for his medicine. "I work for the federal government." He added quickly, "Don't ask for any ID. I don't have any. You're going to have to take my word for it. Have you heard about the shootings at Liberty Hospital?"

Hascol replaced his cap and nodded. "In the morning paper. You involved in that A-rab terrorist stuff?"

Carrigan seized the opportunity. From the corner of his eye, he saw Walker cringe, apparently concerned Carrigan might mention the time travel devices. "These are the two doctors the terrorists tried to kill. All I'm asking is for you to let them stay a couple days. They'll even pitch in and help you out. Shouldn't be any trouble at all." Carrigan felt comfortable committing his companions to work. *Walker loves farms, and Nicholson will feel obligated to help.* "The terrorists have no reason to look here."

Hascol agreed, either a good judge of character or a trusting man. "All right. With the boys away and my wife dead these last few years, I can use the hands and the company. You staying, too, John?"

"Can't." Carrigan touched the tracking device through his pocket, aware his job had scarcely begun. *That time travel device could be anywhere in the world.* He would have at least liked to stay for lunch. The sandwich and soda barely grazed his hunger. *But the longer I delay, the more likely the*

U.M.E.P. soldiers will track us down. Besides, how long before their government plans to send more? "I've got work to do."

Nicholson handed Carrigan the keys to the Omni. As his hand closed over the ring, she gripped his fist. "Wait." Releasing him, she pulled some crumpled bills from her jeans pocket and offered them. "It's not much, but it can't hurt. And take this, too." She removed her beeper from her jeans and handed that to Carrigan as well. "Just in case."

Carrigan accepted the beeper and money absently, without bothering to examine them. He tucked the bills into his pocket and attached the beeper to his waistband, his thoughts elsewhere. *The U.M.E.Ps know the Omni.* He glanced at the Dart and pickup blocking the exit from the driveway. "Ben, I hate to ask for more help, but could I use one of your cars?"

Hascol glanced from his vehicles to Carrigan uncertainly.

"If you don't get it back, you can have this one." Carrigan patted the Omni's hood, then tossed the keys toward Hascol.

Walker looked stricken but, wisely, did not complain.

Hascol caught the keys, and they disappeared into the creases of his oversized hand. "Sure, why not? You wouldn't leave your friends, here, if you weren't coming back. Dart's all gassed up." He unclipped a key ring from his belt loop worked off a single one, and pitched it to Carrigan.

"Thanks." Carrigan snapped the key from the air. Transferring the AK-47 and the pistol from the Omni, he drove the Dart back onto the main street, headed toward town.

*   *   *

Jason Walker watched the Dart disappear amidst the billowing dust of the gravel road, aware the scenario could never have happened in Philadelphia. In his two years in Liberty, Iowa, he had become accustomed to 'carry-out' grocery stores, corn detasseling, and the virtual absence of rush hour traffic. But the easy-going kindness of the farmers on the rural fringes of towns too small to play frisbee across still floored Walker.

Ben Hascol clapped his huge hands across Walker's and Nicholson's shoulders and steered them toward the enclosed back porch. "You two look exhausted. You can use my bed." He patted Walker's back, then addressed Nicholson. "And you can stay in my boys' room."

The three climbed the steps to the screened back porch. Hascol opened the front door, ushering Nicholson and Walker into a tiled kitchen. Simple, wooden cupboards lined the walls. Beneath them, on the east wall to the right, sat a sink and drying rack. Further on the same side, an uncovered doorway opened to a narrow hallway. A combination stove and oven with a blue smoke hood stood to the left of the back entry; a microwave oven occupied the counter space between it and a drab-looking, old refrigerator painted with swirling, blue country designs. Instead of a wall, a white countertop with a wooden base partially divided the kitchen from an L-shaped, combined living and dining room. The front door lay directly across from the one they had entered. Aside from heavily-curtained bay windows looking out over the front, side, and back yards, the room stood relatively empty. Its furnishings consisted only of a hand-carved table with four chairs, a towering bookshelf, and a curio hutch.

Hascol led his guests down the long hallway. A door to the right opened into a tidy bathroom. Directly across from it, a set of carpeted steps led to the lower story. Further, another door led into a blue-walled bedroom, and the hallway ended at the master chamber. "Feel free to use whatever you need. There's food in the fridge. Towels under the bathroom sink." He gestured Nicholson toward the blue room. "So, you and John married?"

Nicholson seemed to take no notice of the farmer's question; and, for a shocked moment, Walker feared the man had addressed him. The same realization must have struck Nicholson. "Huh?" she asked.

"You and John." Hascol pressed. "You two married?"

"Hell, no," Nicholson said with more hostility than Walker felt appropriate. She recovered quickly. "Why do you ask?"

Hascol shrugged. "Just figured when he said his name was John Nicholson what with you being Shawna Nicholson and all."

Nicholson covered. "Oh, well, we're cousins." She added unnecessarily, "*Distant* cousins."

Apparently sensing Nicholson's distress, Hascol backed out. "Don't matter. I was just curious. If you need anything, I'll be out back. I have to remake a section of fence in the near pasture so I can turn my cattle back out. Some trees fell on it during the storm last week."

"Thank you, very much. We really do appreciate your hospitality." Nicholson wandered into the blue-walled room and closed the door.

Hascol inclined his head toward the master bedroom.

"Yes, thanks." Walker parroted, feeling as if Nicholson had already spoken for him. Entering the room, he discovered a queen-sized bed beneath a window, its curtain flapping in the breeze through the screen. Two dressers lined the walls, and the open closet revealed a mixed wardrobe of work clothes and dress shirts. Walker felt as if he was violating Hascol's privacy. Removing his running shoes and socks, he lay atop the bed covers. He closed his eyes, but sleep eluded him. His nerves seemed tied in knots. His usual method of unwinding, envisioning peaceful walks in the woods by his rented home, had been wrenched from him. The forest had lost its virgin purity. He kept picturing Harlowe's twisted body, the droplets of blood splashed across the leaves, and Schreiber's empty death mask.

Walker climbed out of bed. Raising the screens, he slid the glass of the window closed. The curtains dropped into place. The rattle of leaves outside was cut off, leaving only the tromp of Hascol's boots on the tiled kitchen floor. Many thoughts haunted Walker. *We left the medical units without a resident.* He shoved the guilt aside, logically aware no one could blame him for being dragged from the ward at gun point, but still feeling as if he had shirked his duties. *And who the hell is Jack Carrigan?* A new possibility came to him. *Probably a drug runner hunted by a foreign government.* He dismissed the idea. *Yeah, right. A smuggler with a conscience. He saved my life twice, and I do appreciate it. But how the hell can he expect me to believe that outlandish story. Time machines?* Still, Walker had to admit, so far, it was the only explanation that fit facts equally as bizarre.

Walker tried to forget about Carrigan, but his every thought brought him back to one concern or another. His patients reminded him he had abandoned them. His home made him think of the deputies. And Harlowe. *It should have been me.* Jerked wide awake, Walker leaped from the bed. *Fuck it. I can't sleep.* He grabbed his shoes, padded from the bedroom and nearly ran into Hascol in the hallway.

The farmer studied Walker in the dim light funneling into the hallway from the living room windows. "You okay there, Jason?"

Walker sighed. "No. I've been awake twenty-seven hours now, and I still can't sleep. I'm too damn nervous. I'm scared. I'm not used to having people shoot at me." For some reason, it seemed easier to confess his problems to a stranger.

Hascol nodded sympathetically. "What happened, anyway? What is all this terrorist stuff?"

Walker considered and decided what little he knew made no sense at all. He could think of nothing he would less like to discuss. "Can't tell you. Um ... security reasons."

Hascol accepted the denial. "Yeah, I guess I can understand that. But, I expect a phone call after this is all over."

Walker nodded, thinking the only people who deserved an explanation more were Nicholson and himself.

"Well," Hascol said. "If you can't sleep, you might as well come outside for a bit. Ain't often I got extra hands, and building fence by yourself gets to be a royal pain in the ass. Come on out. I'll show you around, get you out in the fresh air a bit. String barbed wire for a couple hours; and, when you come back in, you'll sleep like a log."

"Sure, why not." The invitation sounded perfect to Walker. He liked the outdoors, needed something to get the previous events of the day off his mind; and, though he would never have admitted it earlier, he did not care much for being alone. Sitting on the carpeted floor, he pulled on his shoes. "Let's go."

Hascol, too, seemed glad for the company. He led Walker from the kitchen to the porch and down the steps. He opened the passenger door of the Blazer. "You ever strung barbed wire before?" Without waiting for a reply, he slammed Walker's door closed. Walker watched as Hascol trotted around the truck. Glancing behind him, he noticed an array of shovels, a post hole digger, several rolls of barbed wire, a coffee can filled with U-shaped nails, and a Browning semi-automatic rifle. Further toward the gate lay an assortment of tools, a dented gasoline can, a chain saw, and coiled scraps of wire.

Hascol jumped into the driver's seat, placed the key, and awaited an answer to a question Walker had nearly forgotten in the interim. "Um, no. I've never strung wire. I'd like to learn, though."

The engine stuttered before turning over, and Hascol pulled across his yard onto a lane of tire tracks bordered on the right by the fenced pasture and the left by a tract of trees. "Didn't think so," Hascol said. "Would have taken you for a city kid."

There was no malice in Hascol's tone, but Walker could not help feeling insulted. He tried to establish a fellowship with the farmer. "It's true. I always wanted to grow up on farm. I know it's a lot of hard work and all, but I could stand to be whipped into shape." He raised a pathetically thin arm, suddenly reminded of Tracy Harlowe. *If I had been more fit, she would have let me go, and she'd still be alive.*

"Yeah, well. With the way the economy's going now, farming's no way to make a living. Hell, some of my friends sent their kids off to school so they won't have to tend—" Hascol slammed on the brakes. Grabbing the rifle, he sprang from the truck.

Hascol's first gunshot sent Walker leaping out the passenger's side. He dove to the ground as Hascol fired off three more rounds. Walker hugged the grass, heart racing in panic.

The farmer's voice sounded distant as he clambered back into the Blazer. "Damned coyotes! Coming around dogging my calves for the last two years. Can't never get a good shot at them. Stupid .243, little pop gun, don't do nothing to them anyway." The truck started rolling, then stopped. "Jason? Where'd you go?"

It took Walker an unusually long time to get his limbs working. Flushed, he climbed timidly back into his seat. "Sorry. I'm a bit on edge."

Hascol set the rifle back in its place. "No, I'm sorry. Should have thought of what you'd been through before I did that. You all right?"

Walker swallowed hard. "I will be. As soon as I cough my tongue back up."

Hascol chuckled. Walker joined him, but his own laughter sounded more like nervous choking.

A few more yards of driving along the fence row brought Hascol and Walker to a stretch without the familiar five strands of barbed wire. The wooden columns stood straight as sentinels, but the piled dirt at their bases revealed Hascol had recently replaced them. Hascol stopped the Blazer. "At the far end, there's still one post down." Reaching behind the seat, he passed Walker a post hole digger, then fished a tape measure from his pocket and offered it, too. "Thirty-six inches below ground. Forty-eight above. I'll be attaching wires and getting the ends hooked up to the stretcher on the back of the truck."

Walker accepted the proffered items. Opening his door, he jumped to the ground. The spring air smelled of young plants, wild flowers, and damp. The odor of manure tainted the familiar rebirthing aromas of spring, but Walker reveled in them just the same. He wandered up the fence row, clutching the post hole digger by its two wooden rods, letting the curved, painted red blades drag along the path. He located the single horizontal pole, barbed wire still pulled and twisted awkwardly around it. Its fall had turned its original hollow into a gash. Walker eyeballed a spot halfway between the neighboring posts and jabbed the digger into his chosen site.

Walker faced away from the house and Hascol, looking out over the pastures and timber while he worked. He pushed the posts together, pulling the first divot from the ground. It was small, half the size of his fist. Embarrassed, Walker slammed the digger deeper on his second attempt. The ground resisted, hard as concrete, and the next piece came up no larger than the other. Scenery forgotten, Walker struggled and strained with the hole. Half an hour of frustrated jabbing resulted in a thirty inch hole. Then, the soil became sandy. Each bite sifted through the grooves between the blades, and Walker's efforts gained him no ground.

Sweat trickled down Walker's forehead, and the hospital scrubs clung to his moist chest and legs. He stepped away from the hole, yanking the linen free of his flesh in a gesture of futility. The cloth simply stuck in a different position. "Shit." Raising the lower edge of his scrub shirt, he wiped his brow. He let the fabric fall back into position and tossed back his sodden curls. He considered ignoring the last half a foot and putting the post in the ground, but he suspected Hascol would notice a column six inches taller than the rest. Sighing his resignation, Walker raised the digger for another try.

The sound of the Blazer humming and bumping over the path froze Walker in mid-strike. As the truck pulled up alongside him, its engine cut, and Walker turned to face Benjamin Hascol. The farmer studied Walker's efforts. "Nice job, son. Let me get the last couple inches for you." His tone sounded so nonjudgmental, Walker did not even realize he was being patronized. He surrendered the digger happily.

Hascol widened the hole with a few scrapes of the blades, then stabbed the digger into the hole, removing dirt twice. Taking the tape measure from Walker, he pinned its end to the bottom of the cavity. The metal casing rose to exactly thirty-six inches. Hascol rose. He tapped the button, and the tape retracted with a metallic, sheeting sound. "I got the fence wires hooked up to the back of the truck. As soon as we get this pole in, I'll pull up the rest of the way, and we can start hammering staples."

Walker stared, not daring to believe he had spent

five minutes wresting with a project Hascol completed in as many seconds. *There's no way I'm being any help at all to this guy. He's humoring me.*

Apparently noticing Walker's consternation, Hascol continued talking as he reached for the post. "Don't worry, Jason. Everyone starts a little slow. You saved me the time and trouble of digging this hole while I was getting other things—" He broke off, suddenly, staring toward the house. "Now, how long have they been there?"

Alarmed, Walker followed Hascol's gaze. Two gleaming, luxury sedans sat, parked behind the Omni, one red, the other black. "Oh, God, no."

Hascol glanced at Walker. "You know who that is?"

"No," Walker admitted. The spring breeze seemed chill, and his breathing quickened with fear. "I sure hope it's the F.B.I., but it could be Arabs. And Shawna's in there!"

"Get in the truck." Hascol ran around behind the blazer. He snipped the ties that attached the wire stretcher to the bumper, and the barbed strands fell limp to the ground. Walker fumbled with the handle, opened the door, and climbed into the passenger side as Hascol slid in beside him. The farmer started the engine, turned the truck, and headed back toward his house.

"Where are you going?" Walker's nerves felt taut as guitar strings. "We have to call the police."

Reaching into the back, Hascol retrieved his rifle. "Son, we ain't getting nowhere driving across my pastures. And we don't know yet those visitors ain't just company."

Directly in front of the barn, Hascol threw the Blazer into park. Still clutching the rifle, he clambered out of the truck. Walker exited his own side. He dropped to the ground beside the truck, trying to find the safest place to hide. *Not again. Oh, please God, let it be company.*

The creak of the opening front door drew Walker's attention to the porch. A swarthy face poked out, maned by wavy black hair and a beard. He spoke in heavily-accented but unmistakable English. "We want to talk."

"You're in my house, you damned commie!" Hascol fired. His first shot buried in the door frame. The U.M.E.P. soldier ducked into the kitchen, and the door swung closed. Hascol's second shot drilled through the storm door.

From the living room window, automatic gunfire swept the driveway and tore into the front of the Blazer. Walker screamed, scrambling behind the truck. Hascol threw himself flat to the ground. None of the shots came close to hitting either man, and the round was obviously intended as a warning.

Walker's chest felt squeezed, and a premonition of death made him fear he was having a heart attack. *Not again. Not again. How did they find us this time?*

Hascol's shout sounded tenuous in the resultant silence. "Uh, what was it you wanted to talk about?"

The U.M.E.P.'s reply wafted through a window. "We want the tracking device and Jack Carrigan. You've got twenty-four hours before we kill the woman."

Hascol twisted his head toward Walker. "Jack who?"

Shakily, Walker rose to one knee. "They mean John."

Hascol called back to the house. "We don't know where he's at!"

"Twenty-four hours," the gunman repeated.

Walker's mind raced as he sorted alternatives. So far, almost every decision he had made was wrong. *I hampered Carrigan's escape and was lucky he risked his life for me. I convinced him my house would be safe and got Tracy killed. Now, it's Shawna. I can't afford any more mistakes.* Tears blurred his vision, and Hascol's words scarcely penetrated the wild ringing in his ears.

"Jason, I'm going into town. I'll get as many of my buddies as I can. The police, too. We'll shoot ourselves some A-rabs."

"No!" Walker reached out and caught Hascol's arm. Though uncertain of his own plan, Walker did not like the sound of Hascol's. "They'll kill Shawna. I'm sure."

Hascol rose to a crouch. "What do you suggest?"

Walker considered, afraid to commit to a strategy for fear he might choose wrongly. A memory came to him, words spoken by Shawna Nicholson during a mock code on a resuscitation doll nearly a year ago. *Jason, the main problem with hospital staff teaching by intimidation is that they create interns who believe they must know everything, who are scared to ask for help for fear of being ridiculed. There're too many facts for any one person to know them all. Doctors with limitations don't kill patients; it's the ones who believe themselves perfect who do. In an emergency, the first thing to remember is not to be proud. You're not alone. There's no shame in needing help, only in denying that need.*

Walker gritted his teeth, drawing on his remembrance of the nerve-racking drive that followed

Harlowe's murder. Again, Nicholson's confident voice rose clearly in his mind: *I'm just saying I think it's time to call in a professional, someone who knows how to deal with Arab terrorists. The only person who's shown he can handle those Arabs is John.* Walker's decision followed naturally. *Nicholson put her trust in Carrigan. It's her life at stake; I have to put faith in her judgment.* "Ben, neither one of us is qualified to make that choice. But I know someone who is. A specialist. The only person who knows all the facts, ridiculous as they sound. I have to call Carrigan."

Hascol stared. "You can call him?"

Walker nodded. "Where's the nearest phone?"

Hascol jabbed a thumb toward the barn. "In the garage."

Walker raced toward the barn, Hascol in close pursuit. The huge, cattle doors gaped open revealing stalls, the farthest filled with baled straw. A wall divided it from a standard garage door and the area beyond. Walker and Hascol darted inside the barn. A normal panel, complete with a knob, divided the barn from the garage. Hascol opened it, and Walker ducked through.

A cream-colored Capri filled most of the space. Under ordinary circumstances, Walker might have questioned the number of cars needed by one farmer. Now, he simply attributed it to Hascol's college boys. His gaze passed over deteriorating work ledges, hanging rakes, sickles, pitchforks, and a riding mower before he saw the telephone mounted on the back wall. Walker ran to it.

"What's your hurry, Jason?" Hascol stood in the doorway. "We've got twenty-four hours."

"Not really." Walker dialed out the hospital operator's number and explained while it rang. "There's a limited range on the beeper. He may already be past contact—"

A click sounded during the second ring. Walker clapped a palm over the receiver. "Ben, is this an extension?"

Hascol nodded.

Shit. So they can listen in on any phone conversation we have. Walker chewed his lip impatiently.

The ringing stopped. A woman's voice came over the line. "Liberty Hospital information. Can I help you?"

"This is Dr. Walker. This is an emergency. I need you to page the chief resident in the department of Internal Medicine. That's Dr. Nicholson. I want . . ."

"Thank you . . ."

"Wait!" Jason screamed, aware the operators were quick and efficient and often did not hold for full instructions. "There's more."

"Go on."

"If you don't get an answer, keep trying. It'll be a man. Tell him to call me at . . ." He looked at Hascol.

The farmer rattled off his number.

Walker repeated it for the operator. "And you'd better tell him how to call collect. Be explicit. Lives depend on it."

This time, the operator waited. "Is that all, doctor?"

"Yes."

"Thank you." The line clicked off.

Jason Walker returned the receiver to the cradle. He hunched, shivering against the Capri. And waited.

CHAPTER 11

Hostage

For the sake of privacy, Jack Carrigan had answered Nicholson's beeper from a pay telephone outside the Cedar Rapids Airport; but the noises of the terminal filtered through the cinder block walls. The continuous rumble of conversations too mixed to decipher and the intermittent whoosh of approaching automobiles was punctuated by the sharp slams of car doors and the announcements of flights over the loudspeaker. Carrigan recognized the danger inherent in every contact he made; each call and background sound became a means for the U.M.E.Ps to trace his location. The urge to ignore Jason Walker's summons was strong. *But I got him into this situation. I can at least hear him out.*

Carrigan tucked the receiver between his ear and shoulder and recalled the procedure the woman from the hospital had detailed. He tapped out a zero followed by the ten numbers of Benjamin Hascol's extension. When the operator came on the line, Carrigan spoke distinctly, "I'd like to make a collect call from Jack."

"One moment."

Carrigan heard a ring, followed by Walker's frantic voice. "Hello!"

A second click followed, and Carrigan wondered

just how many people it took to make a single call. As instructed, he waited while the operator spoke. "Collect call from—"

Walker interrupted. "Yes. Yes, I'll accept the charges. Jack?"

"It's me," Carrigan admitted.

Walker's voice communicated the breathy quality of tears withheld. "They've got Shawna."

The muscles of Carrigan's chest knotted. "Got?" he pressed calmly. "Walker, don't talk in euphemisms. Just tell me what's going on."

"The terrorists. They captured Shawna. They're holding her hostage in Ben's house." Walker's already rapid patter accelerated as he considered another danger. "Careful. They may be listening."

The thought had already occurred to Carrigan. He spoke deliberately, hoping his manner might slow Walker's speech and calm him simultaneously. "What do they want?"

"They said they'd kill her if they didn't have you and the tracking device within twenty-four hours."

The death of one woman or the destruction of the world? Carrigan's thoughts clicked smoothly. *There's no decision here, and the Abduls know it. They're desperate. They've lost me, and they're pulling their last trick.* The pressure of the receiver hurt Carrigan's ear, and he transferred it to the opposite side. *The life of a single woman against the welfare of my country. The life of Shawna Nicholson.* Carrigan gripped the phone so tightly, his injured shoulder ached. The choice should have been no choice. The answer was obvious. Yet still, his mind would not let go. *I made this mistake once, and I'm not going to do it again. I sold out Katry. But Katry was a soldier, trained and dedicated, willing to die for our cause and our country. Nicholson is a civilian, dragged involuntarily into war.* Even as the idea arose, Carrigan knew he was lying to himself, at least partially. He recalled Nicholson's insistence on joining him back in her apartment.

Walker's voice went high-pitched with fear. "Jack, are you still there?"

"I'm just thinking," Carrigan said. *Nicholson wanted to accompany me because, despite all her denial, she cares. And, damn it, so do I.* "Walker, have you called anyone else?"

"Like the police?"

"Right."

"No," Walker confessed meekly. "I wanted to. Should I have?"

Carrigan licked his lips, aware his answer to this question would commit him, one way or the other. If he let Walker call in the law, there was no longer any need for a commando. He pictured a uniformed team of gunmen swarming around Ben Hascol's home. There was no way to know if the U.M.E.P. soldiers had brought any future weapons with them. *Surely, explosives, at least. And they must have used a homing device on the Omni to track down Nicholson and Walker.* In Carrigan's mind, there was no question men would die on both sides. *And so will Shawna.* Carrigan weighed his options in the balance and did not like either possibility. Holding one civilian life as valuable as billions was wrong. *But so was Katry's death. And Tracy's.* He smiled. *And who says I can't save Nicholson and the world?* "No. Walker, you did the right thing. For Shawna's sake, let me deal with this." Another realization struck him. "It's possible the anti-terrorist squad might find out you called the hospital. If they phone, send them in the wrong direction."

"But . . ." Walker started.

"Don't question, just do it!" The decision to rescue Nicholson went against Carrigan's training and common sense, and he would not allow Walker to jeopardize a mission that already seemed impossible. "Damn it, Jason. You make a mistake that kills Shawna, and you're going to be running from more than Arabs. Got that?"

"Clearly."

Carrigan sensed sullenness beneath Walker's timid reply, and it pleased him. Anger, no matter how misdirected, was preferable to panic. "Where are you?"

Walker hesitated, apparently fearing eavesdropping. It occurred to Carrigan that Walker might even have called under direct duress, such as a gun at his head. "Ben and I are in his garage."

"Stay put." Carrigan had activated the tracker in the Dart and knew the time travel device was located about 2600 kilometers southwest. The only maps in Hascol's glove compartment detailed the east coast and the midwestern states. He kept his tone casual. "I'm in the Boston Airport. Give me some time to catch a flight into Des Moines and another few hours to drive from there. It'll probably be a good five or six hours before I can get back." Carrigan held his breath, afraid Walker would blow his cover. No doubt, the doctor realized the beepers' signals would never transmit even across the state, but the U.M.E.P. soldiers could not have that information. Carrigan had no way to know how severely he overestimated the speed of 1985 aircraft nor the efficiency of its airports.

Walker played along, sounding appropriately stricken. "Five or six *hours*?"

"It's the best I can do."

Walker conceded. "All right. See you then. And please hurry as much as you can."

Carrigan slammed the receiver back in place. *One step forward, two steps back. I've been in 1985 ten days and still can't seem to get out of Liberty, Iowa.* He punched the plastic ledge around the telephone. *What am I doing? This is crazy.* Another thought rose unbidden. *Well, Diamant always said my insubordination would get the world in trouble.* Laughing at the irony, Carrigan threaded his way between waiting taxis and mini-bus limousines toward the parking lot.

Once committed to rescuing Nicholson, Carrigan did not agonize over his decision. Instead, he let his thoughts run, considering strategies and solutions as he steered Hascol's Dart along the highway. He appreciated the lack of stop signs and traffic signals; their inflexibility confused him. The speed limits gave him less problem. Accustomed to manually overriding the cruise systems, he had become a good judge of velocity, and the Dart wobbled dangerously whenever he took it over sixty mph. The absence of computerized road mapping made him feel continuously lost, and he appreciated the agency training against tampered cars and interposed street plate locators and warnings.

A half mile before the farm town, Carrigan pulled off the road and into one of the deep shoulders that lined Iowa's streets. Carefully, he drew the wrapped AK-47 from beneath the passenger seat and cradled it in the crook of his elbow while he extracted the Smith and Wesson. He jabbed the pistol in his waistband, arranging it as unobtrusively as possible beneath the hem of his T-shirt. The gun left an obvious bulge. Frowning at his efforts, Carrigan clutched the blanketed AK-47 more like a baby than a gun and let the edges of its wrapping hide his hip. *Hardly ideal, but it'll have to do.*

Skirting the town, Carrigan took the direct route toward Ben Hascol's farm. His path brought him through hog- and cattle-filled pastures, fields of corn and soybean, and clutches of timber. Where he saw houses and moving or idle tractors, he avoided them. He slipped through barbed wire fences, unnerved by the side-long, shifty-eyed stares of animals several times his weight. He dodged the pastures as much as possible, clinging to the towering cover the trees provided.

At length, Carrigan followed the patch of woods that bordered Hascol's near pasture, tracing a path to the back of the barn. There, he crouched in silence for several minutes, watching. The only movement he saw was the casual activity of sentries at the windows of Hascol's house, the only sound exchanged conversation between the farmer and Walker, unintelligible mumbles wafting from the garage.

The absence of outdoor scouts did not surprise Carrigan. The U.M.E.Ps knew Carrigan would commit completely or not at all. In either case, the ball was in his court. The house was defensible, the yard not at all. Like him, they could have no way to contact their superiors in 2058. No doubt their numbers were limited; and, though eager to die for their cause, they would not waste men on stupidity.

Carrigan eased around to the side of the barn

opposite the house. A run of barbed wire separated him from the barnside pasture, the strands stapled to the wall. Catching the second wire from the top, he stepped over the middle wire and ducked between them, cautiously working the gun through the hole. He discovered a cattle door leading from the barn into the pasture. A peek between slats revealed the door opened onto a pathway between stalls. Gingerly, he uncovered the AK-47. Back pressed to the frame, he edged the door ajar with his toe.

The maneuver was answered by the click of a rifle chambering a round. Carrigan froze, keeping the AK-47 on semi-auto. *Can't waste bullets. And the instant either of us shoots, I lose surprise on the U.M.E.Ps in the house.* Quietly, he carefully eased back toward the woods to hide.

Ben Hascol's voice sounded through the opening, soft but filled with threat. "Whoever you are, come through that door, or I'm going to shoot right through the wood. One of them bullets'll find you."

Ben. Relief spiraled through Carrigan. *If he's armed, the U.M.E.Ps aren't with him.* He hesitated. *Assuming that was his gun and not some guy's standing next to him.* Not wanting the soldiers to recognize his voice, he made no verbal reply. He kept the assault rifle at his side and entered cautiously, glancing in the direction from which Hascol's warning had come. Seeing no one, he turned his head and looked down the barrel of a Browning semi-automatic rifle.

Hascol lowered the gun. "Welcome back, John."

And a friendly welcome it was. Carrigan waved Hascol silent and pointed further into the barn. As they walked past empty, straw-covered stalls toward the garage, Carrigan questioned. "Anyone else here?"

"Just Jason."

A disquieting thought touched Carrigan. "He's not armed, is he?" He imagined Walker shooting in blind panic.

Hascol shook his head. He opened the door separating the barn from the garage. "Jason?"

Walker trotted forward. "God, Jack. I'm glad to see you."

Hascol leaned in the doorway, between Carrigan and Walker. "So which is really your name anyway? John or Jack?"

"Sorry." Carrigan kept away from the garage door windows. "I couldn't tell you before. It's Jack. Jack Carrigan."

"Well, that's not all you didn't tell me." Hascol sounded more offended than angry.

"What do you mean?"

"You said them terrorists wouldn't find this place." Hascol hitched the rifle over his shoulder. "There's more A-rabs in my house than Iran."

"They couldn't have followed us." Carrigan detailed the possibilities he had already considered on the return trip. "Otherwise, they would have chased me and let you guys alone. I'm certain they put some sort of homing device on the Omni hoping you'd lead them to me."

Walker looked shocked, as if he had caught a friend cheating on an exam. "That's dumb."

Carrigan swiveled his gaze to the doctor. "Jason, it's hard to argue with success."

"No." Walker shook his head rapidly to indicate Carrigan had misinterpreted his comment. "I mean, if they had access to the car, why didn't they just hook up a bomb? And why didn't they put a homer on the Porsche?"

Carrigan fielded the questions in reverse order. "They probably never got a chance to wire the Porsche. The only opportunity was when we left it parked in Shawna's apartment lot, and I don't think they ever doubted they had us cornered then." Carrigan tapped his fist against a stall wall, realizing he was wasting valuable time in conversation. "An explosive would have been stupid. If I happened to be in the car, they'd destroy this." He pulled the tracking device from his pocket. "Or they might have thought I'd secreted it on you. Jason, even if you don't buy my story, you have to believe this is what they're after. They'll gladly kill me. I'm a trained enemy and a hell of a lot easier to handle dead. But they're not going to take a chance with this device; and, until now, I've kept it on my person."

Walker latched onto Carrigan's last statement. "Until now? Looks like you've still got it to me."

"No." Carrigan reached around Hascol and offered the device to Walker. "You do."

"Me?" Walker shrank from the device. "Why me?"

"Because, so far, you're the only person I've met in this era with a normal self-preservation instinct. You know when to run, and you're not afraid to call for help. Take it." Carrigan tapped the tracker against Walker's forearm. "If I'm not back in one hour, smash it beyond repair." The option did not appeal to Carrigan. Destroying the tracking device was a temporary solution, a delay during which he hoped the Americas and her allies could prepare for the U.M.E.P.'s attack. Without the tracker, the enemy soldiers would have to search for the time travel device, a long and nearly hopeless process. But either they or someone else would uncover it eventually. Once found, the news would reach the U.M.E.P. soldiers, and they would claim it by coercion or violence. And, there was always the possibility the U.M.E.P.s in 2058 would develop another tracker before the Americans could destroy the remaining time travel device in their own era. *The only permanent solution is for me to take out the 1985 machine. It'll be decades before the U.M.E.P.s can afford to develop another, plenty of time to prevent them from implementing their plan.* Carrigan sighed, again realizing what his decision to rescue Nicholson had put at stake.

This time, Walker accepted the tracking device. "What do you mean 'if you're not back in an hour?' Where are you going?"

Carrigan removed the 9 mm Smith and Wesson and its attached silencer from his waistband. "I'm going in to rescue Shawna." To test the mechanisms, he pressed the release, removed the spent magazine, and slid it back in place. Pointing the barrel at the floor, he worked the slide, then pulled the trigger on the vacant chamber.

"Going in?" Walker stared. "By yourself? Are you crazy?"

Before Carrigan could remind Walker that "going in by himself" was precisely what he was trained to do, Hascol spoke. "Only if he takes an empty gun. I ain't no government spy, Jack, but I know that thing don't work without bullets."

Walker stuck with his original point. "There's at least half a dozen Arabs. How are you going to handle—"

More interested in Hascol's comments, Carrigan interrupted. "Yeah, I know. But what can I do? The only ammunition I have is half a clip in the rifle."

"Well," Hascol turned his back on Walker. "You can use my B.A.R. if you want." He patted the Browning.

Carrigan shook his head, too well-trained to consider such a thing. "Too big for inside work. I'll have to turn my back getting it through windows, and it'll hang up on everything. Jobs like this are what handguns were made for."

Hascol grinned. "Actually, they were made for cavalry, but I get your point. I just don't understand why you didn't stop at some sporting goods store while you were out there. You could have filled up both them guns."

Hascol's words floored Carrigan. "Sporting goods store? You mean, I could just walk into some public place and buy ammo?"

Now, Hascol appeared startled. "You know, Jack. There's some things you do real good, but they gotta start teaching you more stuff in that secret agent school."

"It's a long story." Carrigan put Hascol off. "Just tell me where's the closest place I can get ammo."

Hascol stroked his chin. "If you mean before going in, Liberty'd be about as near as any."

Twenty minutes back to the car, a half hour drive each way, another twenty here plus whatever it takes to find the store and make the purchase. Carrigan shook his head. "No time. I'd lose any surprise I might have gained by lying about the airport." The oddity of the farmer's word choice struck him then. "You got ammo inside?"

"Boxes. Every different kind I use. My Dillon reloader's in the basement, and there's 9 mill. hardball in the catch bin."

The mention of a familiar product riveted Carrigan. *Could it be the same Dillon?* It seemed possible. *My XL 850 is getting pretty old.* Instead, he focused on the more important matter of the bullets. "Steel or tungsten jacket?"

Hascol gave Carrigan a suspicious look. "Copper."

"Copper." It seemed a poor choice to Carrigan, but any bullet was better than an empty magazine. He motioned Hascol from the doorway. "I need to know the layout of the house. You wouldn't happen to have a knife on you?"

Hascol fished a Swiss Army knife from the front pocket of his overalls. "What do you need it for?"

Carrigan avoided Walker's stare, aware a man dedicated to saving lives would not care much for what he had to say. "It's quieter than an AK-47."

Hascol returned the pocket knife, rummaged through the clutter on the garage utility shelves, and retrieved a six inch hunting blade in a leather sheath. Stepping through the archway, he handed the knife to Carrigan. "You sure you don't want my gun?"

Carrigan accepted the knife and stashed it in his pocket. Silhouetted and hampered by a rifle's size, he would never even make it to the house. "No, you keep that. I've already got a weapon that's too big and makes too much noise. They're using the same weapons as me. If I can't get to your reloads, I can collect some ammo from them." He grinned. "Besides, it won't hurt for me to have a gunner covering me out here." He said it more to make the farmer feel useful than from any real belief the Browning could protect him against AK-47's.

"Okay." Hascol traced figures on the wall as he spoke. "Upstairs, you got the living room, dining room, and kitchen hitched together." He drew a square to indicate the western side of the house. "The hallway goes off the other way." He indicated the area east of the back door. " 'Bout halfway, there's the bathroom." He pointed south. "And the stairs to the basement to the north. Next to that, my sons' room, and the hall ends into my bedroom. That's upstairs."

"Windows?" Carrigan asked.

"Three in the living room, facing each direction. One in my bedroom looks south, toward the barn, here. My boys' faces north. Want the downstairs?"

Carrigan mapped the area in his mind. "Uh-huh."

Hascol flattened his hands and lowered them in planes to simulate steps. "Down the stairs, there's a family room directly under the living room. Couches, TV, that stuff. The rest's unfinished. There's a storage area beneath my sons' room divided from the rest of the basement by a half wall. Under the bathroom's the area for the furnace and hot water heater. There's no door between there and the family room, but there's walls so the opening's just like a normal doorway not a big, gaping hole. Does that help you?"

"A lot. Is that all?"

"Yep." Hascol caught himself. "Nope, almost forgot. Downstairs under my bedroom beyond the heater there're two small rooms. One used to be my wife's sewing place. The boys kept their camping gear in the other, and the reloader's there. The rooms have got normal doors. Carpets and curtains, too." Anticipating Carrigan's next question, he continued. "Three windows in the family room, the basement type, looking out north, south and west. Each of the back rooms has a window facing east."

Based on his current knowledge, Carrigan tried to second guess the U.M.E.P.'s strategy. *The most defensible place to hold Shawna sounds like the family room downstairs. She'll need at least one guard, probably more. There'll be gunmen at the windows facing all directions. No way to know how many soldiers they have; but some, at least, will need to sleep. In shifts, probably.* Carrigan slipped the pistol back into his pants. He set the AK-47 on the floor near Hascol's feet. "Here goes."

"Wait." Walker plucked at the tracking device through his pocket. "Can I call you some back up? The police or someone?"

"Give me a full hour. Don't contact anyone in the meantime. If I'm not back, destroy that device, get yourselves out, then call anyone you want. If it's less than an hour and you know I'm dead, destroy that device anyway. If the terrorists come out after you, *destroy that device.*" Carrigan headed toward the gate through which he had entered, further emphasizing the importance of his decree with a warning. "Hascol, I can't explain now, but a lot more than a woman's life is at stake. I'm disobeying my last orders being here. If I make it back and my superiors ever find out I delayed this mission for Shawna, I'm up for insubordination at best, more likely treason. If Walker tries anything besides what I just said . . ." He paused, allowing Walker to catch the full effect of his words. "Shoot him." Without awaiting a reply, he slipped out the door into the pasture.

Hoofprints pocked the ground, baked into gashes and craters. Carrigan ducked through the barbed wire fence and slipped into the woods. Picking his way as quietly as possible, he followed the tree line south, around Hascol's near pasture. There, it turned east, forming a boundary between the empty meadow and a neighboring corn field. He continued, avoiding the tangled, spring-green vines and closely packed trunks for sparser pathways, always keeping the denser growth between himself and the house. At length, he came upon a patch of timber behind the house at the level of its eastern wall. He crept into it, peering between the trees and across a grassy knoll to where another wooded lot blocked his view of the house. To his left, he could see a downed section of pasture fence, to the right, a young alfalfa field.

Seeing no movement in either direction, Carrigan sprinted across the meadow into the second forested region. He flitted just close enough to catch a glimpse of white shingle through the branches. He dropped to the ground and wriggled toward the edge of the woods. Sticks stabbed into his chest, and moldy leaves clung, wet, to his tee shirt. His weight on his arms made his injured shoulder throb, so he favored the left side of his body.

A cautious crawl brought Carrigan to the boundary of the woods and yard. Twenty meters of open grass and young oaks stretched between him and the back of the house, a propane tank and a pile of firewood the only objects large enough for cover. He assessed the windows. This close to the master bedroom, it would be impossible for a sentry to see

Carrigan through the living/dining room windows on the western end of the house without leaning out the opening. Since the U.M.E.Ps had no way to know when or if Carrigan would arrive, and a head protruding through a window would make a perfect target, Carrigan doubted the guards would do such a thing. The southern window in the master bedroom stood in a direct line with Carrigan's approach, and he could make out the outline of a man and gun against the pane.

Carrigan traced out his route with his eyes. His next goal was the propane tank fifteen meters away, but the sentry would surely spot Carrigan crossing the open ground in front of it. Gathering his knees beneath him, he waited.

Five minutes passed into ten. Carrigan's muscles cramped and his gaze blurred from staring, but still he did not move. Finally, the figure in the window disappeared, perhaps in response to a command or to use the bathroom or simply adjust position. Carrigan did not hesitate. He sprinted into the yard and dove beneath the propane tank. Now, he lay far enough beneath a natural line of sight from the window to make it unlikely for the guard to look in his direction, provided his run had gone undetected. Grimly, he waited, counting seconds until five full minutes passed. Then, he scuttled from the tank to the corner of the house, pressing his back to the cinder block.

Carrigan dropped to all fours. He peered around the corner, scanning the eastern wall and the two casement windows to the small, downstairs rooms Hascol had described. Sneaking closer, he gradually widened his view, tensed for the first glint of a gun barrel. Seeing none, he risked a full glance.

Through a crack in the curtains, he saw a tiny chamber. A card table held a dust-choked sewing machine, and cardboard drawers labeled with magic marker lined one wall. Otherwise, the room was empty. Encouraged, Carrigan took the same approach with the window beside it.

This time, Carrigan saw sloppy heaps of camping gear. A packaged tent leaned against a box filled with canteens, a canvas-covered mess kit, several types of rope and cord, matches, tent stakes, and an ancient compass. The reloader perched on a table, the blue components and jutting lever classically Dillon. A man slept atop a sleeping bag in the corner near the door, his arm draped across an AK-47. Carrigan backed away, weighing alternatives. *If I go through the sewing room window, I won't risk him seeing me, but I'll have to come in on him blind. He might hear me slipping through the other room and have moved or prepared by the time I open his door.* Withdrawing Hascol's knife from his pocket, Carrigan unsheathed it and set it to the trim holding the camping room's windowpane in place. The knife sliced between caulking and glass. Carrigan pried, and the trim came free in chunks. He continued, gaze locked on the U.M.E.P's hand near the gun. The fingers lay, relaxed and curled.

At length, Carrigan chiseled out enough caulk to loosen most of the pane. He eased it from the window and positioned it on the grass by his knee. He studied the U.M.E.P. soldier again. A lock of dark hair had settled over closed lids, and parted lips revealed clean white teeth and the tip of a tongue. His chest rose and fell slowly and naturally beneath his light-weight tan jacket. Carrigan trapped the hilt of the knife against his palm with his thumb and silently lowered himself through the window.

As soon as Carrigan's feet touched the floor, he turned toward his enemy. Measuring a careful path around the camping gear, he worked his way to the U.M.E.P.'s head.

The man stirred. His fingers closed over the stock of the AK-47.

Carrigan sprang forward. He clapped his left hand over the man's mouth, plunged the blade into his throat, and tore. Blood splattered the familiar uniform. The soldier struggled, ripped free, and tried to scream. A hissing sound emerged from his mangled windpipe. Then, he sank to the floor, dead.

Carrigan wiped his blood-smeared hands on the U.M.E.P's shirt, cursing his incompetence. *He should never have pulled away from me. Sometimes it's the small sounds that spell the difference between life and death.* He searched the corpse quickly and discovered a handful of plastic explosive with a watch-sized timer, a loaded 9 mm Smith and Wesson, and two extra magazines. He replaced his empty magazine with the one from the U.M.E.P's weapon and shoved the explosive and the extra ammunition in his pockets. Then, he slid the AK-47 out the window for later retrieval.

Carrigan pressed his back to the wall beside the door. He grabbed the half dozen rounds laying in the Dillon's catch bin and slipped them into his pocket with the other ammunition. He kept the pistol clutched in his right hand, reached his left to the knob, and loosed the catch. He waited, listening for sounds of discovery. Hearing none, he inched the panel open and glanced through the crack.

Drab, gray walls enclosed a square room. Copper pipes and wires ran along the ceiling, and a wooden cabinet held the furnace in the center of the room. Another door, next to the one Carrigan looked around, led into the sewing room. Without opening the camping room door further, he could not see the finished family room Hascol had described nor the storage area with the half wall that, by report, lay off to his right. Sheathing the blade, he returned the knife to his pocket.

Soundlessly, Carrigan slid through the door and ducked behind the furnace cabinet. He kept the sewing room door to his back. To his right, a plywood wall rose to chest height, dividing off the storage room. Directly opposite the door from which he had emerged, an archway opened into the family room. Carrigan's angle did not allow him to see through the entryway. As well, the walls and cabinet hid him from anyone in the chamber. Garbled noise leached through the doorway, barely recognizable as unaccented, American voices. Carrigan caught every few words and was not able to make sense of what he heard. Then, a louder, more vivid bass cut over the others, in Arabic. The difference in quality between the sounds convinced Carrigan the ones he heard first came from a mechanical device, probably a television.

Carrigan dropped flat to the cement floor. Wriggling forward, he peered around the cabinet and into the family room. A short-weave carpet covered the floor, patterned like tiles. A television perched on a hand-made cabinet in the southwestern corner. Images flickered across the screen. An overstuffed, royal blue couch spanned the area between the doorway and the television. Two men sat on the cushions, the backs of their heads visible over the rear panel of the couch. A matching chair stood catty-corner to the couch and separated by an end table. A U.M.E.P. soldier occupied the seat, his side toward Carrigan, his face turned toward the television. A black wood stove filled the northwestern corner of the room, the mantel above it covered with vases and ceramic animals. From the slope of the ceiling in his room, Carrigan could tell the stairs rose from the northeastern side of the room, dividing the family room from the storage area.

Carrigan elbowed back behind the cabinet. He had expected the U.M.E.P. soldiers to hold Nicholson prisoner in the family room; but, this time, his assumptions had fallen short. Second-guessing enemies was risky at best, especially when pitting a sketchy description against first hand knowledge. The couch blocked his view of his enemies' hands, but it seemed only safe to assume they had weapons within easy reach.

Rising to a crouch, Carrigan circled the southern side of the furnace, keeping the western wall between himself and the U.M.E.P. soldiers. He squeezed up against the barrier, his pistol steadied in both hands. Closer, the sounds from the television resolved into a car commercial. *Killing zone*, Carrigan reminded himself. *If anyone screams, it's all over*. Lowering the pistol, he stepped into the doorway and calmly took the time to aim.

Carrigan's first bullet tore through the ear of the man in the chair. The U.M.E.P. slumped, hand halfway to his gun. Carrigan fired the next two rounds in rapid succession, each a clean shot through the back of the skull. Leaping forward, he put a second bullet into each head for certainty. Eyes locked on the stairway, he rummaged through the dead men's clothes. He took as many extra magazines as his pants pockets could hold, then peeling a tan jacket from one of the corpses, he pulled it over his bloody T-shirt. *A glimpse of uniform around a corner might make the others hesitate before shooting.* He ejected the magazine and its remaining bullet from his gun and replaced it with a full one.

Crossing the room, Carrigan hugged the wall that met the staircase. At the base of the steps, he glanced into the storage room. The disarray of boxes, mops, and tools held no interest for him, and he looked only long enough to establish the absence of gunmen before turning his attention to the steps. A dozen wine-colored carpeted stairs rose to a hallway. Beyond it, Carrigan could see the closest half of a bathroom, its interior dark. As he climbed, he held the Smith and Wesson close to his chest, carefully placing his feet at the base of each step where he was less likely to elicit a creak.

Carrigan stopped on the third step from the top. Voices wafted to him from the combined kitchen, dining, and living rooms to the right, rapid Arabic he did not try to decipher. He heard no sound from the bedrooms to his left. Crouched, gun readied, he ascended one more step. The elevation gave him a clear view of the kitchen, its appliances, and the counters dividing it from the carpeted living and dining rooms. Just west of the kitchen stood a table. U.M.E.P. soldiers sat in three of the chairs, enjoying steaming plates of food. Shawna Nicholson shivered in the last seat while another man stood behind her, holding an AK-47 near her head.

Carrigan was unable to see the remainder of the

living room. Before he could duck back behind the wall, the standing guard shouted in Arabic. "At the stairs!" The assault rifle swung toward Carrigan.

Nicholson screamed. Carrigan squeezed off a desperate shot that went wild, then sprinted for the master bedroom, prepared for an answering spray of gunfire. Apparently, the U.M.E.Ps hesitated for fear of hitting their companions in the bedrooms. Instead of bullets, shouts wafted from the living room.

Carrigan skidded into the bedroom, recalling the sentry's window position from his outside glimpse. He took in the chamber at a glance. The queen-sized bed held an awakening U.M.E.P. soldier. Beside the bed, the window guard whirled, raising his rifle. Carrigan fired at the sentry's chest. Without waiting to see if he hit, he shot the soldier on the bed, then turned back and put a second round through the collapsing U.M.E.P. near the window. Carrigan sprang back to the doorway. In the hall, a U.M.E.P. soldier used Shawna Nicholson as a shield, the barrel of his AK-47 poking from beneath her arm. He spoke in English. "Carrigan, throw down the gun. Get in plain sight and raise your hands."

Carrigan dropped back out of view. *Got to get out of here.* The U.M.E.P. on the floor lay still. The one on the bed moaned, groping blindly for his rifle. Carrigan glanced at the window, not liking his options. Taking as much of a running start as he could, he bounced onto the bed and dove for the window. His shoulder snapped the wooden divider between the panes. Glass shattered, slashing his skin. He plummeted to the ground and landed on his back. The fall jarred agony through his wounded shoulder and the breath from his lungs. He rolled toward the house, gasping, and flattened against the wall. Fighting pain, he raised the pistol, waiting for someone to lean far enough through the window to take a shot at him.

A head poked cautiously through the hole. Carrigan crouched, pressing solidly against the concrete to keep himself as small a target as possible. A single rifle shot cracked, echoing, from the barn, followed by a second and a third. The head in the window snapped back inside. Taking advantage of Hascol's covering fire, Carrigan dashed over the open ground to the patch of timber. Without slowing, he crashed through the brush. Sweat stung the gashes in his back. His lungs ached; and, aggravated by the fall, his bullet wound felt on fire. He covered ground swiftly and soon worked his way back to the barn.

Carrigan had scarcely rejoined Hascol and Walker when one of the U.M.E.P. soldiers stepped onto the screened back porch. Hascol aimed the Browning through the barn door, but Carrigan slapped a hand to the barrel. "No, Ben. Let him talk."

Hascol lowered the weapon. Walker studied the slashes and smears of blood across Carrigan's back.

The U.M.E.P. shouted from the door, his thick voice betraying outrage. "Bad move, Carrigan. She's dead." Without another sound, he turned to leave.

Walker made a wordless noise of pain. Hascol's grip tightened on his gun. Carrigan's heart quickened, but he maintained composure. "Wait! Don't shoot her."

The man hesitated in the doorway. He turned

with the unhurried grace of a dancer. "You've got thirty seconds to get us the tracking unit." He started counting immediately. "One, two, three, four . . ."

"Hold on!" Carrigan shouted, assessing the layout of the backyard. "It's yours. Just give me time to figure out a way to keep it an honest trade."

The soldier glanced inside, as if to confirm the possibility. "All right," he shouted. "But think right where you are. You move, and she's really dead." He waited.

Walker whispered. "Are you actually going to give them the device?" He seemed torn between relief for Nicholson and fear for the consequences he did not quite understand.

Carrigan frowned. All his training went against risking so many lives for so little. Once the U.M.E.P.s uncovered the location of their target, they would prove nearly impossible to stop. Still, Carrigan did already have a vague idea of the location of the time traveling device, and he might be able to take another stand against the enemy. *With help from the local authorities* Carrigan brushed aside the possibility. *By the time I convinced them of my story, if ever, the U.M.E.P.'s would take the machine and be long gone.* Carrigan trained his mind to another prospect. *I've only got a pistol, a half-loaded assault rifle, and a semi-automatic; but we might be able to keep the U.M.E.P.s from leaving the house.* None of the ideas seemed viable, but Carrigan knew he had no other choice except to sacrifice Nicholson. *And I'm not doing that.* He addressed Walker's question. "Yeah, I'm going to give it to them. I've still got options. Once they kill Shawna, she has none."

"Well?" the man on the porch pressed.

'Okay." Carrigan pointed to one of the oak trees near the barn. "We'll put the tracker in the crook of that branch and train a gun on it. You send one of your men out to get it: unarmed. Once he signals you we haven't cheated, you release Shawna. Your guy runs back. Shawna comes here. We're even."

The U.M.E.P.s deliberated in silence.

Carrigan added. "I see anything on your man that looks like a weapon, I blow away the tracker. Same goes if anyone else leaves that house or Shawna's not freed."

The soldier glanced toward the barn. "What guarantee do we have you won't kill our man?"

Carrigan rolled his eyes. *My innate respect for human life.* He controlled his annoyance. "I'm not going to do anything stupid until Shawna's out of your range." He did not care that he implied he would become foolish after Nicholson's release; there was a certain probable truth to that insinuation. Carrigan whirled to face Walker, but the doctor had disappeared. *Walker's got the tracker, and he's about to do something crazy.* Sudden apprehension gripped him, immediately transformed to anger. "Jason?"

Hascol pointed toward the opposite end of the barn.

Aware Nicholson's life hinged upon his remaining in place, Carrigan gestured Hascol after Walker. "Get him."

Hascol nodded once, then trotted to the doctor's side. Walker's voice sifted softly to Carrigan's ears. "Ben, I set something down here I think might help. Belonged to a friend of mine."

Of course. Walker's words brought Carrigan's

thoughts back to Nicholson's apartment. He pictured Tracy Harlowe fumbling a tracking device look-alike from an end table, then placing it in her pocket.

Shortly, Walker returned. "Jack ..." he started.

"I know," Carrigan interrupted impatiently. "I'll cover you. Put it out there." He inclined his head toward the oak."

Walker passed the ergometer from hand to hand. "Me?"

"You're safe. They're not going to take a chance now, not when they think they're getting what they want. But if I go out, it'd probably be worth it to kill me and get the tracker from you and Ben." Realizing Walker could use some praise, Carrigan obliged. "That switch thing was a smart idea, Jason. You're all right."

"Thanks." Walker sounded more nervous than pleased, and he stared at the oak without looking up. He sighed, glanced briefly toward the sky, as if in prayer, then passed the real tracking unit to Carrigan. Stiffly, he walked to the oak, planted the ergometer on the branch, and darted back to the barn. Once there, he clutched his chest and leaned against a stall, seeming as surprised as relieved to make it back alive.

The U.M.E.P. on the porch trotted down the steps to the driveway. Carrigan waved Hascol over. "Keep your aim on his chest. If I tell you, shoot to kill. Otherwise, let him go." Carrigan hugged the door frame just inside the barn, pistol trained on the ergometer. He watched the U.M.E.P. soldier advance, scrutinizing him for the bulge of weapons, watching his walk for any evidence he was hiding a side of his body. Discovering nothing suspicious, Carrigan allowed the man to reach the tree.

The U.M.E.P. soldier plucked the device from the branch, but his gaze settled on the opening to the barn. Piercing, dark eyes met Carrigan's, traced the gun in his hand, then returned to the ergometer.

Carrigan kept the Smith and Wesson trained on the device, aware Nicholson's life hung on the U.M.E.P.'s ignorance of the tracker. Though refined by Americans, the U.M.E.P. had financed the project and probably had at least a vague description of its function and design. It occurred to him that, if the Arab tested the device, the clarity of the display or its current numbers might clue him to the switch, and it was all over for Nicholson. "Don't activate it," he warned. "I'm not letting you know where the time unit is until Nicholson's free." He clutched the gun grip tighter, acutely aware how swiftly and unobtrusively a button could be pressed.

At the oak, the U.M.E.P. turned the ergometer over in his hands, and the eyes of every man on both sides remained desperately affixed on him.

CHAPTER 12

Showdown

Jack Carrigan braced his pistol in both hands, watching the U.M.E.P. soldier at the oak tree in Benjamin Hascol's backyard. Against the opposite side of the barn door's frame, Hascol's rifle barrel remained steady, trained unerringly on the Arab. Gradually, the U.M.E.P. raised the ergometer in a stiff gesture of triumph and started back toward the house.

"Freeze," Carrigan commanded, gaze locked on the man's hands. A nominal piece of plastic explosive, tossed casually, would level Hascol's barn and everyone in it. "Don't move until your buddies release Shawna. Try anything, you're dead and the tracker's toothpicks."

The U.M.E.P. soldier stopped. "Free the *woman*," he shouted toward the house in Arabic, using the vulgar term the U.M.E.P.s reserved for foreign females.

Carrigan considered shooting the man on principle, but he placed Nicholson's life above her dignity. Soon, the back door opened. Pushed from behind, Shawna Nicholson stumbled out, barely catching her balance in time to keep from plunging down the steps.

The U.M.E.P. messenger tensed to run.

"Let her get down the steps," Carrigan warned.

The man opened his mouth as if to protest, but he obeyed in silence. As Nicholson fled down the stairs, the U.M.E.P. made a break for the house. More from caution than concern, Carrigan followed the soldier's flight across the yard and between the sedans his fellows had left parked in Hascol's driveway. The U.M.E.Ps had no reason to gun down Nicholson. As a hostage, she had value. Killing her now would only serve to enrage Carrigan and compel him more fully to oppose their cause. Alive, she was a weapon they could use against him again, if necessary.

Nicholson dodged between Walker's Omni and the lead sedan, then raced for the barn. Carrigan caught her damp and shivering arm at the door and spun her safely inside. He waited until the U.M.E.P. messenger disappeared into the house before turning to comfort Nicholson. But she clung to Walker, locked into his embrace, her face buried in his chest.

Carrigan balled his free hand to a fist. *Great. I risked billions of lives and endured a back full of glass splinters so the woman can show her gratitude to the one man who never fired a shot in her defense.* He battered this thought aside for a practical realization. *A day or two, and I'll be back in 2058 or dead. Why shouldn't Jason and Shawna fall in love?* Still, he could not shake the feeling the doctors would form an incompatible couple, one attached to duty and serenity, the other drawn to the adventurous.

A foreign blasphemy from the house redirected Carrigan's attention. *They know.* "Hurry!" He grabbed Walker's wrist and pulled him toward the pasture door. "We have to get out of here. Fast."

Walker and Nicholson scurried after him. Hascol remained in position. As Carrigan jabbed through the cattle door, rifle reports slammed against his ears. *What the hell?* He ducked through the barbed wire, then held the strands apart for the doctors. By the time Nicholson, then Walker wriggled through, Hascol had joined them, the Browning still gripped in his hands.

"I'm parked about a half mile south of town," Carrigan told Hascol. "You lead, I'll tail gun. Keep us in cover. And what the hell were you shooting at?"

"Cars." Hascol flailed into the woods, kicking aside twigs and brush. "Shot out two tires on each of theirs. Never knew anyone to carry more than one spare. It'll take time to start mine and Jason's without the keys. That ought to slow 'em down a bit."

Nicholson ran behind Hascol, and Carrigan prodded Walker faster as they went. "Good idea."

Hascol continued blazing the trail through the woods. "Worked on them kids as was joy riding my cows and leaving their empty six packs."

Carrigan tucked the Smith and Wesson in the pocket of the U.M.E.P. jacket and leaped a deadfall lightly as a cat. "You think pretty quick. Ever been in the army?" In Carrigan's era, every man and woman put in two years of military service after high school, but he recalled his teachings about the war-time draft, unable to place the precise years when it was banned, reinstituted, and became archaic.

"Korea," Hascol said, skirting a pasture Carrigan had crossed in the opposite direction.

Carrigan stiffened, his first thought that Hascol had served a foreign government. Then, he remembered the old convention, to name wars by their location instead of years, back in the days when battles were fought for politics and territory rather than industry, and in battles rather than raids.

"Lost my oldest in Vietnam," Hascol continued, his voice nearly drowned by the doctors' panting.

Too much hospital work, not enough fitness. Carrigan nudged Walker, encouraging him to close the widening gap between him and the farmer; the commando wanted to hear the rest of Hascol's story.

Hascol steered his companions through a field of green weeds. "Brian weren't no hero, but he loved his country and he tried. Used to send back letters saying he wished he was as brave as this other boy or that guy. He was a good kid, just didn't have none of that natural dexterity or grace under fire. You know the type."

Carrigan studied Jason Walker's back. Recently he knew the type too well. "Yeah."

"Well, to me, Brian was a bigger hero than any of them other guys. He worked hard for everything he got and was shot in the trenches doing his duty." At the end of the field, Hascol slipped back into the timber. He waited until his companions darted between the trees before continuing. "The city types likes their people graceful and pretty, men and women. Lucky for guys like me and Brian, hard work gets more reward on the farm." He added hastily, as if in defense, "Not that our people's all ugly or nothing. Just takes all kinds, I guess."

Carrigan recognized a trunk leaning in the branches of another tree. By the landmark, he knew he was nearing his car, and he took the lead. Hascol's words turned his thoughts to Walker, and he felt a twinge of guilt about his impatience with the doctor-in-training. *Jason's made a lot of mistakes, but he's trying. And he did save my life. Now, if I can just get him off the battlefield and back into the hospital, I'll have a lot more respect for his abilities.* He kept to the tree-lined edge of a corn field, its rows scarred by tire tracks, and the road eased into sight. "The car's in the ditch there." He pointed in the general direction. "Of course, it's yours, Ben, but I'd like to keep using it."

Hascol made a throwaway motion. "Hell, take the old rust bucket. You're going to have to come back for your car anyway, and I'm more worried about my house." He flipped up the Browning until the barrel rested on his shoulder. "I'm going into town to get some backup. We'll get those A-rabs out."

Carrigan smiled, guessing the U.M.E.P. soldiers had probably already vacated the house. "Good luck and be careful." He clasped Hascol's beefy hand between his own. "Thanks for your help. Sorry for the trouble. I'll try my best to make sure any damage gets covered."

"I'd appreciate that. Now, you better get moving." Hascol nodded to Walker and Nicholson in turn, whirled and headed toward town.

Seeing no other vehicles on the road, Carrigan waved his friends to the Dart. He climbed into the driver's seat, waiting until Walker slipped into the back and Nicholson in the passenger's side before cranking the ignition. He pulled out of the ditch and back onto the road, headed away from the farm town. "All right, first thing. We need a map of the west coast."

Nicholson reached toward the glove compartment, but Carrigan caught her hand. "I've checked there." He glanced to Nicholson. She avoided his eyes but did not pull away, and Carrigan accepted that as the most positive signal he had received from her.

Walker flopped a magazine-sized, soft-covered book across the back of the bench seat. "Well, you apparently didn't look under the seat. It's a road atlas."

Though accustomed to computerized maps and automatic readouts of routes and directions, Carrigan guessed Walker's find would serve his purposes. Keeping his eyes on the street, he released Nicholson, fumbled the tracking device from his pocket, and handed it to her.

Nicholson gave Carrigan a quick glance. "I thought you gave this to the Arabs."

"I'll explain later. Hit the button."

Nicholson complied. "2615.426 K? And it's flashing. What does that mean?"

Carrigan explained. "Shift it around until the light goes steady."

Nicholson manipulated the device. "Okay."

"What direction is it facing?"

Nicholson glanced out at some landmarks. "I don't know. South, I guess. That way." She pointed forward and toward the left.

"Southwest," Walker corrected.

Carrigan nodded. The direction corresponded to

his own attempt to activate the device earlier. "Hit the button again."

Nicholson stared at the device. "17SW. What's that stand for?"

Carrigan ignored the question. "Now, Walker, can you find us on the map?"

Walker flipped through the pages, then set the open book on the top of the bench seat between Nicholson and Carrigan. "Approximately."

"Measure off 2600 klicks at 17 degrees south of west, and tell me where that puts you."

Walker chuckled. "I don't hardly have to think about it. That'd put us in California, probably somewhere in the vicinity of Los Angeles. Is that where the . . . um . . . time machine is?"

"Yeah." Carrigan tried to phrase his next bombshell carefully, but chose the direct approach instead. "This time, you two will have to come with me. I can't afford to get delayed again. Besides, I need your help with 1985 stores, transportation, geography and such. After I go back to 2058, I'm going to need someone to destroy the time travel unit." He touched his pocket to reassure himself of the presence of the plastic explosive, then mumbled the last part, still feeling uncomfortable discussing money. "And, I'll probably need currency." He awaited Walker's protests.

Nicholson responded first. "Of course, we're going. I hate those Arabs more than I've ever hated anyone in my life, and I'm going to see this through. It's already cost me more money than I want to think about." Her fingers fell against Carrigan's sleeve, then she pulled away as if embarrassed. "They said some pretty awful things about you, Jack. They told me you're a mass murderer

running from the law and you killed 12,000 innocent people. They told me you use women, you're
a traitor to your country, and you murdered your
own wife."

Nicholson's last comment struck too close to
home. Carrigan shook his head. "They're lying, trying to turn you against me."

"I know that." Nicholson sounded insulted.
"They blindfolded me at times. They kept threaten-
ing me, and they weren't gentle." She ran her finger
along fresh bruises that striped her arms.

Carrigan's instinctive caution kicked in. "Did
they take anything from you, then return it?"

Nicholson considered. "They did take my wallet.
As far as I can tell, they only removed the cash."
She added, apparently seeking the happier side of
the situation. "At least they left my credit card."

Carrigan had found the information he sought.
"Shawna, take a look at that card of yours. And
anything else you routinely carry. A real close
look."

Obligingly, Nicholson emptied her wallet, scrutinizing the contents. "What am I looking for?"

"A bump that doesn't belong there."

Nicholson pawed through her things for several
moments. "Here. On my MasterCard. What is it?"

"Throw   it   out   the   window,"   Carrigan
commanded.

"My credit card?"

"Throw it out the window."

Nicholson rolled down the glass and pitched the
plastic outside. It thumped against the back passenger window, then flew beyond sight. Walker
cringed, as if awaiting an explosion.

Nicholson watched its flight then turned her attention back to Carrigan. "Now why did I do that?"

Carrigan explained. "So the Abdul's can't track us. It only made sense that they'd wire you, just in case. People bathe, clothes change, but everyone carries his credit at all times."

Nicholson looked behind the car, though they had long left the credit card in the dust. "I wish you'd told me it wasn't something lethal. I would at least have cut the card up so no one could buy anything." She considered briefly. "Not that they could have gotten much. It's maxed out for the month." She let her gaze sweep Walker as she returned to the proper position in her seat. "Jason has to come with us, too, of course." She winked at him. "We'll need his credit card."

"It's nice to be wanted," Walker grumbled. "My credit's limited. Even so, two months' salary doesn't cover the bills you could rack up."

"Look, I'll take care of it." Carrigan turned onto the entrance ramp of the main highway to Cedar Rapids. "I can't remember the exact years, but I know enough Kentucky Derby winners to include two or three coming up in the next few races. Make some wise bets, and you'll have all the money you can spend."

Walker muttered something unintelligible into his arm.

Nicholson twisted her neck toward him. "Jason, the Arabs also mentioned the time machine and 2058. If Jack's making this up, he did an incredible job covering his story. Anyone who would go to that much trouble deserves to be believed."

Carrigan changed the subject. "Jason, see if you can get a bit more exact with our destination. And what's the fastest way to get from here to Los Angeles?"

"F-14 fighter jet," Walker said. At Nicholson's scowl, he elaborated. "Available to us, it's a plane. Head back to Cedar Rapids airport. I assume that's where you called from before, though how you expected six bucks and change to get you anywhere, I'll never know." He addressed Nicholson. "Check the glove compartment and see if you can get me a pen and a straight edge."

Nicholson groped through the maps, screwdrivers, and manuals in the glove compartment before emerging with a pencil and an index card.

Accepting the implements, Walker set to work. The Dart had nearly reached the airport before he spoke again. "Uh, Jack, you might want to hope I'm wrong here."

Carrigan tossed a glance over his shoulder. "Why's that?"

"Because, according to my calculations, that time machine is somewhere in the middle of Southern California. It's one big city. That machine's probably embedded in 500,000 tons of concrete."

Carrigan shook his head. "There're safeguards against that. We'll narrow it down as we get closer. We'll also need to buy weapons, something high-powered and legal, just in case."

Nicholson glanced to Walker. "How much credit did you say you have?"

Walker simply moaned.

Dr. Jason Walker's Visa card bought air fare; a Remington 7400 semi-automatic rifle; five extra, extended clips; spare ammunition; a rented Ford Escort; several picks and shovels; and ten hours of sleep in the LaJolla Marriott. Now, dressed in the protective, unobtrusively colored uniform of the U.M.E.P. over a clean T-shirt and crouched before the chain link fence that enclosed San Diego Naval Air Station, Carrigan felt as if his life had turned full circle. This time, it was 1985 instead of 2058, he used a bolt cutters rather than a laser torch, and his companions consisted of two awkward civilians instead of flawlessly trained commandos.

Night cloaked the desert into a flat expanse of gray interrupted by the skeletal outlines of manzanita and creosote. In front of Carrigan, the fence rose, capped with barbed wire, its links weathered and pocked. Walker had assured Carrigan the fence would be devoid of security systems, that some parts of the base would lack even this flimsy barrier, but the encouragement did not make the first cut any easier. Behind Carrigan, the Escort lay, dark and silent, in the gloom. Walker and Nicholson watched the road in either direction to warn Carrigan of approaching vehicles.

Carrigan set to work, snipping steel and peeling, opening a hole wide enough for the Escort. Since Nicholson's release, he had seen no sign of the U.M.E.P. soldiers, but he was not wholly lulled by their absence. Between leaving the Dart and the Smith and Wesson in the airport parking lot, buying the tickets, purchasing five hundred dollars worth of gun and ammunition and having it bore-sighted in the store and the time spent sleeping in the hotel, they had left an easily followed trail.

The hole widened gradually. At length, Carrigan stretched, gave a low whistle to summon his companions and headed back toward the Escort. Nicholson and Walker met him at the car. Walker took the back seat, Carrigan and Nicholson the front. Carrigan started the engine. The headlights cut a path through the night, bathing the slashed edges of fence. He pulled up onto the road then through the manufactured opening and onto the desert grasslands of San Diego Naval Air Station.

Nicholson rubbed at her naked arms to warm them. "I thought California was supposed to always be hot."

"Night in the desert can get cold," Walker said. "Even this close to the Pacific there's no moisture to trap the heat and—"

Not interested in hearing Walker's reply to what Nicholson obviously intended as a rhetorical question, Carrigan interrupted. "Here." One hand on the steering wheel, Carrigan shifted magazines from the jacket pockets to his pants and worked the uniform jacket over his shoulders, exposing the matching tee shirt beneath it. Though thin, the uniform's synthetic fibers were constructed to keep the human body comfortable at temperatures ranging from over fifty to less than negative twenty degrees. Though Walker had removed the larger glass fragments from Carrigan's back at the hotel, the movement shifted the remaining bits painfully deeper. He swerved around a clump of brush.

Nicholson accepted the jacket and pulled it across her back. "At least you didn't blindfold me and take my shoes. My feet would freeze."

The reference escaped Carrigan, and he wondered if it was another 1985 expression he could never understand. "I'm not known for that."

Walker seemed equally confused. "What brought that on?"

Nicholson clarified, placing her left arm then the

right through the uniform sleeves. "That's what the Arabs did. When they caught me. They blindfolded me, took my shoes, and made me walk up and down the stairs." She snorted at the ludicrousness of the strategy. "Like I wouldn't know where I ended up."

Now the relevance came to Carrigan in a flash. "They took your shoes."

"Yeah."

"And gave them back?"

Walker put the pieces together first. "Shit. You don't think they stuck trackers on those, too? Do you?" His tone pleaded for the reassuring answer Carrigan could not give.

"I believe," the commando said, "you can count on it."

Nicholson tugged at her laces. "What an idiot!" she berated herself. "I can't believe I was so—"

Carrigan cut her off. "Don't worry about it now. If they've tracked us this far, there's no turning back. Better to let them think we're still oblivious." *Not that it matters.* He shared some of his thoughts aloud. "We left a credit trail any novice hacker could follow anyway. I never doubted they'd find us, one way or another. They don't need the tracking device if we lead them directly to the travel device."

Walker contradicted. "I don't know how credit works in your time . . . or cops or airlines. But I know enough about 1985 to believe some of those stores haven't even processed our purchases yet. Surely every police unit in Iowa has their description by now, and Arab terrorists don't go unnoticed. Unless those Arabs have another time machine at their fingertips, they'll have to catch a later flight from a different city. And Ben probably bought us some time, too."

Carrigan doubted they had as long as Walker thought. *Their government probably armed them with money and details of firearms transport and purchasing, at the least.* However, he saw no need to worry his companions. The U.M.E.P. would catch them when they did. More likely sooner than later. He glanced at the Remington. *I'm going to be sorely outgunned.* "Now, activate the tracking unit."

Nicholson removed the device from her jeans pocket. "3.282 K. Ahead and to the right."

"And down?" Carrigan added.

Nicholson shook her head. "Level. Ahead and to the right."

Carrigan adjusted his course. "Now?"

Nicholson waved him further toward the right.

Again, Carrigan shifted. "Let me know when we're about ten meters."

"On course. Keep going."

Carrigan detailed his plan as he drove. "We'll have to dig the machine up. Once we've got it free, I'll program it back to 2058." An image of his apartment rose in his mind, the familiar disarray and softly painted colors. His job had paid well; his government-alloted credit allowed luxuries others could not afford: a car, a state-of-the-art computer/communications system with security access, a personal, self-contained exercise unit. "I'm not sure how long it will take me to encode, a good ten minutes at least, maybe an hour or more. I'll give you some sort of signal before I activate it. I'll time the explosive for two minutes." He patted his pocket. "That should leave enough time for me to clear and you to drive safely away without leaving enough extra time for someone to deactivate it. If anything goes wrong, do whatever you can to destroy that machine." The Escort approached an incline, and Carrigan started up the slope. *The time travel device is buried on a hill. That explains why the tracker didn't indicate a downward coordinate.* "Oh, one last thing. Jason, do you have a pen?"

Walker hesitated less than a second. "Got one."

"Write this down: Alysheba. Sunday Silence. Ferdinand."

Walker wrote before questioning. "What's that mean?"

"Those are the Kentucky Derby winners I promised. Each won the race in the late eighties, but I may not have them in order."

"Thanks."

Nicholson interrupted, appropriately serious. "We're at 0.011 K. Straight."

Carrigan slowed to a crawl. "Stop me at five meters."

Shortly, Nicholson touched Carrigan's arm. "We're at five. Now, the light goes steady at ahead and down."

Halfway up the slope, Carrigan slammed into park and pulled the emergency brake. Leaving the headlights on, he clambered out of the car and set the Remington 7400 on the ground. Walker poked shovels and picks, one at a time, through the open door, and Carrigan stacked them. He waited for the others to exit the car, then handed a shovel to each, saving the two picks for himself and Walker. Nicholson found the location where the tracking unit indicated the time travel device was directly beneath the soil, and they started digging.

Chill air raised goose bumps on Carrigan's arms; but, as he dug, exertion warmed him until the breeze felt pleasurable. Steadily, the hole widened and deepened, and the pile of dirt beside it formed a noticeable mound. A half hour later, Walker shouted in triumph. "I hit something solid!"

The headlights sheened from a corner of silver-colored plastic. "Hang on." Carrigan sidled over and studied the object, relying on his memory of the other device to calculate its positioning in the dirt. "We're not going to be able to uncover the whole thing. I think if we chip around the side that Jason's standing on, we ought to find the door." Using the pick, he hammered at the ground beside the unit.

Nicholson sucked air through her teeth with a sharp sound. Carrigan glanced at her, then followed her pointing finger back the way they had come. A set of headlights bumped and wove over the tract, headed for them.

U.M.E.P.s. "Get to the car. Now!" Carrigan tossed Walker the keys, pulled the plastic explosive from his pocket and reset the timer for one minute. *Whatever else, I have to destroy that machine.* Then, another thought occurred to him. *What if it's not U.M.E.P.s? If it's military security and they see an explosion, they might shoot first and question later.* It was a logical assumption, based on Carrigan's past experiences rather than 1985 standards.

Nicholson and Walker raced for the car. At the door, Walker turned. "Jack?"

"Get in and go!" Carrigan grabbed the rifle and ducked behind the dirt mound. "Dodge them. Get out through the hole and go home."

Nicholson paused halfway inside the passenger door. "But—"

"Damn it, don't argue with me!" Carrigan screamed. "Let me handle this."

The car doors snapped shut, the engine growled, and the Escort spun, leaving Carrigan in darkness. He cocked the Remington, dropped to his belly behind the dirt pile, and steadied the gun on its surface. He held his breath, watching the taillights as the Escort looped around the approaching vehicle. *A patrol would have no reason to think I'm here. If it's Navy, they'll intercept the car. If it's U.M.E.P.s, they'll come for the machine.* The Escort jerked erratically, never heading in one direction long. *Good, Jason's scared. It'll make him a tough target.*

The strangers' headlights continued unwaveringly toward Carrigan. *No question any more. It's U.M.E.P.s.* As the car rumbled forward, Carrigan realized he could no longer destroy the time travel device until the battle was resolved. *That machine is the only thing that'll keep them from using explosives against me.* The thought seemed ludicrous. *So what if they kill me? It's a suicide mission.* Carrigan raised his head for a better look over the mound, suddenly aware he did not want to die. He was not afraid of death, but he was trained to survive. *And that training may see me through this yet.*

The car jounced toward him, visible only as a paired set of lights. Carrigan let it come within a hundred meters before squeezing off his entire first clip at the windshield. He left the headlights intact. Closer, they should spotlight him; for now, they outlined his targets.

The car slowed. The doors were flung open, and

shadowy shapes rolled out to disappear into the darkness. Carrigan reloaded, cursing the wasted opportunity. Apparently, the driver remained inside because the engine roared, and the car raced toward Carrigan.

Shit. They'll run me over. Carrigan aimed between the headlights, shooting desperately. The first slug missed. the second hit with the plastic snap of grill work. The car continued, quickly narrowing the gap. Carrigan loosed a third round and a fourth. The car ground to a halt, stuttering and banging, headlights clearly outlining Carrigan against the hill behind him.

From the bottom of the slope, a spray of automatic gunfire strafed the mound, splashing Carrigan with sand and chips of rock. Half-blinded, he shot for the headlights. The first round missed. The second shattered the glass, and one light winked out. He fired his last four shots for the other bulb, and the hill plunged into darkness.

Carrigan reloaded. Another wave of gunfire chewed into the dirt pile. He kept his eyes up as he loaded, counting and memorizing muzzle flashes. *Six Abduls.* Carrigan aimed for the remembered site, waiting, suddenly glad for the hill behind him. Halfway up it, his position was reasonably defensible. *The top would be even more so, but I can't leave the cover of the dirt or the time travel unit.*

Below Carrigan, the shots became less coordinated. He aimed for a muzzle flash and pulled the trigger. A scream rose above the rattle of gunfire, and that gunner went silent. Carrigan aimed and shot again, uncertain whether he had hit.

The whine of a car engine emerged between the scattered echoes of the rifles. Carrigan glanced to his left. A pair of headlights rolled toward them. Another car, behind and to the left of the new-comer, revealed the first as a sedan painted light blue and white with an unlit roof bar similar to the one on the police car that had investigated the accident at the Liberty stop sign a day ago. Carrigan could just make out the words "Air Police" on the side panel.

Carrigan held his fire as the cars approached. The U.M.E.P.s also stopped shooting until the first sedan came within 50 meters. Suddenly, one auto-matic rifle opened up on the car. Bullets belled as they drilled through metal. The engine shut down. The sedan slowed, its carriage pinging as it bounced over the brush, then lurched to a stop. The follow-ing car swerved aside. Then, a hurled explosive struck the leading vehicle, and it erupted. Flame rose, yellow and orange through the darkness; smoke roiled, filling the air with the odor of gasoline.

The second car wheeled, roaring back the way it had come. Bullets chased it, and Carrigan shot the gunner. The man screamed. His muzzle flashes dis-appeared, and two more guns fired wildly from the darkness below him, raising tiny explosions of dirt from the mound. *Two down, three at the most. Two shooting. Where's the last one or two?* Carrigan re-turned fire carefully. *They're moving. They get above me on that hill, and I'm dead.*

Come on. Show yourselves. Carrigan stopped shooting, eyes probing the darkness for some sign of movement. *Got to relocate. Otherwise, they've got me pegged in a crossfire.* He slithered sideways, sacrificing cover for unpredictability. His hand touched a bush, and he sidled behind it. Movement touched the corner of his vision. He turned his head in time to see a figure belly-crawling across a lighter-colored patch of dirt. Carrigan swung his rifle around, aimed for the man's chest, and pulled the trigger.

The muzzle flash revealed Carrigan's open position as surely as a flare. Without waiting to see if he hit, he dove, rolling, back toward the dark cover of his dirt pile. Bullets tore into the ground where he had been. Dislodged sand stung his face. He scuttled behind the mound amid the ceaseless sputter and roar of the automatic rifles. Once there, he reassessed the location of his enemies. He traced the yellow streaks from the guns. *Two below, one alive to the right.* Carefully, he swung the barrel of the Remington toward the third. As if on cue, the U.M.E.P. soldier on the hill ceased firing.

Moving again. Carrigan held his shot, not wanting to reveal his position on a desperate guess. He searched for shadows against the adobe and scattered plants, listened for the subtle rattle of brush or the scrape of cloth against clay. But the night swallowed sound as well as sight, and the relentless pop of gunfire covered the softer noises he sought. *If he gets behind me, it's over.* Frantically, his gaze tore through the darkness, sketching the outline of twisted brush, the side of the hill, and a distant eucalyptus.

The realization of defeat crept over Carrigan. *No choice anymore.* He pulled the plastic explosive from his pocket, finger tensed over the button that activated the timer. *One minute and it's all over for me and the time travel device.*

For the first time, Carrigan hesitated. The country and causes for which he had struggled, suffered, and killed remained strong within him, justified for the people and nation he served. But his reasons to die seemed faded, obscured by the knowledge of forests, pastures, and open spaces and the realization that he could live with the guilt he could not banish. He pictured Shawna Nicholson, red-brown hair framing intelligent features, her blue jeans and tee shirts accentuating the right bulges, lines, and curves. Like all the soldiers of the underground wars, Carrigan knew he could never become a hero; the monuments and history books would not hold his name. The people he saved would continue to drink and dance beneath the threat of war, never knowing the blood spilt to preserve their lives and their luxuries. *All I ever wanted was not to die in vain.* Carrigan's finger tensed on the button.

One of the U.M.E.P. soldiers paused to reload. Rhythmical thudding slaps emerged beneath the chatter of the other gun. Thinking back, Carrigan realized he had heard it for some time, hushed and safely distant, dismissed for the more significant noises of the guns and the repositioning snipers. Now, he recognized it as helicopters, their rotors loud and ungainly, the turbines high-pitched hissing unrecognizable as any craft he knew from the twenty-first century.

Carrigan looked up and to his left and pinpointed the two helicopters by their red and green navigation lights and the larger, white funnel-shaped search beams raking the ground as they came. The last U.M.E.P. gun fell silent as they, too, assessed this new threat. Again, Carrigan tried to put himself in the U.M.E.P.'s place. *They know they have to kill me fast and get out.* As if to confirm the thought, the gunners at the bottom of the hill opened fire again, a wild, desperate volley in the hope of a lucky shot. One of the U.M.E.P. soldiers sprang free of his cover, and rushed Carrigan.

Carrigan aimed as the helicopter spotlights closed. A voice blasted over the loudspeaker. "This is a United States Government restricted area. Throw down your weapons. Stand up and place your hands behind your head. You are under arrest." The searchlights panned over the U.M.E.P.s at the base of the hill, revealing sweat-sheened, dark features and tan uniforms. "This is a United States Government restricted area . . ."

Carrigan shrank back behind the mound, the explosive clutched in his left fist, the Remington resting on the dirt pile. *U.M.E.P. on American military soil. They can't afford to be arrested.* Carrigan watched. *If this was still 2058, the U.M.E.P.s and I would already be dead.*

". . . Throw down your weapons . . ."

The U.M.E.P. stopped in mid-charge, raised his rifle and fired on the helicopter, aiming for the center of the body. The other U.M.E.P. joined in, gunning for the engine deck. The voice went silent. The volume of the whining turbines decreased as the engine of one vehicle quit. The helicopter plummeted, its rotors still spinning, turned toward the shore breeze from the west, and glided to the ground in perfect autorotation.

The other helicopter paused as its companion maneuvered down safely, then swept in on the U.M.E.P. soldiers, guns blazing. The night filled with the battering explosions of an M-60 machine gun. Dirt splattered and flew, and the standing U.M.E.P. crashed to the ground. The searchlight hung over the bloody, bullet-pocked earth, then panned up the hill toward Carrigan. As the beam slid toward him, Carrigan realized his options had disappeared. *I have to destroy that time travel unit. Otherwise, the Americans will study it and the U.M.E.P.s will send more men after it, maybe an army. There'll be one hell of a war. Modern U.M.E.P. artillery against 1985, primitive American war machines.* As the light touched him, Carrigan pressed the detonator timer and tossed the explosive into the hole. Then the light snapped fully on him and the loudspeakers started again:

"Drop your weapons, stand up, and place your hands behind your head. You're in a United States Government restricted area. You are under arrest."

Carrigan gripped the Remington by the barrel and, with exaggerated motions, tossed it away. The gun slid, rattling across loose dirt and spun off into the darkness. Raising his hands in surrender, Carrigan made a great show of standing and clasping his fingers behind his head. Balancing the need to get out of range of the explosion against the danger of running and possibly drawing the helicopter's fire, Carrigan started to walk away. *Thank God, it's over.*

From behind Carrigan a single gunshot rang out. The bullet tore through Carrigan's back, drawing a line of agony through his chest. He slammed to the ground, hitting his face before he realized he was falling. The searchlight whipped away toward the sniper, and the world blurred into darkness. Carrigan gasped for air. Pain tightened every muscle in his body, and he tasted blood. His thoughts swirled. *Gotta get away.* But, suddenly, he could not remember why. *It's going to blow. Something's going to explode.* He clawed to his knees, air rasping through his throat.

Carrigan scrambled forward. *Got to keep moving.* He dropped to his hands and crawled. His lung felt on fire, and every breath was anguish. He tried to keep them quick and shallow, but reflex drove him to desperate, excruciating gasps. The words over the loudspeaker pounded his eardrums, the voice of God, obscured to nonsense by the harsh ringing in his ears. Then, the buzzing overcame reality. The reports of gunfire dulled and blended to a distant thunderclap of noise. Carrigan fell to his side and rolled down the hill. Brush and rock bruised his hips and shoulders, and he fought for every mouthful of bloody air.

The explosion hammered Carrigan's ears, and the ground quaked beneath him. The spotlight swung over the area again. The edge of a beam found Carrigan. Then, the ringing deepened into his skull. His vision faded to winking points of light, and darkness closed over him completely.

CHAPTER 13

New Beginning

Two weeks later, Shawna Nicholson returned to Liberty Hospital. She sat, alone, at the study table in the resident's lounge and marveled at how everything seemed exactly the same. The same cartoons, articles, and family pictures decorated the dingy, yellow lockers lining the dingier, yellow walls. The same mail cubicles stood in three rows by the doorway; Dr. Mehrhoff's correspondence overflowed onto the floor, as always. The same eight pairs of Dr. Cherry's dress shoes lay wedged beneath the table. Nicholson leaned over the page on transient ischemic attacks in her Internal Medicine textbook. Behind her, beneath the wall telephone, the apartment-sized refrigerator would hold its customary assortment: unidentifiable molds in the back; brown bag lunches scattered throughout; containers of yogurt, milk, and candy saved from on-call dinners, and the rare sample of blood or urine slipped in with the food. The glass and metal cabinet by the mailboxes held scrubs in two sizes, too small and too large; every medium disappeared as fast as it could be replaced.

Nicholson tried to concentrate on strokes, but, even after the ninth reading, the words did not register. It seemed impossible for the world to continue as if nothing had happened. After the struggle for life and death, the hospital routine seemed hopelessly bland, its dry, continuous battles against illnesses and injuries lacking meaning. The aggravation of lung cancer and heart disease patients who sucked cigarettes beneath their oxygen masks muted to gentle irony. And Shawna Nicholson felt as though she no longer fit in the realm she had helped create.

The clack of an opening lever seized Nicholson's attention. She glanced across the table to watch Jason Walker fling open the narrow, metal door of his locker. It crashed against the neighboring locker, and he pinned it there with his right hand. Carefully, he removed a textbook, set it on the table behind him and reached for another volume.

Nicholson leaned her elbows on her book, glad for the company of the one person who might understand how she was feeling. "Jason, how have you been?" Nicholson winced. It was a stupid question, the kind friends and relatives asked with knowing looks and nervous coughs.

Walker stacked a second text on the other and paused with a paperback fellowship directory in his hands. "As well as can be expected. It's my first day back, you know."

"Mine, too."

A long silence ensued, interrupted only by the crackle of shuffling papers as Walker continued to remove objects from his locker. The long hush did not seem awkward or uncomfortable, and Walker's question several minutes later did not appear out of place. "Does everything seem different to you?" He turned and regarded Nicholson directly.

Nicholson closed her book. "Actually, I was

thinking just the opposite. That it all seems almost painfully the same."

Walker hesitated, trying to verbalize his thought. "But less satisfying."

Now, Nicholson considered. "Yeah, that's it. Less satisfying." The attitude seemed impossible to verbalize, as if the events of the past few weeks made the concerns of the rest of the world petty. "I keep thinking about how mothers go on yelling at their kids for spilled milk, never realizing ..." She trailed off.

Walker straightened his books into a neat pile. "So you think Jack succeeded?"

Nicholson slipped two fingers into the pocket of her dress pants and flicked the tracking device to the table. She touched the button. The display remained blank. The red light blinked rapidly as if seeking, and she knew from past attempts changes in orientation would not affect the signal. "The time travel device is gone. That's what he wanted to do."

Walker stared at the square of black plastic. "You've still got that thing? Aren't you afraid some lunatic Arab will come after it?"

Nicholson shrugged. "What for? There's no machine to find anymore. I was more concerned the F.B.I. would take it and somehow use it to construct another time machine. That scares me."

"So they questioned you, too?"

"Over and over."

Walker returned to his locker and started a tower of papers beside the books. "What did you tell them?"

"The truth, mostly." Nicholson hugged her internal medicine textbook and leaned back in her chair.

"Like we discussed on the plane, I left out the 2058 stuff. I just left it with Jack never regaining his memory."

Walker nodded, and Nicholson took this as a signal he had done relatively the same thing. She continued. "What'd you decide about the Derby?"

"You mean the winners Jack gave us?"

"Yeah."

Walker balanced a hand on his books. "I'm not going to bet. This may sound stupid, but I keep getting images of Twilight Zone episodes. You know, the ones where some guy goes back in time and does something tiny. Like kick his dog. And the entire course of history gets changed in some apocalyptic fashion. It's got me spooked." He threw the question back to Nicholson. "How about you?"

Nicholson had already decided not to bet, though for different reasons. "Me neither. It feels too much like cheating."

"Yeah," Walker repeated. "Like cheating." He continued sorting papers.

The oddity did not escape Nicholson's notice. "Jason, why are you cleaning out your locker? You're not leaving, are you?"

"For a while." Walker sighed. "I love medicine, and I think I can be good at it. I just need some time to pull myself back together." He turned to Nicholson, clutching a mixed handful of unused needles, a reflex hammer, and old laboratory reports. "I pooled my vacation time, and the department gave me an extra four weeks. I'm going to spend the next two and half months farming." Nicholson started to speak, but Walker anticipated her next question. "With Ben Hascol."

"Really?" It seemed like a great idea to Nicholson, a chance to make up for the damage the Arabs had inflicted on the farmer's home and time to think things over without risking patient lives.

"Really," Walker confirmed. "What about you? Your residency's almost finished. Where are you going next year?"

Nicholson had heard the query so many times from friends, residents and family, she had begun to hate it. She felt like a child in a roomful of adults, smothered by the inevitable questions: "How old are you? What grade are you in? What are you going to be when you grow up?" as if people were their ages and occupations; and, without a job, they ceased to exist. "I still haven't decided. They've offered me a staff position here. There's a group practice in Madison I've been looking at, and something new has come up." She chewed at a fingernail, recalling the surprise she had received in the mail the day before. "Randy wants me to take a position in Berkeley and get back together with him."

Walker set his supplies carefully on the table. A capped, 20 gauge needle rolled toward the edge, and he caught it before it fell. "Randy? Randy Oakley? The ophthalmologist you were living with?"

Nicholson nodded.

"Are you going?" Walker sounded disappointed and oddly concerned.

Nicholson revived her memories of Oakley. She pictured his tall, thin frame, his features chiseled and ringed by wheaten hair. But there, the recollection ended. His wooden personality and passionless sex faded into the same, dreary obscurity as her calculus lectures in college. "Going? To appease some jerk's carnal urges until he can find a virgin to marry? No thanks." Nicholson's words surprised her. Only the day before, she had given the proposition serious consideration. She looked at Walker, and noticed his cheeks were flushed as he turned back to his cleaning. She tried to soften her description. "I think I finally learned the difference between loving something beautiful and loving something *because* it's beautiful. I only wish I'd figured it out before I hurt Jack."

Walker placed a heap of journals beside his books and dropped a backpack to the nearest chair. He slammed the locker, and it closed with a hollow, metallic clang. "The longer I talked with the feds and the cops, the more I liked the guy. Patriotic to his country and loyal to his friends. I couldn't help it. He came off sounding like some sort of hero." Walker shoved books, papers and magazines into the backpack. "Jack was all right."

Nicholson dropped her text book to the table and leaned forward. "Was? You think he's dead?"

Walker shrugged as if the answer was obvious. "How many Arabs did you say there were?"

"After the dead were counted? Six?"

"One man with a rifle against half a dozen with explosives and machine guns?" Walker shouldered his backpack. "You have to admit the odds don't sound too good." He rested a foot on the seat of the chair. "You know, I combed the newspapers. The government's got it hushed up tight. I couldn't find a word." He examined his toes, as if embarrassed. "I even checked those sensationalist rags in the grocery checkout lanes. You know the ones:

Spider Gives Birth to Human Child. Twin of Alien Love Slave Shares Sex Through ESP."

Nicholson laughed, hoping to put Walker at ease. "I did the same thing. Found nothing there, but I did dig up a two paragraph blurb in one of the reputable San Diego papers. Something about the Naval Base doing some weapons and explosive testing. I guess that appeased the neighbors."

"Yeah, well. See you, I guess." Walker shuffled toward the door. He stopped, one hand against the frame and half-turned. "I hope you decide to stay. You'd make a great addition to the staff." He sounded too sincere for a blind platitude.

"Thanks." Nicholson watched Walker shifting from foot to foot in the doorway, and knew he wanted to say something more. She encouraged him. "In any case, you better come back. You handled your first code like a pro, and you'll make one fine doctor."

"Thanks," Walker returned. He paused thoughtfully. "I'm really sorry about Tracy. I saw in the papers they found her body. I . . . well, I feel like it's my fault."

Grief returned to Nicholson, cold and sharp as a knife, and with it, her medical school psychiatric training. *If I'm not careful, I'll ingrain that guilt even deeper.* "I know. But it isn't. Your fault, I mean. Not any more than the young woman who blames her miscarriage on the single glass of wine she shouldn't have drank or the fellow who thinks he got cancer because he didn't go to church last Sunday. Tracy made her own decision. She didn't deserve to die, but there's not many people who do." Nicholson bit her lip.

Smooth as they sounded, the words came only
with great difficulty.

"I guess that's one of the things I have to work
out." Walker slipped into the hallway and disappeared from sight.

Nicholson listened to the thud of Walker's re-
treating footfalls until they dwindled beneath the
clack of word processors from the room next door.
*If anyone can pull Walker from his confusion, Has-
col can.* Heaving a loud sigh, she leafed open her
text.

The beeper at Nicholson's hip shrilled. From
habit, she tapped it off before the second tone. The
display flashed 8-3-9-4, an unfamiliar number, and
Nicholson pressed the button for a second look.
The same digits paraded across the monitor.
Though unusual, it was not the first time one of
the residents had paged from the library or a hall
telephone, or someone from orthopedics or pediat-
rics called for a rare consult. She rose, reached for
the wall phone behind her, removed the receiver
and tapped out the number.

A woman answered on the second ring. "Liberty
Hospital information."

"This is Dr. Nicholson. Did you page me?"

"Yes, doctor. There's a delivery man here at the
booth with a package."

A package? Nicholson frowned, wondering if
some thoughtful coworker or neighbor had sent
flowers. "I'll be right down."

Nicholson hung up and paused in consideration.
Her parents had been supportive, allowing her to
stay with them while the workers repaired her dam-
aged apartment, lending comfort in the wake of
Tracy's death. It did not surprise Nicholson that

her mother might choose to soften the first day back at work with a gift. Nicholson turned and walked into the hallway.

The medicine resident's lounge sat beside the fire door and almost directly across from the ward on second floor west. Nicholson worked the opening bar with both hands and took the concrete steps to the ground floor. Once there, she wove through the crowded hallway to the main entrance.

The information booth occupied a corner, to the side of the rows of padded chairs. The angle of Nicholson's approach brought her first within view of the windows surrounding the doorless opening. Outside, she saw spring sun reflecting from white sidewalks. Inside, the beams cutting through the panes puddled warmly on the tiled floor. At the door, the security guard helped an elderly man from a car into a wheelchair. People in hospital gowns or street clothes sat, chatting, or crisscrossed through the halls en route to the pharmacy, cafeteria, or various clinics and wards. Closed between cinder block walls and glass, Shawna Nicholson felt as if she had spent her life trapped in a plastic bubble while other people fought the important battles; the problems of her every day existence faded to trivia.

As the slant of the hall changed, Nicholson came upon the information booth. Two women, one middle-aged, the other elderly, sat behind a marble counter fielding telephone calls while a haggard man herded three preschool children into a huddle before the booth and waited for one of the women to get free. Beside them, a man leaned against the wall, watching the flow of hospital traffic from beneath a white cap pulled so low it eclipsed his eyes.

A black beard jutted from his chin. He clutched a cardboard box webbed with packing tape. He wore blue jeans and an unlettered, dark green tee shirt beneath a light jacket rather than any recognizable company uniform. Still, the woman who had paged Nicholson said the delivery man was waiting, and no one else passed the description.

Nicholson approached the man. Closer, she saw hollow cheeks in an otherwise handsome face. "I'm Dr. Nicholson. Is that for me?"

The man's eyes swiveled toward her. He straightened, studied her in the fluorescent lighting, then handed her the package.

Nicholson took the box. For its size, it seemed almost weightless. She tucked it beneath her arm, waiting for him to produce a clipboard or sheaf of papers.

The man simply stared.

Nicholson grew uncomfortable beneath his scrutiny. She readjusted her dress shirt, unobtrusively glancing down to make certain none of her buttons had popped open and her fly was zipped. "Do I need to sign something?"

The man nodded. "Outside."

Something in the man's voice stopped her cold. Nicholson had never accepted a package at the hospital before, but his suggestion struck her as odd. She examined him more closely. The muscled sweep of his body and casual alertness of his stance jarred with the foreign contour of his face. She focused on an eye beneath the shadow of his cap's brim, and recognized the deep, Siamese cat blue the surgery resident had remarked on the first time he saw Jack Carrigan with opened lids. Excitement squeezed in on Nicholson, hemmed by disbelief. "Jack?"

The man blinked twice in rapid succession. His brow wrinkled. "Excuse, me, doctor?" His tone conveyed confusion.

Nicholson flushed, feeling foolish. *Oh, no. I'm going to spend the rest of my life calling every blue-eyed man I meet 'Jack.'* "Outside, you said? At your truck?"

"Yes, ma'am." He started toward the entrance.

Nicholson followed him uncertainly. The windows enclosing the doorway accorded a perfect view of the drive-up area and the fountain. Three cars parked or idled on the macadam, but she saw nothing that could pass for a delivery truck. *Something's wrong here.* Fear balled in her stomach as the man trotted through the entryway with a careless nod to the security guard. Curiosity kept her moving. *I'll confront him near the door; the guard can intervene if he tries anything.* Package still clutched against her side, she trailed him out into the cool, damp air of spring.

Once outside, the delivery man strode along the sidewalk toward the parking garage.

Quickening her pace, Nicholson caught up to him about thirty feet from the entrance. "All right, stop. I don't know who you are or what you want, but you're going to tell me before I go any further from the hospital."

The man went still. He threw a glance behind them at the security guard and the stream of traffic flowing through the opening. Apparently satisfied no one was watching, he removed his cap. Feathered, black hair tumbled to the nape of his neck. Gently, he peeled the false beard from his chin.

Without the beard, the shape of his features softened remarkably. It was Jack Carrigan. He had the
gaunt, sallow look of someone who had undergone
a week of chemotherapy, and his skin looked paler
than Nicholson remembered. But there was no
longer any question. "Is there somewhere quiet we
can talk?" he asked softly.

Nicholson hesitated, uncertain whether to laugh
or cry. She looked at her watch, but it was a wasted
gesture. The instant she let her arm drop, she had
already forgotten the time. "Of course." She led
him along a path between the hospital and the
parking garage. Emotion warred within her. She
wanted to ask a thousand questions, yet to spare
him the pain answering might cause. The urge to
protect him seemed natural, and also ludicrous. Finally, she settled on the sort of open-ended query
that allows patients to direct the conversation to
what concerns them without feeling threatened.
"What happened?"

Carrigan swept his hair back under the cap and
slanted the brim over his eyes. He did not replace
the beard, and that lapse pleased Nicholson. Had
she been less absorbed anticipating his answer, she
would have told him he was not the type who
looked good with facial hair. "We exchanged a little gunfire," Carrigan explained. "I spent some
time in a military hospital."

Nicholson led the way around Liberty Hospital
toward town. She felt certain Carrigan was hiding
some fact beneath simplicity, from the look of him
a serious injury, but she did not press. "Did the
government question you?"

Carrigan smiled. "Oh, yeah. I got to thinking
about how Jason reacted to my explanation. Then,

I realized how many clues I missed when I couldn't remember things; the possibility of time travel never occurred to me. It sounds so impossible, I knew only one of two things could happen." Nicholson and Carrigan crossed along the edge of a metered parking lot. "Either they'd think I was lying and try to torture the truth from me . . ."

Nicholson cringed, hoping the United States government did not operate that way.

". . . or they'd believe me, in which case they'd want me to play oracle. You know, to tell them what missions would succeed or fail. When and how to fight their wars." He regarded Nicholson directly. "That kind of stuff scares me. I love my country, but changing history. . . ?"

They came upon a college recreational building and skirted it. Ahead, the sound of cars whooshing across the road by the riverside touched Nicholson's ears. In the past, when she needed time alone, she had climbed into the gully of the river to its lower banks, lulled by the lap of the water and the chatter of wind through treetops. She nodded to indicate she understood Carrigan's point. Just talking about future wars unnerved her. "What did you do?"

"I pretended I still had amnesia." Carrigan paused as they turned the building's corner to enter the open area before the road. A concrete and macadam street bridge spanned the river, its raised sidewalks brimming with students. At Nicholson's gesture, he continued toward the highway. "I was carrying a legal weapon and obviously shooting in self-defense. When the soldiers asked me to surrender, I didn't resist. The only crime they had me for was trespassing." He chuckled. "And now jail break."

"Jail break?" Startled, Nicholson unconsciously shifted between Carrigan and the road, now wishing he had left on the beard. "You broke out of jail?"

Carrigan stopped on the shoulder, awaiting an opening in the flow of traffic. "Not exactly. I waited until they moved me to a lower security area, then escaped." His gaze tracked a car, and he grew ominously serious. "I'm not going to prison. I didn't do anything wrong."

Signaling Carrigan to follow, Nicholson darted through a hole in the pattern of cars. Again, she suspected a lot of unspoken information, and she understood. To a claustrophobic, a cell might seem more frightening than death. She waited on the shoulder until Carrigan came up beside her, then jogged toward the river. Neither spoke again until they crossed the sparsely wooded area between the street and the river, slid down the grassy hill, and sat on the dirt and stone banks. Clear waters burbled over smoothed stones, and scraps of algae clung to sticks and rocks jutting to the surface. Where the river widened and deepened, mallard ducks turned lazy circles in the river.

"I've got something for you, too." Nicholson set the package beside her, withdrew the tracking device from her pocket, and offered it to Carrigan. She measured his reaction carefully, wondering if the unit would remind him of the era he had misplaced, his last relic of a world once his.

Carrigan accepted the object without comment. He touched the button. As before, the display lay flat and dark. The red light winked a rapid, lost cadence.

Nicholson shook the package. Nothing dislodged or rattled, and she realized it was empty, a prop to draw her to the information desk. She pushed it aside, organizing Carrigan's information. "So now you're stuck in a strange time and running from the law."

If Carrigan saw things the same way, he seemed strangely unperturbed. He watched the ducks, grinning like a child. "I doubt it. How much government money can they spend chasing a trespasser?" He shifted closer to the river and ran a hand through the waters, rubbing his fingers as if he expected to find grit or oil. His gaze followed the canopy of oak and poplar trees and the blue sky visible between the branches. "Sometimes things work out for the best." He stood, holding up the tracking unit until it caught the light of the sun. Turning it sideways, he snapped his wrist toward the open portion of the lake. The plastic cut air, neat as a frisbee, skipped twice across the water's surface, then sank. The ducks paddled away, then darted toward it, apparently accustomed to people hurling food.

Carrigan reached down a hand.

Nicholson caught a grip on his wrist and let him hoist her to her feet.

"How about dinner at The Choice in Cedar Rapids tonight?" Carrigan flinched away as he asked the question.

Afraid she might have hurt his arm, Nicholson released him. "Are you all right?"

"I'm fine. It's just the last time I invited you to The Choice, you hit me."

Nicholson stared at the pale angles of his features, met strong, blue eyes with a sparkle of mischief, and allowed herself to enjoy the attractiveness of his face without guilt. "I didn't hit you for the invitation. I hit you for what you did." She caught him into an embrace, drew him close; and, this time, she made a pass at him.

Carrigan didn't struggle.

Kate Elliott

The Novels of the Jaran:

DAW

S. Andrew Swann

☐ **FORESTS OF THE NIGHT** UE2565—$3.99

When Nohar Rajasthan, a private eye descended from geneti-
cally manipulated tiger stock, a moreau—a second-class hu-
manoid citizen in a human world—is hired to look into a human's
murder, he find himself caught up in a conspiracy that includes
federal agents, drug runners, moreau gangs, and a deadly
canine assassin. And he hasn't even met the real enemy yet!

☐ **EMPERORS OF THE TWILIGHT** UE2589—$4.50

New York City, sixty years in the future, a time when a squad
of assassins was ready to send an entire skyscraper up in
flames to take out one special operative. Her name: Evi Isham,
her species: frankenstein, the next step beyond human, her
physiology bioengineered to make her the best in the business
whether she was taking down an enemy or just trying to stay
alive. Back from vacation and ready to report in to the Agency
for a new assignment, Evi suddenly found herself on the run
from an unidentified enemy who had targeted her for death.
Her only hope was to evade her stalkers long enough to make
contact with her superiors. But she would soon discover that
even the Agency might not save her from those who sought
her life!

DAW

Cheryl J. Franklin

The Tales of the Taormin:

☐ **FIRE GET: Book 1**   UE2231—$3.50

Only the mighty sorcerer Lord Venkarel could save Serii from
the Evil that threatened it—unless it became his master. . . .

☐ **FIRE LORD: Book 2**   UE2354—$3.95

Could even the wizard son of Lord Venkarel destroy the
Rendies—creatures of soul-fire that preyed upon the living?

☐ **FIRE CROSSING: Book 3**   UE2468—$4.99

Can a young wizard from Serii evade the traps of the computor-
controlled society of Network—or would his entire world fall
prey to forces which magic could not defeat?

The Network/Consortium Novels:

☐ **THE LIGHT IN EXILE**   UE2417—$3.95

Siatha—a non-tech world and a people in harmony—until it
became a pawn of the human-run Network and a deadly alien
force. . . .

☐ **THE INQUISITOR**   UE2512—$5.99

Would an entire race be destroyed by one man's ambitions—
and one woman's thirst for vengeance?
